Praise

Melissa Craig mysteries.

'A clearly gifted and knowledgeable writer, never less than
engaging and

'Gently old-
anguish'

'Full of sharp insights with an unexpected twist in the tail. A
satisfying read'

Val McDermid, *Manchester Evening News*

'She
atten

'Enga
from

'All t
insigl'

'Fres
array

The Fourth Suspect

Betty Rowlands

NEW ENGLISH LIBRARY
Hodder & Stoughton

First published in Great Britain in 2001
by Hodder and Stoughton
First published in paperback in 2001
by Hodder and Stoughton
A division of Hodder Headline

A New English Library Paperback

10 9 8 7 6 5 4 3 2 1

A CIP catalogue record for this title
is available from the British Library.

ISBN 0 340 75081 2

Printed and bound in Great Britain by
Mackays of Chatham plc, Chatham, Kent

Hodder and Stoughton
A division of Hodder Headline
338 Euston Road
London NW1 3BH

About the author

In 1988 Betty Rowlands won the Sunday Express/Veuve Clicquot Crime Short Story of the Year Competition. Her success continued with the publication of nine previous acclaimed Melissa Craig mysteries. She is an active member of the Crime Writers' Association and regularly gives talks and readings, runs workshops and serves on panels at crime writing conventions.

She lives in the heart of the Cotswolds where her Melissa Craig mysteries are set and has three grown-up children and four grandchildren.

Prologue

'He was just sitting there with his head on his arms and for a moment I thought he'd fallen asleep. I'd made him a cup of tea and I went to put it on the bench beside him . . . and then I saw—'

Sylvia Ross broke off and tightened her grip on the cup of tea a young policewoman had made for her. She had barely tasted it, but she was thankful for its warmth and the comfort of having something for her shaking hands to cling to. Her gorge rose at the awful memory: the staring, wide-open eyes, the thin lips curved in a rictus that was almost a sneer, the pool of blood congealing beneath the head as it lay pillowed in the crook of his arm.

The senior of the two women detectives who had come in response to the emergency call leaned forward in her chair, put a reassuring hand on Sylvia's arm and said, 'Mrs Ross, I realise that you're in a state of shock and I won't ask you too many questions just now, but there are one or two things I need to know straight away. Just take your time over your answers.' She had introduced herself as Detective Inspector Mollie Adair; she had coal-black hair and bright blue eyes set in a pale, oval face and she seemed absurdly young to be in charge of a murder enquiry. The word *murder* echoed and re-echoed in Sylvia's brain as if an old-fashioned gramophone needle had stuck in a groove. Her husband, Frank Ross, had been murdered, struck down as he sat at his bench in the shed he had fitted out as a workshop, the bench where he spent so much of his spare time making the toys he sold in aid of church funds.

'You said you came home at about four o'clock,' the inspector prompted gently. 'Can you remember what time you left?'

Sylvia made a desperate effort to force her brain to function, to think clearly. She switched her mind back, saw herself clearing the table after lunch and carrying the dishes into the kitchen, heard Frank say in his dry, flat voice, 'I'll be in the workshop for a couple of hours or so,' and her equally flat reply, 'I'm going into town to do some shopping.' Aloud, she said, 'It must have been about ten to two — I caught the two o'clock bus.'

'And your husband was in his workshop when you left?'

'That's right.'

'Did he say he was expecting anyone?'

'No.'

'Was there anyone about — someone in a car, perhaps —

2

when you left? Or did you see anyone drive away as you came home?'

'I didn't notice . . . no, I don't think so.'

'So when you got home you put away your shopping, made a pot of tea and took a cup out to your husband. What time would that have been?'

'Five o'clock.'

'Did you realise right away that he was dead?'

Sylvia felt another wave of nausea; she gagged, put the by now lukewarm tea on the occasional table at her elbow and covered her mouth with her hands. 'Yes, of course,' she gulped. 'When I saw his face . . . he had to be, he looked so dreadful—'

'What did you do then?'

'I ran next door, to Mrs Menzies.' Sylvia indicated with a slight movement of her hand the middle-aged woman sitting quietly beside her on the couch. 'She came back with me into the house and called 999. That's all I remember.'

Inspector Adair turned her attention briefly to the neighbour, who had not uttered a word so far but sat with a comforting arm round Sylvia's thin shoulders. 'What time would that have been, Mrs Menzies?'

'I don't recall exactly. It was a little after five . . . I'd switched on the radio to hear the news.'

'And you came back here with Mrs Ross straight away and called 999. Can I take it you've been here with her ever since?'

'Of course — she was in no fit state to be left alone,

after what she found in that shed. A dreadful sight, not one I ever wish to see again. Whoever could have done such a thing I simply can't imagine.' Being directly addressed had the effect of transforming Mrs Menzies from a silent listener to an active participant in the interview. 'Such a good, upright citizen, a churchwarden, a real pillar of the community. No one would think he had an enemy in the world – but I'm sure the police will catch the wicked person who did it,' she went on, giving Sylvia a consoling squeeze. 'And if I can be of any help in your enquiries, Inspector Adair, you have only to ask.'

'Thank you, Mrs Menzies, I may want a word with you later. There are just one or two more points I want to clear up with Mrs Ross and then we'll leave her in peace for now.' The detective transferred her gaze to the widow, looking her full in the face. 'I'd just like to make absolutely sure I've got this straight. You say you got home about four o'clock, but didn't go out to the shed with your husband's tea until an hour or so later?'

The expression in the blue eyes, unblinking and hard as glass marbles, sent a cold trickle running down Sylvia's back. She ran her tongue over lips that felt suddenly dry; her throat seemed to have seized up, making her reply almost a croak. 'He always had his tea at five o'clock. Usually, he came indoors for it, but as he hadn't I took it out to him.'

'What did you do in the meantime?'

Sylvia shut her eyes, trying to remember. 'I unpacked the shopping and put it away . . . and then I . . . I think I sat down and read the evening paper for a little while.'

'I see. And when you went out with the tea and saw your husband lying on the bench, you were in absolutely no doubt that he was dead?'

'Hasn't she just said so?' interrupted Mrs Menzies indignantly.

'We have to make certain about every detail,' said the inspector with a trace of impatience. 'Now, Mrs Ross, just a couple more questions. 'You didn't touch him, or try to move him?'

'I don't think so. It was such a shock, you see . . . I can't remember exactly what I did before I ran next door.'

'Did you touch anything else?'

'I don't think so,' Sylvia repeated. She felt her agitation rising again. 'I really don't remember. Please, do I have to answer any more questions?'

'No, that's all for now, but I may want to speak to you again in a day or two, when you've had time to recover from the shock. Will your friend stay with you, or would you like us to send a counsellor to keep you company?'

'She'll be staying at my house tonight,' Mrs Menzies announced before Sylvia had a chance to speak.

'Fine. What about your family – is there anyone you'd like us to contact?'

There was a long silence. Then Sylvia said hesitantly, 'I have a daughter, but I haven't seen her for a long time. I suppose she ought to be told.'

'Do you know where she lives?'

'No, but I know how you could get in touch with her.

She's a writer, you see. Her publisher will have her address.'

'Right.' Inspector Adair reopened the notebook she had been about to put away. 'What's her name?'

'It's Melissa. I don't know what her other name is now – I mean, she may be married – but she writes under the name of Mel Craig.'

Chapter One

Melissa Craig flexed her arms, put her clasped hands behind her head and leaned back in her chair with a sigh of mingled weariness and satisfaction. On the desk in front of her lay the first draft of her latest novel. It read well and she was pleased with it; pleased, too, that she had had the courage of her convictions and finally closed the door on the career of her fictional detective, Nathan Latimer, despite the blandishments of her editor and numerous letters from fans pleading for more mysteries. The misgivings of her agent, Joe Martin, had been harder to resist, but once she had convinced him that she had had enough of murder – and had written one highly successful literary novel which had been short-listed for a prestigious award – he had given her every encouragement. *Dear Joe, what a rock you are*, she thought as she got up and went over to the window to gaze out at the familiar landscape of field and woodland.

It was late April; the pastures were a vivid green after the winter rains and the trees and hedgerows were bursting with new life. Another Cotswold spring to give thanks for. She put the draft back in its folder and glanced at her watch. Ten to eleven; time for coffee. She went downstairs and filled the kettle.

She drank her coffee and ate a couple of ginger biscuits standing at the kitchen window, admiring the colourful show of spring flowers in the little garden that she had tended with such love and diligence since moving into Hawthorn Cottage some five years ago. So much that was significant in her life had happened during that time: the end of her affair with Aubrey, whom she had left languishing in London; her enduring friendship with Iris Ash, an internationally acclaimed artist who owned the adjoining Elder Cottage but was now Iris Hammond and spent most of her time in France, where she and her husband Jack ran a flourishing arts centre; her sometimes turbulent relationship with Kenneth Harris, the doughty former detective chief inspector with whom she had crossed swords so many times over her involvement in the cases he was investigating. For Melissa's acquaintance with murder was not confined to the pages of her bestselling novels. Time and again, circumstances and her own fascination with real-life crime and criminals had conspired to bring her uncomfortably — sometimes dangerously — face to face with the real thing. One more reason, she reflected, why she had so resolutely sent Nathan Latimer into honourable retirement. Her fiftieth birthday was looming; it was time she opted for a quiet life.

She had finished her coffee and was reaching for the cafetière for a refill when she heard the sound of a car outside, its tyres crunching on the gravelled track which linked the pair of semi-detached cottages to the lane leading to the village of Upper Benbury. Moments later the doorbell rang; through the spyhole that her son Simon, during his latest visit from his home in New York, had insisted she have installed in the solid oak inner door, she recognised Detective Sergeant Matthew Waters of the Gloucestershire CID, an old friend and former colleague of Kenneth Harris. Ken had retired from the force and gone to America to join a firm of private investigators, but the two still kept in touch.

'How nice to see you, Matt,' Melissa exclaimed as she ushered him into the narrow hall and closed the door behind him. 'I'm just having my elevenses — would you like a coffee?'

'Thanks, that'd be lovely.'

'Come into the kitchen and tell me the latest news. It seems ages since I saw you.'

'It is quite a while,' he agreed.

'Are the local villains keeping you busy?'

'Pretty well.'

'What brings you here today?' She waved him to a chair, but he ignored the gesture and went over to the window. He stood there for several moments without speaking, his back turned towards her. There was something about his attitude and the uncharacteristic brevity of his replies that she found vaguely disturbing. A sudden fear gripped her and she said, 'Is something wrong? Has something happened to Ken?'

He turned away from the window and sat down. 'Ken's fine so far as I know. I haven't heard from him lately – have you?'

'I saw him a month or so ago when I was in New York visiting Simon. We're still good friends.'

'I'm glad about that.'

'So what brings you here?' she repeated as he once more lapsed into silence. She handed him a mug of coffee, invited him to help himself to milk, sugar and biscuits, replenished her own mug and sat down opposite him. 'Is it just a social visit, or do you need my help over some case that's got you all baffled?' she added flippantly.

He smiled faintly at the banter, but did not respond. He spooned sugar into his coffee and stirred it for what seemed an unusually long time before saying quietly, 'Mel, you may think this is an odd thing for me to ask, but have you been in touch with your mother and father lately?'

The question was so unexpected that for a moment she could only sit and stare at him with her mouth open. So far as she could remember, she had never referred to her parents in his presence. She had confided to Ken the history of her brief, passionate affair with Guy Craig, the car accident in which he had so tragically died and the discovery soon after that she was to bear his child, but she could not imagine that he would have told Matt or revealed that, so far from giving her the support she desperately needed, her own parents had summarily thrown her out.

The memory of the angry scene — her father's cold, terrifying rage, her mother's tearful, almost craven acquiescence in his harsh judgment — made her shiver, despite the warmth of the kitchen and the sunshine outside. Several seconds passed before she found her voice. 'No,' she said, and the words seemed to be coming from outside herself, from somewhere a long way off. 'We . . . lost contact many years ago. Why do you ask?'

'We've had a message from Thames Valley CID, asking us to contact you on behalf of a Mrs Sylvia Ross who claims to be your mother.'

'My mother's name is Sylvia Ross. What does she want with me?'

'She has asked the police to let you know that your father is dead.'

'Don't tell me she's invited me to the funeral!' The remark escaped before she had time to think; she saw Matt's keen blue-grey eyes widen, knew that she had shocked him and felt a need to justify herself. 'That must have sounded bitchy, but the fact is that my father ordered me out of the house for getting pregnant without benefit of clergy and I never saw or heard my mother making the slightest effort to persuade him to change his mind. I wrote and told them when Simon was born, hoping that they might have relented and want to see their grandchild, but the letter came back to me unopened, "Return to

Sender" written on it in my father's writing. That was nearly thirty years ago and I haven't had any contact with them since – for all I knew, they might both have died. There are no relatives on either side who would have told me.' The revelations came in a flood that she was powerless to control; when at last she fell silent she was trembling so violently that coffee spilled from her mug on to the table.

In an uncharacteristically demonstrative gesture, Matt reached across the table and put a steadying hand on her arm. 'Mel, I'm so sorry, I had no idea,' he said gently.

'Of course you hadn't – why should you? It isn't something I like to talk or even think about.' She closed her eyes, comforted by his sympathy and the warmth of his touch. 'What was it – a heart attack?' she asked after a moment or two.

'Worse than that, I'm afraid. Mel, this is going to come as a nasty shock, but he didn't die a natural death. He was murdered.'

'Murdered!' The word hit her like a blow to the stomach. 'How? What happened? Was he mugged, did he disturb a burglar or what?' The questions came tumbling out with no coherent thought behind them.

'I haven't any details, but it seems it was a deliberate attack, and' – Matt cleared his throat and hesitated before going on – 'I understand from the officer in charge of the investigation that your mother is under suspicion.'

✳   ✳   ✳

After Matt Waters left, having extracted a promise that she would call him immediately if she needed any help, Melissa went up to her study and sat for a long time at her desk, staring at the blank screen of her computer. She was conscious of nothing but a strange sensation of numbness which brought with it a sense of guilt. Her father had met a violent death, yet she felt no grief, no sense of loss. For the first twenty years of her life he had been everything a father should be, but the loving relationship they once shared lay buried under the almost thirty years of silence that had followed his rejection of her for falling short of the standards of morality that he had set for her. Nor could she, in her present state of shock, bring herself to feel any warmth or sympathy towards her mother, who had done nothing, so far as she was aware, to plead for compassion and forgiveness for her only child. *What right have you to make demands on me?* she thought resentfully. *What comfort and support did you give me in my hour of need?*

From time to time she glanced at the sheet of paper on which Matt had written an address and telephone number, but she instinctively shrank from making the move that would bring about the first contact with her mother. She found herself wondering what her life had been like during those thirty years. Did she never think of her daughter and her grandchild? Surely she could have made some attempt to get in touch without the knowledge of her sternly puritanical husband? But there was one over-riding question beside which all the others seemed trivial, the question that she only dimly realised lay at the root of her reluctance to pick up the telephone. Was her mother indeed a murderess?

She had no idea of the time, but was suddenly surprised to realise that she was hungry. A glance at the clock on her desk told her it was half past twelve; she had been sitting there for over an hour. She would have something to eat before deciding what to do. She went mechanically about the task of heating the portion of soup she had taken earlier from the freezer. Home-made tomato soup to a recipe Iris had given her. If only Iris, with her down-to-earth wisdom and undemonstrative affection, were here now. She was only a phone call away. Or Simon; it was about eight in the morning in New York and he was probably at home, having his breakfast, reading the Saturday morning paper . . . but what was the point in calling either of them? It wasn't just someone to talk to that she needed, it was a human presence.

Her hand had reached for the phone and called the number almost before her brain was aware of giving the command. 'Joe, thank God you're there!' she gasped as he came on the line.

'Mel, what is it? Are you ill?' The concern in his voice, the love that she knew was there for her, had been there for so long, patiently waiting until she was ready to accept it, was enough to bring her deadened senses back to life.

'No, I'm all right, but . . . Joe, I've just been told that my father has been murdered and the police think my mother killed him.'

'Good heavens, how appalling! How? When?'

'I don't know any details. Matt Waters came to tell me. Joe, I need you . . . can you come?'

'Where do . . . that is, where does your mother live?'

'In a village – well, it's a small town really – near Reading.'

'Are you there now?'

'No, I'm still at home.'

'Stay there. I'll leave right away and be with you in a couple of hours.'

'Bless you!'

It was only then that she broke down and wept.

Chapter Two

'That's it,' said Melissa, pointing. 'Ironic, isn't it? All these years we've lived less than two hours' drive apart, yet we might have been on different planets.'

'Not ironic – tragic,' Joe replied soberly. He pulled into the kerb and switched off the ignition. For a few moments the pair sat in silence, contemplating the neat, brick-built, bay-windowed house. Built, like the others in the street, in the style of the 1930s, it was set back a short distance from the road behind a low privet hedge and linked to a detached garage by a slatted wooden door across a covered passageway leading to the garden. The police had strung their familiar blue and white tape across the white-painted gate and a uniformed police officer stood on guard. A woman pushing a pram with a bag of shopping swinging from its handle gave the car and its occupants a quick, curious glance as she passed; on the opposite pavement, a small group of women paused in their gossiping and stared.

The officer spoke into her radio. 'Announcing our arrival, I suppose,' Melissa said. 'She's probably been told to look out for us.'

Joe did not appear to have heard the remark. 'So this is where you grew up, Mel – number twelve, Brimley Road.'

He spoke as if it held some significance for him, but she was quick to put him right. 'Oh no, I never lived here; our house was some way away, in a different part of town. I've no idea when they moved – as soon as possible after I left, I imagine. They probably couldn't bear the shame of having a fallen daughter.' She spoke lightly, but felt a stab of bitterness at the memory.

'From the way you directed me, you seem to know the neighbourhood pretty well,' he commented.

'My best friend at school used to live not far from here and I came to her house quite often. It was very nice inside, but I remember feeling almost sorry for her, living in a house that looked like all the other houses and knowing hardly anyone except the next-door neighbours. We lived in a cul-de-sac where every house was different and it was like a small village – everyone knew everyone else. I had a crush on Sheila's elder brother when I was about fourteen,' Melissa went on reflectively. 'He was called Dermot; he was quite keen on me too, took me to the pictures a couple of times when I was supposed to be out with a girl friend. My father found out and forbade me to see him again, which meant that I wasn't able to go to the house any more and I wasn't even allowed to invite

Sheila to ours.' This time, she could hear the bitterness coming to the surface.

'Your father even stopped you seeing your best friend?' Joe exclaimed in disbelief.

'He was always very protective of me. I suppose it's natural with a daughter.' Melissa closed her eyes tightly for a moment. 'Sheila and I saw one another at school, of course, but we were in different forms and somehow it was never the same after that.'

'Poor kid!' He took her hand and squeezed it.

She returned the pressure for a moment, then unclipped her seat belt. 'Let's not talk about that part of my life any more,' she said briskly and got out of the car. She glanced along the street; there were cars parked here and there, but the woman with the pram had disappeared and the others, as if ashamed of their blatant inquisitiveness, had begun to disperse.

'You know,' Joe remarked as he locked the car and joined her on the pavement, 'I was half afraid there might be reporters waiting. You're quite a celebrity and it's amazing how these things get out.'

'The same thought occurred to me,' she admitted.

The policewoman greeted them courteously and asked them for some form of identification. 'Every effort has been made to keep your name secret, but we've been told to look out for journalists just the same,' she explained as she unhitched the tape to admit them.

'I appreciate that,' said Melissa warmly. The adage that

any publicity was good publicity did not, she felt, apply in this case.

They walked in silence up to the front door, which was protected by a glazed porch. In one corner was a wrought-iron umbrella-stand; foliage plants hung from the walls in matching wrought-iron holders. Joe pressed the bell and they waited. Melissa's heart was thumping. A terrible thought came into her mind.

'Joe, suppose I don't recognise her!' she whispered.

'Don't worry, I'm sure you will,' he whispered back.

The inner door opened and a stout, grey-haired, stern-featured woman emerged, a bunch of keys in her hand. She fixed them with an expressionless stare while she unlocked the porch door. 'That's not her,' muttered Melissa out of the corner of her mouth.

Before either of them had a chance to speak, the woman said, 'I suppose you're the daughter.' She spoke in a flat monotone while eyeing Melissa up and down, ignoring Joe completely.

'I'm Mrs Ross's daughter, yes,' said Melissa stiffly. Already on edge, she found it an effort to conceal her irritation at the woman's manner. 'Is my mother here?'

'She's expecting you. I suppose you'd better come in.' The woman held the door wide open and the two stepped inside. She relocked the porch, leaving the keys hanging in the lock, before closing the inner door. Her body language shouted disapproval; behind her back, Joe and Melissa exchanged uneasy glances.

'Wait while I tell her you're here,' she commanded. She

pushed past them, opened the door to a room at the far end of the hall and announced, 'She's arrived,' adding, without lowering her voice, 'She's brought a gentleman with her.'

There was a pause before a voice from within the room, a voice that Melissa instantly recognised, said softly, 'Thank you, Mrs Menzies. Tell them I'll be out in a moment . . . and thank you once again.'

'Are you sure you'll be all right? You wouldn't like me to make you another cup of tea?'

'That's very kind, but I'll be quite all right.'

'Well, you know where I am if you need me.' Mrs Menzies turned and came back to where Melissa and Joe were standing. 'You heard what your mother said.' She spoke with a touch of resentment which Melissa suspected was down to disappointment at not being allowed to witness the reunion. She fixed Melissa with a look of undisguised hostility and said, this time in a lower voice, 'So you're the one who writes all those nasty books.'

'I'm sorry you think they're nasty.' Thrown by the unexpectedness of the attack, Melissa could think of no other reply.

'I'd have thought there was enough wickedness in the world without people like you making money out of inventing more,' said Mrs Menzies. 'I hope you won't upset your mother by talking about it.'

'We're not here to talk about my books,' said Melissa through her teeth.

'No, that's right. You're here to give some comfort and

support to your mother after the dreadful thing that happened to your father, and don't you forget it. That man was a saint,' Mrs Menzies went on. Her eyes glittered, her voice dropped to an angry hiss. 'He deserved a loving, dutiful daughter – and what did he get?' Without waiting for a reply, she strode to the front door and let herself out of the house, leaving Melissa trembling with anger.

'The interfering old harpy! How dare she talk to me like that!' she muttered in Joe's ear.

He gave her a quick hug. 'Don't let it get to you, Mel,' he said softly.

A voice called from behind them. 'Lissie? Is it really you?'

They turned to see a woman standing in the open doorway, one hand resting on the frame as if for support. It flashed through Melissa's head that her mother was smaller and slighter than she remembered. She had developed a slight stoop, her cheeks had hollowed and deep lines ran from nose to chin, but her skin was surprisingly firm for a woman of seventy, her hair was only lightly sprinkled with grey and the warm brown eyes that her daughter had inherited were still clear and bright.

There was a catch in Melissa's voice as she replied, 'Yes, Mother, it's me.'

'It was good of you to come.' Sylvia's eyes flicked briefly towards Joe. 'Aren't you going to introduce me?'

'This is Joe Martin, my agent . . . and my very dear friend. He kindly drove me here.'

'How do you do, Mrs Ross,' said Joe politely. Sylvia gave a half smile, nodded and turned back to Melissa. She seemed to be waiting for her to speak.

Melissa opened her mouth, but could find no words. She took a couple of steps forward and impulsively held out both hands. Sylvia reached out and grasped them; the next moment they were clinging to one another, cheeks pressed together, their tears mingling as they fell.

After a while, Melissa said, 'Why don't we sit down?' She guided her mother into what turned out to be a sitting-room and immediately had the sensation of having moved back in time; although it was a different shape from the one in her old home, it had nevertheless a familiar, yet dream-like quality. The three-piece suite covered in cretonne and the floral patterned carpet were so like the ones she remembered that they could have been the same; well-loved pictures hung on the walls; the firescreen that she and her mother had embroidered together while she was still at school stood in front of the grate beside the brass coal-scuttle which shone as brightly as ever beside the set of matching fire-irons. As in the old house, French windows gave on to a garden; that too was laid out in a style similar to the one where she had played as a child. One glaring difference brought her back to the present with a sickening jolt: the blue and white tape stretched across the door to a brick-built extension to the rear of the garage.

Melissa sat down beside her mother on the couch and took her in her arms, the bitterness and anger for the time being forgotten in the face of so much distress. For several minutes she sat stroking her mother's hair and whispering soothing words in an effort to stem the convulsive sobs racking her body. When at last Sylvia was able to speak, she said brokenly, her face hidden in Melissa's shoulder, 'Lissie darling, I'm so sorry!'

'Sorry for what?'

'For letting you go. I'd never have turned you out . . . I was shocked at what you'd done, yes, but I wanted to take care of you — and the baby — but he wouldn't . . .' Fresh tears poured from Sylvia's red and swollen eyes.

Melissa put her hands on her shoulders and gazed at her in disbelief. 'Mother, what are you saying? I thought it was both of you . . . you never said, you never gave me any comfort—'

'He wouldn't let me . . . he forbade me—'

'I wrote and told you where I was staying, hoping you'd relent. Didn't you get the letter? You could at least—'

'Yes, we got the letter.' Sylvia lay back and closed her eyes. 'He burned it,' she mumbled, almost as if she was talking in her sleep. 'He said if I had anything further to do with you I could leave as well.'

'Oh, dear God!'

Melissa made a helpless gesture with her hands and looked round, expecting to see Joe standing behind the couch. He was not there; in a moment of panic which she knew to be totally irrational she leapt to her feet and called out to him.

'Here I am.' Instantly, he appeared in the doorway. 'I thought you and your mother would rather be on your own so I . . .' His gaze moved beyond her to Sylvia, who had fallen back among the cushions. Her face had the waxen pallor of a dead woman, but her breathing was soft and regular. 'Is she all right?' he asked anxiously.

'She's emotionally exhausted, that's all.'

'Perhaps we should give her a drop of brandy?'

'You won't find any brandy in this house. Maybe some strong tea.'

'I thought that might be welcome so I took the liberty of having a poke around in the kitchen. I'll go and make it.'

'Bless you!'

By the time he returned, carrying a tray with three steaming cups, a jug of milk and a bowl of sugar, Sylvia had opened her eyes. On seeing him she gave a little shocked exclamation, got to her feet and pulled a small table from a nest beside the couch. 'Good gracious, Melissa, what are you thinking of to allow your guest to make his own tea!' she exclaimed fussily as she positioned the table and took the tray from him. 'I expect you'd like some cake with it, or a biscuit.' She bustled out of the room and they heard cupboard doors opening and closing.

'Has she told you what happened?' asked Joe in a low voice.

Melissa shook her head. 'We haven't got round to that yet.'

It was several minutes before Sylvia returned with a plate of assorted biscuits. She had evidently tidied her hair and made a supreme effort to compose herself. 'Here we are,' she said, offering the plate to Joe with a brave attempt at a smile. 'Have one of the chocolate ones – they were always Lissie's favourite, weren't they dear?'

'Fancy you remembering.' The angry scorn that Melissa could not contain brought a spasm of pain to her mother's face. 'Sorry, that just slipped out,' she muttered uneasily.

They drank their tea in silence for a few minutes. Then Melissa said, 'Do you feel able to tell us what happened?'

'To your father, you mean?' Sylvia put down her cup, wiped her mouth with a lace edged handkerchief and glanced doubtfully at Joe, who was sitting in an armchair beside the fireplace.

Quick to read her thoughts, he stood up. 'Perhaps you'd rather I waited in the car—' he began, but before Sylvia could speak Melissa interposed.

'No, please stay,' she said. 'Joe is a very close friend and you can rely completely on his discretion,' she assured her mother. 'And besides, I need his support. This is an ordeal for me as well, you know.'

'Yes, dear, of course it is.' Sylvia sat very still and upright on the couch, biting her lips.

Seeing that she was having difficulty in deciding how to start, Melissa said, 'I don't know anything except that Father is dead and that somebody killed him.' Sylvia nodded, her lips pressed tightly together. 'How did it happen? Was it you who found him?'

'Yes.' The word was the faintest of whispers. 'Yes, I found him. It was . . . terrible.' There was a long pause, during which Sylvia sat twisting the flimsy handkerchief between her fingers. When she began to speak again, her voice was stronger, but toneless, as if she was reciting something she had learned by heart. 'I'd been shopping . . . it was my regular day to go into town. He was in his workshop and a little while after I got back I made a cup of tea and took it out to him. He was slumped on the bench with a terrible wound in his head and the chopper was lying on the floor with blood on it. I ran next door to Mrs Menzies and she came back with me; she said he was dead and she called the police.'

'Is Mrs Menzies a close friend of yours?'

Sylvia looked faintly surprised at the question. 'Not really close, although she's been very kind since . . .' She swallowed hard before continuing. 'We've known her a long time, but she had more to do with Father, really. She's on the PCC and Father is . . . was a churchwarden.'

'She obviously doesn't approve of me. What have you told her?'

Sylvia looked uncomfortable. She stared down at her hands and made no reply. After a moment she said, 'She thinks . . . that is, your father told her . . . he told everybody who asked if we had any family . . . that you'd left home years ago and we hadn't heard from you since.'

'Meaning, he implied that I'd walked out of my own accord. And you let him get away with that lie!' Melissa could no longer control the rage and bitterness. Her own voice cracked as she burst out, 'Mother, how could you?'

'You don't understand. It was the way he was. I felt I couldn't cross him or disobey him. You must remember how strict he was—'

'Strict, yes, and very strait-laced . . . but I never thought of him as a tyrant, not until—' Once again, Melissa's anger was swept aside by a wave of pity. 'Poor Mother,' she said gently. 'What you must have gone through.'

'There were times when I'd have given anything to get away, but I had nowhere to go.'

'There are counselling services nowadays – did you never think of asking for help? Or haven't you a friend you could have confided in?'

'There's Lottie Haynes . . . I met her at the flower club . . . she's very kind, I can talk to her a little but I don't see her so often since I gave up going to the meetings.'

'Why did you do that?'

'Father didn't approve, I don't know why. He just said I wasn't to go any more.'

'How cruel!' Melissa leaned across and took her mother's hands in both her own. 'If only I'd known, you could have come to me. I'd have taken care of you.' The thought of all the wasted years was like a knife in her stomach. 'It's too late to think about that now, but we'll make some plans once this terrible business is over.' Recalling Matt's final words, she hesitated and drew a deep breath before putting her next question, the one to which she dreaded hearing the answer. 'Mother, have you – or the police – any idea who might have killed Father?'

Reluctantly, Sylvia met her daughter's gaze. 'I've really no idea,' she said. After a moment she added, 'I'm afraid they think it might have been me.'

Chapter Three

'You don't look surprised. Lissie, please, I beg you . . . I implore you to believe me. I didn't kill your father!'

'Of course I believe you.' Almost unbearably moved by the plea, Melissa unhesitatingly gave the assurance her mother sought, but in her heart she longed to feel as certain as she willed herself to sound. The pain and frustration of the enforced separation from her only child, followed by years of virtual imprisonment in a loveless marriage, would have been enough to drive many a woman to breaking point long ago. Sooner or later the truth would be known; whatever the outcome, strength and support were what the widow would be needing for a long time to come.

'The reason I'm not surprised is that it very often turns out that a murder victim has been killed by a husband or wife or someone with whom they've had a very close relationship,' Melissa explained. 'That's normally where the police start looking, but of course it doesn't mean they don't consider all other possibilities. I'm afraid,' she went on, picking her words carefully, 'that unless they find some clues that lead them straight to the killer, there will be a certain amount of probing into your relationship with Father.'

'What do you mean? I'm sure everyone thinks – knows, believes – we're a perfectly normal, devoted couple. Father goes to work and I run the home, we go to church – I told you, Father's a churchwarden – we go on holiday, visit friends like everyone else. I don't think anyone has any idea—'

'What you're saying is you've kept up a pretence of being a happily married woman, even though you've just admitted you'd have given anything to be able to leave him? That's right, isn't it?'

Sylvia nodded, her head bowed. 'What else could I do?' she whispered. 'He gets . . . used to get . . . so angry with me if I didn't agree with him on everything. He could be really frightening when he was angry.'

'Yes, I know.' The memory of the final confrontation that had ended with her flinging a few clothes and personal belongings into a suitcase and departing weeping from the house where she had lived all her life hit Melissa like a blow to the face. It took her several moments to bring the surge of pain under control.

'He never became violent, he never raised a hand to either of us,' Sylvia said. It was almost as if she had suddenly switched sides and was trying to defend her late husband. 'And he was so proud of you, you were the apple of his eye and he had such hopes for you. It was a terrible blow to him when you . . . got into trouble.' Her voice thickened with embarrassment as she uttered the old-fashioned euphemism.

'It was a terrible blow to me when my lover was killed,' Melissa retorted angrily. 'Being chucked out like that was the last straw; I think if Guy's parents hadn't taken me in I'd have killed myself.'

Sylvia gave a little gasp and put her hands over her eyes. 'It was only the knowledge that they were looking after you that kept me going,' she whispered brokenly. 'So many times I was on the point of getting in touch with them to ask after you, but I didn't dare, I never felt able to cross him, even in secret.'

'And you kept it all to yourself?' Sylvia nodded. 'You see,' Melissa went on, 'if there doesn't seem to be anyone with an obvious motive for killing him, the police are bound to start probing, asking your friends and neighbours if they ever saw or heard anything to make them think your relationship wasn't as perfect as it appeared on the surface. You mentioned someone called Lottie Haynes – I got the impression you've confided in her.'

'Just a little. It was one afternoon . . . I met her in town and we went for a cup of tea. I was feeling low; it was your birthday, you see, and I—' Sylvia swallowed hard; her chest heaved and she compressed her mouth to contain the emotion that threatened to engulf her. 'I found myself starting to tell her and then I got scared, made her promise not to tell a living soul or say anything that would let Father know I'd spoken about it to anyone. He's . . . was like that with all our private affairs – they had to stay private.'

'Yes, I remember hearing him say things like "We don't want other people to know our business",' said Melissa wryly. 'He was always very fussy about not leaving correspondence or private papers lying around "for nosey people to poke into", he used to say.'

'He was quite right. Some people can be very inquisitive, you know,' said Sylvia, with a further unexpected hint of loyalty. 'Sometimes he brings . . . brought papers home dealing with company business and naturally he wouldn't want them to be seen by outsiders.'

'Oh goodness, I'd forgotten about the company. Father must have been over seventy – had he retired? Who's in charge now?'

'He hasn't completely retired, he still goes to the office two or three times a week.' It was plain from her lapses into the present tense that Sylvia had not yet fully grasped the fact that she was a widow. 'He says there's no one he can trust to run it the way he wants it run,' she added with a hint of pride.

'Well, someone will have to now. Has anyone been in touch with you?'

'I haven't talked to anyone since it happened . . . except Mrs Menzies, of course. She's been looking after me; she sent everyone away except the vicar. He's been very kind but he says we can't do anything about the funeral yet.'

'That's because the police won't release the body until after the inquest. Have they been to see you again?'

'They came this morning. They kept asking the same questions: did I touch anything, how long had I been home before I found Father, that sort of thing. And then they wrote out what they called a formal statement and asked me to sign it. They took my fingerprints as well. They said something about elimination purposes . . .'

'That's right. It's standard practice, so they can establish if anyone else has been at the scene of the crime besides the people who had a right to be there.'

'Of course, you know all about this sort of thing, don't you? I can tell from your books. They're very clever – I never thought you'd turn out to be a writer,' Sylvia added, with a note of pride in her voice that Melissa found as surprising as it was touching.

'You've read my books?' she exclaimed. 'However did you manage that without Father knowing?'

'Lottie gets them from the library and lends them to me. I read them at her house on the days when he's at work.'

'I think I'd like to meet her.' Rather than cause her mother any anxiety, Melissa refrained from adding, 'and have a chat before the police get to her.' Instead, she asked, 'Does she live near here?'

'Not far, but she's away until Saturday.'

'Today is Saturday.'

'So it is. I must give her a ring and tell her what's happened. Oh, it will be such a relief not to have to live a lie any more! I can tell everyone what a brilliant daughter I have, and maybe get to know my grandson as well one day.'

'You know about Simon?' said Melissa in surprise. 'I remember writing to let you know when he was born, but the letter came back unopened.'

The animation that had momentarily lit up Sylvia's face when she spoke of her hopes for the future died away like a snuffed candle. 'He showed me the letter, but he wouldn't let me open it,' she whispered. 'I only know about your son from what I read about you in the papers . . . and on the covers of your books.'

'Of course you shall meet him. He lives in America but we visit one another quite often. Tell me, before you speak to Lottie, what did you mean by not living a lie any more?'

'Only that I can explain about you, that it wasn't your fault that you had to go away—'

'I don't think that's a very good idea.'

'Why not? I want all our friends to meet you, I want them to know how proud I am of you—'

'That's very sweet of you, and I hope it will be possible before too long, but for the time being you must let them go on believing I'm the heartless daughter who left home of her own accord and never bothered to keep in touch with her devoted parents.'

'But that's terrible! I can't bear for them to think badly of you when it isn't true. Mrs Menzies especially; she's a good woman but she can be very hard, she's said some very unkind things—'

'I can imagine,' Melissa said grimly. 'She was pretty rude to me when we arrived.'

'But now Father's gone, why do I have to—'

'Mother, listen to me.' Melissa took Sylvia's hand and gently stroked it, trying to force to the back of her mind the possibility that barely twenty-four hours earlier it had wielded an axe with deadly intent. 'This is going to be hard for you to take on board, but if you let everyone know what hell you've been through these past thirty years, you're as good as admitting you had a very strong motive for murder.'

Sylvia gasped and put her free hand to her mouth, her eyes stretched wide with terror. 'But I didn't do it!' she wailed. 'Lissie, I swear I didn't do it, please believe me!'

'I've already said I believe you, but I'm not the one who's conducting the murder enquiry. Don't you see, to the police it will seem like a classic example of an abused woman finally losing control? You must have read about similar cases in the paper. There was one only the other week of a woman who stabbed her violent husband while he was lying in a drunken stupor. She'd suffered years of beatings and she just snapped.'

'But it wasn't like that with me!' Sylvia pleaded.

'I'm not saying it was. I'm only trying to make you understand how the police would see it if they knew what you've been through. Please, Mother, just leave things as they are for the time being.'

There was a long silence, broken by a ring at the front

doorbell. Sylvia jumped in alarm as if what Melissa had just hinted at as a possibility had already come to pass. She clutched her daughter's hands, whimpering with fear.

'You must try to keep calm,' Melissa urged her.

'Suppose it's the police come to arrest me?'

'It's probably only a neighbour wanting to ask how you are. I'll go and see.'

'No, don't leave me!'

The bell sounded again and Joe stood up. 'Shall I go?' he offered. He had been sitting so quietly in his chair that the two women had temporarily forgotten his existence.

'Would you?' said Melissa. Her mother seemed not to have heard. Joe went out of the room, closing the door behind him. A few moments later he re-entered behind a tall thin man wearing a dark suit with a clerical collar.

Sylvia scrambled to her feet, looking almost dazed with relief. 'Oh, it's you, Vicar,' she exclaimed. 'How good of you to call!' She turned to her daughter. 'Lissie, this is Mr Simmons, the vicar of St Luke's . . . my daughter, Mrs Craig and her friend Mr Martin.'

With barely a glance at Joe, Mr Simmons inclined his head towards Melissa. She sensed disapproval in his unsmiling manner, an impression that was confirmed when he turned back to Sylvia and said coldly, 'I am glad that your daughter has seen fit to stand by you at this dreadful time.' He cleared his throat before continuing, 'It would seem that I have called at an inopportune moment, but I thought you should know that the inquest on Frank's death will be held on Wednesday.'

'Thank you,' said Sylvia. She had recovered her composure and even managed a smile. 'It's good of you to let me know.'

'Not at all. Will Mrs Craig be able to accompany you?' His tone implied that he would not be surprised to learn that she might find it inconvenient.

'Of course I will. I'll be staying with my mother until this terrible business is cleared up,' Melissa said firmly.

'I'm glad to hear it. Well, that's all I came for, but you know where to find me if you need me, Mrs Ross.'

'Thank you.' Sylvia held out a hand and he took it briefly.

'Goodbye for now, and God bless you. There's no need to see me out.' With a brief nod towards Joe and Melissa, he left the room. In the silence that followed they heard the front door closing quietly behind him.

Barely two minutes passed before the bell rang again. As before, Joe went to answer. This time, it was the police.

Chapter Four

Sylvia's face was ashen as she made the introductions.

'This is Detective Inspector Mollie Adair,' she said shakily. 'And Detective Constable Sharwood, I think — is that right?' Receiving a confirmatory nod, she went on, 'My daughter Mrs Craig and her friend Mr Martin.'

Melissa's reaction on meeting Mollie Adair was, without her realising it, the same as her mother's had been: at first glance the detective appeared far too young to be in such a responsible job. A closer look, however, revealed fine lines round the eyes and mouth and flecks of grey in the neat, glossy black hair. Her manner, too, had a certain gravitas and her voice, clear and resonant with a touch of the local accent, held a note of authority.

Sylvia gestured towards the couch in a mute invitation to the newcomers to sit down. She shot a glance at Melissa, who moved to her side and took her hand, saying,

'I hope this won't take long, Inspector. As you can imagine, my mother is still in a state of severe shock.'

'We appreciate that, but there have been certain developments and we need to ask her a few more questions,' said DI Adair. She turned back to Sylvia and said, 'You probably remember, Mrs Ross, that we took certain items away for forensic examination.' Sylvia nodded. 'You may also recall my asking you, on the day of your husband's murder, whether you touched anything at all between finding his body and sending for us.' Another, barely perceptible nod. The inspector referred to her notes. 'At the time you claimed to be so shaken by your discovery that you had no recollection of your movements or actions during that period.'

Melissa felt the grip on her hand tighten and she quickly interposed, 'Surely, there's nothing remarkable about that, Inspector? Such an unnerving experience would be traumatic for anyone, let alone a woman of my mother's age.'

'Undoubtedly. However, with hindsight, people often recall details which escape them at the time.' Without taking her eyes off Sylvia or altering her tone, Inspector Adair managed to convey the impression that she did not welcome the interruption. 'According to the statement you signed this morning, Mrs Ross,' she went on, 'you are certain, on reflection, that you touched nothing. Is that right?'

'I think so.'

'You only think so? You're still not sure?'

Sylvia shook her head with an air of total bewilderment. 'I told you at the time, I couldn't remember anything at first between seeing him lying there and finding myself ringing Mrs Menzies' doorbell. When I thought about it afterwards, I remembered dropping the cup of tea and screaming. Then I just rushed out of the shed in a panic.'

'Yes, we found the broken cup and remains of the tea on the floor. We also found an axe with traces of blood on it. Neither your original statement, nor the one you made this morning, mentions seeing an axe. Does that mean you didn't notice it?'

'I suppose I couldn't have done.' Sylvia passed her tongue over her lips. 'Is that what was used to kill him?'

'We believe it is, although we have to await the results of further tests before we can be a hundred percent certain. Examination by our scenes of crime officer shows that an attempt was made to wipe away any fingerprints – an attempt that was only partially successful because although the handle was clean an identifiable thumbprint was found at the base of the blade.' There was a pause during which Melissa saw something like panic in her mother's expression. Her own heart seemed to stop as the detective continued, 'It was your thumbprint, Mrs Ross. Can you account for that?'

'I . . .' Sylvia looked despairingly at Melissa and then back at the detective.

'I don't remember . . . I don't understand.'

'I also have to inform you that you were seen by a

neighbour entering your husband's workshop a little after four o'clock, yet according to your statement you did not go out there until five o'clock when you took him his tea. Have you anything to say about that?'

Sylvia looked frantically round the room as if seeking some way of escape. 'There must be some mistake,' she whispered at last.

'We'll just have to establish who's making the mistake, won't we?' said the inspector drily. 'The neighbour said she thought you were wearing a floral dress – is that right?'

'I think so.'

'I seem to recall that when we responded to your 999 call you were wearing a plain coloured dress. Did you change after coming back from shopping?'

'I suppose I must have done. I don't remember.'

'Can you remember what shoes you were wearing?'

'I think so.'

'I'm afraid I must ask you to let me have them for forensic examination. The floral dress as well. Where is it, please?'

'It's . . . do you want me to fetch it?'

'Constable Sharwood will go if you tell her where to find it – and the shoes.'

There was a hunted look on Sylvia's face as she muttered, 'The dress is in the sink in the utility room and the shoes are in the hall.'

The constable left the room and returned moments later with a pair of fawn court shoes in one hand and a plastic washing-up bowl containing a saturated garment in the other. 'It was soaking in cold water,' she announced. 'I've left the water in the sink – it's a pinkish colour, could be blood.'

Inspector Adair's expression hardened. 'You're certain these are the things you wore on Friday, Mrs Ross?' she said.

Sylvia jumped at what for a moment looked like an escape route. 'No, on second thoughts, perhaps I wore a different dress,' she said eagerly.

'You have another floral dress?'

'Not exactly floral—'

'Or one that could be mistaken for a floral dress from a short distance away, perhaps?'

Sylvia gave a deep sigh and bowed her head in an attitude of utter dejection. 'Not really.'

'Bag everything up for the SOCOs to examine, Carole. We'll get one of them to come back for a sample of water from the sink.' Inspector Adair got to her feet. 'Mrs Ross, I'm arresting you on suspicion of the murder of Frank Ross. You do not have to say anything . . .'

Mother and daughter listened in a stunned silence to the formal caution before Sylvia burst out, 'But I didn't do it!' The piteous denial was addressed to her daughter rather than the policewoman.

Melissa's mind was in turmoil; she heard herself saying, 'Try not to worry, I'm sure this can be cleared up quickly,' but her mind was seething with doubt even as she uttered the words.

Sylvia clutched her arm; she was plainly in a state of

terror. 'Will you come with me?' she begged. 'Will you help me to . . . will you stay with me while they ask their questions?'

'Of course I'll come with you, but you're entitled to have your solicitor with you during the interview and to consult him in private beforehand. I think it would be better if you called him right away.'

'I don't have one. At least, there's Mr Bell, the company solicitor, but I hardly know him.'

'The police will arrange for you to consult a duty solicitor—'

'I don't want a stranger, Lissie.' Sylvia's eyes were wide and staring, her voice cracking. Melissa winced as her mother's thin fingers dug into her flesh. 'You know about these things, you can advise me what to say. I'd rather have you with me than anyone. Say you'll come with me, Lissie, I need you!' The plea ended on a thin, high-pitched note that was almost a scream.

'All right, if you're sure that's what you want.' Melissa gently freed herself from the clutching hands and drew Sylvia to her feet. 'Come along, I'll help you get ready.' She turned to Inspector Adair and said, 'I take it there'll be no objection if I act as my mother's adviser?'

'If that's what she wants I've no objection.'

'Are you sure you're okay?'

Joe's voice seemed to come from a long way off. Melissa opened her eyes. They had stopped at traffic lights immediately behind the car containing the detectives and their suspect, who sat in the back seat and from time to time turned her head to cast an anxious glance behind her, as if to reassure herself that her daughter was still there.

Joe repeated his question. Melissa combed back her hair with her fingers and said, 'I just hope I've done the right thing by agreeing to this. Maybe I should have insisted that she got professional advice.'

'She's more likely to confide in you than in a stranger.'

'I know, that's what worries me. I've got this awful feeling that she's keeping something back and the thought of what I might be going to hear scares me rigid.'

Without taking his eyes from the road ahead, Joe reached for her hand. 'This is beastly for you, Mel. I wish I could say something to comfort you.'

'Just having you with me is a comfort. Joe, do you think she did it?'

He gave her hand a gentle squeeze. 'My dear, I simply don't know. I have the same impression as you – that she's hiding something, I mean – but it doesn't necessarily mean she's guilty. There could be another explanation.'

'I hope to God there is. I'll have to try and get her to tell me the whole story before the interview starts.'

'I take it you'll have an opportunity to do that?'

'Oh yes, I'll have the same right to private consultation as a solicitor.'

The lights changed and they moved off. A few minutes later they reached the local police station, a modern building separated from the road by a grassy bank dotted with flower-beds. In the afternoon sunshine it presented a pleasant, almost an attractive, aspect which was totally lost on Melissa. The police car disappeared round a corner and Joe followed a sign indicating the visitors' car park. He pulled into an empty space and switched off the engine.

'Do you want me to come in with you?' he asked.

'I've no idea how long this is going to take. In any case, you won't be allowed in the interview room – you'll just be kept hanging around.'

'So how would it be if I waited out here in the car?'

'If that's all right with you.'

They sat waiting until the detectives reappeared with Sylvia, a small, pathetic figure wrapped in a coat that seemed too big for her, walking between them. A couple of shallow steps led to the station entrance; she stumbled and they each took an arm to guide her through the door.

'See you later,' said Melissa. Before getting out of the car she leaned across and kissed Joe on the cheek. 'Thanks for your support,' she said softly.

She reached the reception desk just as a uniformed sergeant was being briefed by Inspector Adair. Minutes later, Melissa found herself alone with her mother in a small interview room. In the middle was a table topped with grey plastic and a grey plastic chair was placed on either side. The two women sat down facing one another; a uniformed officer put two polystyrene cups of tea in front of them and left without speaking.

The moment the door closed behind her, Melissa

leaned forward and said, 'Mother, I want the truth and I want it now. Did you kill Father?'

Sylvia's mouth fell open. 'Lissie! How could you ask me that after I swore to you that I didn't?' she demanded indignantly. 'I thought you believed me; you said you believed me.'

'I know I did, and I want to believe you, but it's quite obvious you've been lying to the police and I want to know why. What are you hiding?'

Sylvia cast a furtive look towards the door and lowered her voice. 'Do you think they're listening?' she asked fearfully. 'Or perhaps this place is bugged.' Her eyes swept the room as if in search of a hidden microphone.

'You can be sure that this interview is absolutely private,' Melissa said impatiently. 'Look, Mother, I want to help you, but I have to know the truth. Exactly what happened the day Father died?'

'I've told you.'

'It seems you've told me, and the police, a pack of fairy stories so far.' Melissa could feel her self-control under pressure, hear her voice taking on a note that was almost hectoring. With an effort, she controlled her rising anger, forcing herself to speak more gently, telling herself that bullying would get her nowhere. 'Just tell me the exact truth and I'll advise you to the best of my ability,' she said.

'All right. It's very simple, really. I did go out to the shed about ten past four to tell Father I was back. He always wanted to know where I was, what I was doing,' she added with a touch of resentment.

'So what did he say?' prompted Melissa as her mother seemed disinclined to continue. 'Come on, they'll only let us have so much time before starting the interview.'

'He didn't say anything. He was dead.'

Melissa could hardly believe her ears. 'You're saying you found him almost an hour before the time you told the police? Or the time you went round to Mrs Menzies?'

'I had to give myself time to think. You see, I saw the axe on the floor, covered in blood. I picked it up and I . . . Lissie, this is terrible, please don't think badly of me, but for a moment I thought, if I'd had the courage, I would have killed him myself, years ago. I held the axe up above his head, imagining how it would have felt . . .' Sylvia's voice faded to nothing and she buried her face in her hands.

'Stop it!' Melissa almost shouted in horror at the revelation, then lowered her voice for fear of being overheard. 'You mustn't think like that, not for a moment, d'you hear me?' The bowed head nodded. 'Pull yourself together and tell me the rest of it.'

'All right.' Sylvia sat up and drank several mouthfuls of tea, swallowing slowly and deliberately between each one before speaking. When she did, the words came slowly but steadily, with little or no hesitation. 'It was just a moment of madness and when it passed I put the axe down, and then I thought, if the police find my finger-prints on it, and if they ever find out about how things were between Father and me, they'll think straight away that I really did do it. There was some clean rag on the bench and I wiped the handle and put the axe on the floor where I'd found it.'

'And then what?'

'I went back indoors. It may sound strange, but I felt quite calm. I looked at myself in the hall mirror and I saw blood on my face and on my dress and there was some on my shoes as well. I washed my face, wiped the shoes, changed into a clean dress and put the soiled one to soak in cold water. I was going to wash it in the machine with some other clothes, but time was getting on and I thought, I'd better take tea out at five o'clock and then I can make out that's when I found him. I meant to see to the washing later, but of course, once Mrs Menzies took charge, she was with me all the time and I thought she might find it odd if I . . .' Without warning her temporary composure collapsed and she clawed at Melissa's hands, her eyes streaming and her mouth working. 'Lissie, I'm telling the truth. Say you believe me, please!'

'Yes, Mother, I believe you.' Melissa's brain felt numb; she gave the assurance mechanically.

'What do I say to the police?'

Melissa closed her eyes and tried to think clearly, but she felt totally out of her depth. 'I wish you'd agree to talk to a solicitor—' she began, but her mother interrupted with a desperate, almost hysterical cry of 'No!'

'Then I think you'd better tell them the truth about what actually happened, only for God's sake don't say anything about waving the axe around or having murderous thoughts, just say you picked it up without thinking

and then panicked when you remembered about finger-
prints. And whatever you do, don't let on about how
things really were between you and Father — or between
Father and me. Do you understand?'

'Yes, I understand.'

'Shall I tell them we're ready?'

'I suppose so.'

'You haven't finished your tea.'

'It's got cold, I don't want it.' Sylvia pushed the cup
away. She grasped the edge of the table and stood up,
swayed and sat down again. 'I don't feel very well,' she
mumbled. Melissa was just in time to catch her as she
toppled unconscious from her chair.

Chapter Five

Rather than wait in the reception area, where two warring neighbours who had been arrested for breaches of the peace were continuing to exchange insults despite the desk sergeant's repeated commands to 'Shut it!', Melissa slipped out and rejoined Joe in the car. 'She passed out and they sent for a doctor,' she told him. 'He's with her now and he's sent for an ambulance; he's talking about keeping her in hospital overnight for observation. She's still under arrest of course so a police officer will have to go with her.'

'Has she come round or is she still unconscious?'

'She was only out for a few seconds, but she's still pretty woozy.'

'That's understandable. I doubt if the reality has completely sunk in yet. I noticed she kept using the present tense when speaking of your father, as if she hadn't grasped the fact that he's gone.'

'She's grasped it now all right. She suddenly took hold of my hand and said, "Lissie, you'll find out who did it, won't you?" Fortunately, the doctor arrived at that moment so I didn't have to reply, but you can see how her mind's working, can't you?'

'Of course. You've written a string of highly successful detective stories and even helped to clear up one or two real-life mysteries. It must seem a perfectly logical request from her point of view.'

'I suppose so. Joe, I can hardly believe what she's been telling me. She admits handling the axe and says she'd have done it herself if she'd had the courage and she held it up over his body because she wanted to know how it might have felt.'

'Good heavens!' Joe exclaimed. 'I hope she's not going to admit that to the police.'

'I've warned her not to, but she's in such a fragile emotional state that I'm terrified she'll blurt it out under questioning.'

'Well, let's hope they do keep her in hospital overnight. With any luck she'll be calmer by morning.'

'God, I hope so. I'll have to try and have another go at her before the interview.' Melissa sat back in her seat with a sigh of utter weariness. 'I can't bring myself to think about it for the moment.'

'What happens now?'

'I said we'd follow the ambulance to the hospital – if that's all right with you?'

'No problem.'

'I'll see her settled in and get the initial report. After that, I don't know . . . I just don't know.' Very close to tears, she covered her eyes with her hands. He put an arm round her, drawing her close. Thankfully, she leaned against his shoulder, fighting the hard ball of emotion that threatened to explode in her chest. 'Joe,' she said when she had succeeded in bringing it under some kind of control, 'what should I do?'

'You want my advice?'

'More than I've ever wanted it in my life.' She inhaled deeply in an effort to calm herself, drawing comfort from his strength, the warm texture of his tweed jacket, the clean tang of his breath. 'It's all been too much; I feel as if I'm being dragged down in a maelstrom.'

Very gently he smoothed her tousled hair back from her forehead. His fingers were cool and dry, his touch inexpressibly comforting. 'Let's start by being practical,' he said. 'I know you were planning to stay at the house with your mother, but I assume that's out of the question now.'

'Even if the police were to allow it, that's the last place I'd want to be.'

'So why, once she's settled at the hospital, don't we find a hotel with a bar and a decent restaurant? You'll feel better when you've had a drink, something to eat and a night's rest. We can discuss what to do next in the morning.'

She raised her head and looked at him in surprise. 'We? I thought you said you were planning to spend tomorrow with Paul.'

'Only nine holes and lunch at the club.' Golf was one of several interests Joe shared with his twenty-four-year-old son. 'I spoke to him on my mobile and explained the situation while you were in the nick. You don't seriously imagine I'd leave you to cope with this lot on your own, do you?'

This time the emotion spilled over unchecked and she cried on his shoulder for several minutes while the hand gently stroking her brow sent a mute assurance of un-failing love and support. When she was calmer she sat up and dried her eyes, just as an ambulance drew up in the forecourt. One of the crew, a tall blonde young woman in a green track suit with 'Paramedic' embroidered in yellow across the chest, jumped out and hurried up the steps into the building while her similarly clad colleague opened the rear doors, lowered a hoist and brought out a wheelchair before following. A few minutes later they reappeared with a white-faced Sylvia, wrapped in a blanket, walking unsteadily between them. They guided her to the chair where she sat with her eyes closed while they manoeuvred it on to the hoist.

As Joe started the engine in readiness, Melissa jumped out of the car, ran across to her mother and took her hand, ignoring DC Sharwood who was standing by. 'I'll see you in the hospital,' she said. 'Joe and I will be following in the car.'

Sylvia's eyelids fluttered open for a second. 'You won't forget?' Her breath came in short, shallow bursts and the words were so faint that Melissa had to lean close to her mouth to catch them. 'Find out who did it, Lissie . . . promise me.'

'I will, of course I will.' With DC Sharwood steadying the wheelchair the hoist was raised, the doors were closed and the ambulance drove off. Melissa stood for a few seconds and watched it go before hurrying back to the car, wondering how in the world she was going to set about keeping her promise.

'She's had some kind of shock?'

'You could say that. Yesterday she found my father's body and an hour or so ago she was arrested for his murder.'

'I see.' The young doctor's expression hardly changed and Melissa had the impression that in his experience murder and mayhem were nothing out of the ordinary and that it would have taken something far more dramatic to shake his composure. 'Well, Mrs Craig,' he said, 'so far as I can establish from a preliminary examination, there's nothing physically wrong with your mother that a mild sedative and a good night's rest won't put right. She's asleep now and she'll be kept under observation till the morning. I'll come and see her again then.' He gave Melissa a keen look. 'You look pretty shattered yourself. Do you live near here or would you like to stay in the hospital overnight? We have facilities for accommodating close relatives.'

'That's very kind of you, but I have a friend with me.

He's talking about finding a hotel – can you recommend one?'

'The Beverley Court is within walking distance and I'm told it's quite comfortable; someone on reception will direct you. Let the ward sister know where to find you, just in case. Don't worry,' he said in response to Melissa's anxious glance, 'I'm sure she'll be fine in the morning. You take care of yourself now, have something to eat and try to get some sleep. A brandy at bedtime works wonders!' he added with a twinkle.

To her surprise, she found herself returning the smile. 'Thank you, that sounds like good advice,' she said.

He stood up and glanced at his watch. 'Now, if you'll excuse me, I have another patient to see.'

Melissa rejoined Joe in the waiting-room where she had left him and sank wearily into the chair next to his.

'Well, that's your main worry off your mind,' he said briskly when she had relayed the doctor's report. 'Let's go and find that hotel.'

'What about you? What are you going to do? I mean, you didn't come prepared for an overnight stay . . .' Melissa was aware of an unexpected wave of embarrassment at the way the situation was developing. She had been holding Joe at arm's length for so long that it had become almost a ritual. Ever since the day he agreed to act as her agent their friendship had steadily grown and ripened, but when his marriage ended and he made her aware of his true feelings towards her, she had instinctively shied away. In any event, at the time she had still been involved with Aubrey, although already beginning to chafe at his over-protective ways. Without allowing herself to consider what her own sentiments might be, she had used light-hearted teasing as a form of defence. Admittedly, their relationship had subtly altered since the parting with Ken Harris, yet she was still wary of allowing it to develop in the way he so obviously wanted.

Overnight, the scenario had changed for ever; her life had been thrown into confusion with a violence that left her struggling against a tide of conflicting emotions which had thrown up one inescapable, uncompromising truth: her feeling for Joe was stronger than she had ever realised, although even now she was not quite ready to admit that it was love. She knew that his commitment to her was total; he had dropped everything, sacrificed time with his son, to be with her at this time of crisis. She found herself imagining how it would be to share his bed through the coming night, then pushed the thought away. This was hardly the time; to yield to him now would seem like gratitude and he deserved better than that.

As if reading her thoughts, he said quietly, 'Never mind me, the important thing is to get you settled. If the Beverley can't fix us up with a couple of acceptable rooms, we'll find a hotel that can.' He stood up, took her arm and drew her to her feet. 'It's only a step away so we might as well walk; it'll do us both good to stretch our legs. We can come back for the car once we're booked in.'

'Whatever you say.'

The Beverley Court turned out to be a large, attractively converted Edwardian house where they were offered two prettily furnished rooms overlooking a large garden. 'Hard to believe we're only half a mile from the town centre, isn't it?' the porter commented as he put down Melissa's case and handed her the key. 'It's nice and quiet too – we're just far enough away from the main road not to be bothered by the traffic.'

'That's good news,' said Joe.

'Right sir, that's the lady settled. Your room's next door.'

'See you later,' said Joe and the two men withdrew. Left alone, Melissa wandered over to the window and looked out. A wide expanse of lawn with an ornamental pond in the middle was surrounded by beds of flowering bulbs that made glowing pools of light among the patches of dappled shade cast by a protective ring of trees. Immediately below, relaxing in cushioned garden chairs on a flagged patio, some of the hotel guests were taking advantage of the mild evening to enjoy a pre-dinner drink in the late April sunshine. Three couples – two apparently in their twenties, their companions middle-aged – were laughing at the antics of a group of toddlers chasing one another round the pond. Grandparents enjoying the company of their children and grandchildren, no doubt. A stab of pain at the thought of what might have been made her turn sadly away.

Presently, refreshed after a bath, she went down to the bar where she found Joe seated at a table in one corner, a half-full tankard in front of him and a menu in his hand. He stood up and pulled out a chair for her.

'What will you have to drink?' he asked.

'A gin and tonic, please.'

He went to the bar, ordered the drink, signed for it and brought it to the table. He sat down, raised his own glass and said gravely, 'Here's to a happy outcome of a dire situation.'

'I'll certainly drink to that.'

'This menu doesn't seem at all bad.' He handed it over and said, 'You look better.'

'I feel better. It's wonderful what a good long soak can do.' She studied him for a moment and then said, 'You've changed your shirt. You never told me you brought an overnight bag with you.'

He shook his head. 'I didn't. The hospital shop is remarkably well stocked.' He passed a hand over his chin. 'They even had my regular brand of shaving cream.'

'That was a bit of luck.'

Every line of his face was familiar yet somehow his eyes, clear and deep-set beneath strong brows, his clean-cut features under neatly trimmed brown hair and the whiteness of his teeth when he smiled, struck her in a new light. It was almost as if she were seeing him for the first time. Something in the way he looked back at her hinted that he felt the same. It was a moment to cherish, to store in the memory.

One day, when all this was over, they would share

it openly. Meanwhile, there was her promise to her mother, rashly given, extracted under emotional duress, but a promise none the less. She would do her best to keep it.

Chapter Six

They sat studying the breakfast menu and Joe said, 'What are you going to have?'

'I'm almost ashamed to say this after last night's dinner, but I think I'm going to go for the full English,' Melissa replied.

'I'll have the same,' said Joe. He gave their order to a waitress hovering close by.

'Tea or coffee?' They both opted for coffee. 'Brown or white toast?' They both chose brown. 'Help yourselves to juice and cereals from the buffet,' the woman said and withdrew to the kitchen.

As they returned to their table with glasses of fruit juice and bowls of cornflakes, Joe remarked, 'It was a good dinner, wasn't it?' He glanced round and added, 'This is an attractive dining-room, don't you think?'

'Very pretty,' she agreed.

They sat down again and he asked, 'What sort of a night did you have?'

'Not bad, considering. How about you?'

'It took me a while to drop off, but once I did I slept soundly enough.'

They fell silent, handing one another milk and sugar, eating their cornflakes, sipping their juice. Melissa was conscious of an atmosphere of restraint that seemed to be affecting them both. She had become aware of it the previous evening. They had been so relaxed at first, so comfortable in one another's company. She had been grateful to Joe for taking the lead, deliberately steering their talk away from the events of the day and focusing instead on her new book and her ideas, still in the embryonic stage, for the next. After dinner they had taken a short stroll, avoiding by unspoken consent the path leading to the hospital; on returning to the hotel they went to the bar where, following the advice of the hospital doctor, Melissa had a glass of brandy as a nightcap. It was only then that conversation dried up, as if they both recognised that the sensation of well-being was a sham, a protective fence they had been hiding behind. It was a relief when, seeing her stifle a yawn, Joe had suggested they turn in, saying, 'We'll discuss our next move in the morning.'

At her door, he had taken both her hands in his, kissed her on the cheek, murmured, 'Goodnight, my dear. I hope you sleep well,' and turned away — but not quickly enough to hide the look of longing in his eyes. For a split second she had been on the point of calling him back, but at that moment a group of other guests had appeared on the landing, chatting, laughing and exchanging goodnights. By the time they dispersed Joe had entered his own room and closed the door behind him.

She brought her mind back to the present and signalled her readiness to face the inevitable by saying, 'I crashed out almost immediately, but I've been awake since before six, trying to decide what to do next.'

'Any conclusions?'

'Oh yes, I've made up my mind to do a bit of ferreting around. After all, I did promise to try and find out who really killed my father.'

'Do I take it that you believe your mother's version of what happened?'

Melissa put down her spoon and finished her juice before saying slowly, 'I wish I knew. My memories of her are all of someone kind and gentle who wouldn't hurt a fly, but when I think of the emotional pressure she must have been under for all this time . . .'

'Enough to drive anyone to murder, is that what you're saying?'

'It wouldn't be the first case of its kind.'

They were interrupted by the waitress arriving with a jug of coffee. Melissa filled two cups and passed one across to Joe. She drank hers black; he tipped milk and sugar into his and stirred it thoughtfully before saying. 'Whether you believe she did it or not, I can understand your not wanting to leave things as they are.' His mouth twitched in a mischievous smile as he added, 'Anyway, it'll do you good to go round rattling a few cages – better than sitting at home brooding.'

She smiled back and said, 'It won't endear me to DI Adair.' It was good to begin fixing her mind on practical things. 'I'm glad you feel that way, though. I was almost afraid you'd advise me to let things take their course.'

'Even if I had, you wouldn't have done anything of the kind.'

'How well you know me!' The tension was slipping away and she felt herself unwinding. 'My, that looks good!' she added as the waitress deposited two well-filled plates in front of them. They ate in silence for several minutes before Joe said, 'So whose cage do you propose to rattle first?'

'The obvious person to start with is the company solicitor, Mr Bell – there'll be all sorts of business matters to see to – but as today's Sunday that will have to wait till tomorrow. Incidentally, I've made up my mind about one thing: whether she likes it or not, Mother will have to agree to taking proper legal advice. I'm simply not competent to handle the responsibility, and in any case I'll be too busy running around sleuthing on her behalf.'

'That makes sense. So, have you any plans for today?'

'I thought I'd try and contact Lottie Haynes. It seems to me that she probably knows Mother better than any of her other acquaintances.'

'Good thinking.'

They finished their breakfast and Joe said, 'I guess

you'll want to find out how things are at the hospital before you do anything else.'

'Yes, of course. I imagine that as soon as she's discharged, she'll be taken back to the police station. I'll phone the ward sister right away to find out what's going on.'

'What would you like me to do about the rooms? Shall I book for another night?'

'It might be an idea.'

'See you in reception, then.'

It was all so matter-of-fact, they might have been discussing some everyday situation that touched neither of them personally. Something was missing; it was like the occasional interval during a howling gale, as if it were holding its breath while preparing for the next onslaught. Any moment now the wind, metaphorically speaking, would rise again to buffet her senses; the feeling of detachment was nothing but a lull in the storm.

She made her call, put on her coat, checked her handbag and prepared to go downstairs. As she closed her room door behind her, the enormity of the task she had undertaken hit her with the force of a typhoon.

'I need my head examined!' she muttered to herself as she descended the carpeted staircase to the entrance hall, where Joe was waiting for her.

'They say she had a comfortable night and ate a good breakfast,' Melissa reported as they walked to the hotel car park. 'The doctor is going to see her shortly and Sister thinks he'll probably discharge her. She didn't actually say, "into police custody"; I got the feeling she was going to but checked herself at the last minute to spare my feelings.'

'It's the only thing they can do, isn't it?' said Joe.

'I suppose so. I just hate the thought of her having to spend a night in the cells.'

'Maybe it won't come to that. From what you've told me, the evidence against her is purely circumstantial and the explanation she gave you seems quite feasible.'

'I'm sure it is, provided she sticks to the facts and doesn't reveal the way she felt towards my father.'

The sister greeted Melissa with a pleasant smile and led her to a side ward where her mother sat, fully dressed, on the edge of the bed. There was a faint but healthy tinge in her cheeks and her expression was intelligent and alert.

'Good morning, dear, how lovely to see you!' she said, lifting her face for a kiss. 'The doctor says I can go home, but I'm afraid I have to go back to that horrid police station first. They're sending a car for us. I've been telling the officer' — she cast a glance to a corner of the room where a weary faced DC Sharwood was slumped in an uncomfortable-looking armchair with plastic upholstery and wooden arms — 'that it's all a terrible mistake and I'm sure it can be cleared up quickly. She's worn out, poor thing; she had to spend the night there, watching to make sure I didn't get up and run away!'

For a moment, Melissa could only gape in astonishment at the extraordinary change in her mother's demeanour.

Then she sat down beside her and said, 'It's wonderful to see you looking so much better.'

'Oh, I'm fine now. I'm sorry to have been such a nuisance. What about you, Lissie? Where did you spend the night?'

'Joe booked a couple of rooms in a hotel quite near the hospital.'

'Joe? Oh yes, that nice gentleman who came with you; your agent, did you say?'

'My agent, and a very dear friend.'

This is unbelievable, Melissa thought. *Here she is, waiting to be hauled back to the police station to be questioned about her husband's murder, and yet she can chat away to her long-lost daughter as if she hasn't a care in the world.* Aloud she said, 'Mother, we have to talk.' She glanced at the bleary-eyed young detective in the corner and said, 'Would you mind leaving us alone for a few minutes?'

Looking relieved at the opportunity to move, DC Sharwood stood up, flexed her shoulders and said, 'No problem. I'll wait outside.'

As soon as the door closed behind her, Melissa said, 'Before we go any further, there's something I want you to do for me.'

'Yes, dear?'

'I want you to agree to be represented by a solicitor.'

'But why?'

'Because I'm afraid I might not be able to give you the best advice – I'm simply not qualified. And in any case, I'm going to be busy running around trying to find

Father's killer. You made me promise, remember? I can't be in two places at once.'

'Yes of course, I quite understand.'

'So you'll do as I ask? As soon as you get back to the police station, you must refuse to answer any questions until you've spoken to a duty solicitor. And by the way—' Melissa cast a glance towards the door; through a glass panel she could see DC Sharwood's back a few inches away. She lowered her voice to a whisper, put her lips close to her mother's ear and said, 'Don't say a word to anyone, anyone at all, do you hear me, about having had murderous thoughts towards Father.'

Sylvia's expression as she looked her daughter straight in the eye was one of total bewilderment. 'Murderous thoughts . . . towards Father?' she exclaimed. 'Whatever are you talking about, dear?'

'Don't you remember telling me that when you discovered his body you picked up the axe and held it over him, wondering how it would have felt—'

'Lissie! Have you been having nightmares?' Sylvia stroked the back of Melissa's hand as if to comfort her. 'Poor girl, all this must have been so upsetting for you.'

'Mother, you distinctly said you'd often wished you'd had the courage to kill him.'

'I'm quite sure I never said anything of the kind,' said Sylvia in a voice of shocked horror. 'I can't think what put the idea into your head.'

'Are you telling me you didn't pick up the axe?'

'Of course I didn't.'

'So how do you account for your thumbprint on the blade?'

'Well, for goodness' sake, it was our axe, wasn't it? I must have handled it lots of times, tidying up after Father had been chopping wood for the fire.'

'And it wasn't you who wiped the prints off the handle?'

'Of course not – it must have been Father's killer. I suppose he never thought to wipe the blade as well.'

'What about the blood on your dress and shoes?'

'When I saw Father lying there I thought he'd fallen asleep and I put my hand on his shoulder to wake him, and then I felt something sticky on my hand and I realised it was blood. There was blood on the floor as well and I'd trodden in it. It was terrible.' Sylvia looked at Melissa with a piteous, pleading look on her face. 'I could see at once that he was dead.'

'And you went back indoors, changed your dress and put the bloody one in to soak, and cleaned your shoes – and then waited until five o'clock before going out there again to "discover" the body?'

'I was in shock, dear, don't you understand? I must have done all that mechanically, in a kind of dream. Perhaps I was telling myself that when I went back to the shed I'd find Father was perfectly all right, that I'd had some sort of nightmare.'

'And this is what you're going to tell the police?' By this time thoroughly bemused, Melissa could only stare at her mother in blank amazement.

'Of course. It's the truth.' Sylvia's eyes as she met Melissa's were as clear and guileless as a child's.

'But you will insist on seeing a solicitor, won't you?'

'Yes, dear. I just promised, didn't I?'

There was a tap on the door. DC Sharwood popped her head inside and said, 'The car's here to take us to the station, Mrs Ross.'

Sylvia stood up. 'I'm ready,' she announced. 'The sooner we get this stupid mistake cleared up, the better.' She directed a fond glance in Melissa's direction and said proudly, 'My daughter knows all about detective work – she's going to help you find the real killer.'

Joe was waiting for Melissa in the hospital car park. She climbed in beside him and said, pointing to the police car waiting at the main entrance, 'They're taking her back to the station now.'

'We'd better follow, then.'

As he started the engine and drove slowly forward, she said, 'You'll never guess what she's been saying this morning – I simply couldn't believe my ears!'

He listened in silence while she told him of Sylvia's extraordinary volte-face, then asked, 'So what do you think really happened?'

'I think what she told me before passing out was probably the nearest we're going to get to the truth. I suspect that at some time during the night – or maybe this morning, when she woke up after a good long sleep and was able to think more clearly — she just decided, consciously or unconsciously, to shut her mind to it. I found her completely calm and rational, but there was a hint of "that's my story and I'm sticking to it" about her manner that makes me think she's deliberately concocted what she believes is the most credible version of events.'

'You reckon the redoubtable DI Adair will go for it?'

'We can only wait and see. I wish Mother hadn't blurted out all that rubbish about my helping the police, though. You should have seen the patronising look that young detective gave me. You can imagine the DI's reaction, can't you?'

'She should be very relieved to learn that Mel Craig is on the case!' said Joe with a chuckle. Back in the car park at the police station, he said, 'Would you like me to come in with you?'

'Please, but I've no idea how long I'll be.'

'My time is yours,' he said with an exaggerated air of gallantry that broke the tension.

'Assuming they let me talk to her again before she sees the duty solicitor, I'll ask her for Lottie Haynes's address. I've got a hunch she might be able to give me a lead or two.'

Chapter Seven

When Melissa rejoined Joe in the reception area at the police station she found him listening sympathetically to a sad-faced woman explaining that she was waiting for news of her teenage son, who had been arrested for attempted burglary during the night. 'It's only since his Dad walked out that he's been in trouble; he got in with the wrong crowd and started taking drugs,' she confided with a despairing shake of the head.

'Poor thing, I can imagine how she feels,' Melissa said as they made their way back to the car. 'Several of Simon's friends at university were on drugs and I lost a lot of sleep worrying that he might get involved. Thank God, he had more sense, but it can happen to anyone.'

'Yes, I know,' he agreed. 'Georgina and I had the same concerns about Paul.'

It was the first time in a long while that he had mentioned his ex-wife. Disconcerted by a totally unexpected stab of jealousy, Melissa quickly changed the subject. 'Mother's asked to see the duty solicitor, which could mean a longish wait while they get hold of one,' she told him. 'Meanwhile she wants some clean clothes so I'd like to go back to the house to collect a few things for her.'

'No problem. Do you have a key?'

'Oh yes.' She held up the small bunch the custody sergeant had handed over. 'The scenes of crime examiners have finished at the house. Father's workshop is still out of bounds, but otherwise we're free to come and go as we please.'

'Did your mother give you Lottie Haynes's address?'

'I said I'd need to talk to a few people and asked for her address book. She told me where to find it; I didn't mention Lottie's name in case someone overheard and reported to DI Adair.'

Joe gave a knowing grin as he unlocked the car and held the door open for her. 'Making sure you keep ahead of the pack!' he said slyly.

The teasing words had the stimulating effect of a rush of adrenalin. For the past twenty-four hours her emotions had been subjected to such a battering that she had been planning her strategy with a kind of detached logic which suddenly gave way to an eagerness to embark on the task she had so reluctantly undertaken. Almost cheerfully she replied, 'You could say that.'

He settled in the driver's seat, clipped on his seat belt and started the engine. 'Right. Let's go.'

It felt strange, letting herself into the house where her

parents had lived for so many years but which had never been her home. Leaving Joe in the hall, Melissa went upstairs on her own. Feeling almost an intruder, she moved slowly from room to room, every so often pausing to touch a piece of furniture, an ornament or a picture that she had known all her life, trying to visualise them in the settings that she remembered from long ago. Her mother had explained the layout of the house and told her where to look for the things she wanted in the room she had unthinkingly referred to as 'our bedroom'. Instinctively, Melissa left that errand until last.

When she was a child her parents' room had been forbidden territory unless she had express permission to enter. Today, even though she was there on her mother's behalf, she experienced a sense of guilt as she pushed open the door, as if afraid of being challenged by the stern voice of her father and scolded for disobedience. Everything looked uncannily familiar: the big double bed covered with an old-fashioned counterpane and matching eider-down; the walnut suite, arranged almost exactly as it had been in the other house; the tallboy with her father's brushes placed carefully at right angles; the double-fronted wardrobe against one wall and the dressing-table with its triple mirror under the window. Her heart was thumping uncontrollably as she opened drawers and snatched out items at random, unwilling to remain there a second longer than necessary.

The scent of coffee greeted her as she hurried down-stairs. Joe was in the kitchen, rinsing out a bottle at the sink. 'I thought you could do with some elevenses,' he explained.

'What a lovely thought!' she said gratefully.

'We'll have to drink it black, I'm afraid – the milk's gone off.' He turned and caught sight of her face. 'Are you all right, Mel?' he asked in concern. 'You're as white as a sheet.'

'I'm fine, really. It was just a bit traumatic, being in their bedroom; it was almost as if Father's ghost was there watching me.'

'Here, drink this.' He filled two mugs from a cafetière and put them on the table.

'In a moment. I'll have to find something to put these in. Ah, this will do.' While speaking she had been rummaging in an old shopping bag full of plastic carrier bags hanging on a hook. She pulled one out and stuffed the items of clothing inside before sitting down and picking up one of the mugs, thankful to realise that her pulse rate was returning to normal. It leapt again at the sound of an imperious ring at the front doorbell.

'I'll go.' Joe put down his own coffee and got quickly to his feet, but even before he left the room the bell sounded again. 'I'll bet it's Mrs Menzies,' he predicted.

His guess was correct. His polite 'Good morning' as he opened the front door was brushed aside by a sharp, penetrating voice asking for Mrs Ross and demanding to know what was going on. The next moment Mrs Menzies marched without ceremony into the kitchen with Joe, trying to explain that Mrs Ross was 'not here just at present', trailing in her wake. She took in the cafetière and the steaming mugs in one sweeping, contemptuous glance and sniffed, 'I see you're making yourselves well at home.'

'Can we offer you some coffee?' said Joe. 'I'm afraid there's no milk—'

'No thank you. I was just getting ready for church when I noticed your car. I saw Mrs Ross driving off with those two detectives yesterday and she never came home. I phoned last night and again this morning but there was no reply.' The look she directed at Melissa held a hint of a challenge and her voice was heavily laced with sarcasm as she said, 'Is it too much to ask to be told what's happened to her?'

Melissa managed to control her resentment at the woman's hectoring manner, recognising the genuine concern that lay behind it. 'The police wanted to ask my mother some further questions—' she began, but was quickly interrupted.

'Hasn't she already answered enough questions? Where were they taking her?'

'To the police station. Joe — Mr Martin — and I went with her. Unfortunately she collapsed soon after we arrived and she spent the night under observation in hospital.'

Mrs Menzies drew a quick breath at the word 'collapsed' and her manner was noticeably less aggressive as she said urgently, 'Is she all right? Is she still in hospital?'

'She's fine now,' Melissa assured her. 'She was discharged an hour ago and taken back to the police station.

Mrs Menzies, I know you're a very good friend to my mother, and at the moment she's badly in need of her friends.' She hesitated for a moment before saying. 'The fact is, the police suspect her of having killed my father.'

'What rubbish!' Mrs Menzies gave an indignant snort. 'Why on earth should she kill such a wonderful man, a devoted husband? That Adair woman must be out of her mind.' She glared at Melissa with something of her original hostility. 'You must do something about it, do you hear me? Find out who really did it. It's obvious you know a lot about detective work or you couldn't write about it the way you—' As if aware that she had betrayed a closer acquaintance with Melissa's 'nasty books' than she would care to admit, she broke off in confusion, a tinge of dull red creeping into her sallow complexion.

Joe cleared his throat, picked up the cafetière and took it over to the sink where he made a great play of rinsing it out. Sharing his barely concealed glee at the involuntary lapse, but making a superhuman effort to conceal the fact that she had even noticed it, Melissa said quietly, 'It so happens that my mother has asked me to do just that. It would be nice to think that I could count on your help.'

'Of course. I'll do anything I can — anything.'

'That's good to hear. First of all, we have to go back to the police station to take some things she's asked for. We'll be leaving in a minute; would you like me to give her a message from you?'

'Just give her my love,' said Mrs Menzies gruffly. It was

plain that she was genuinely moved by her neighbour's awful predicament. 'Tell her I believe in her innocence.'

'I'm sure she'll be comforted to hear that. I plan to visit a friend of hers later on, a lady called Lottie Haynes. I believe she lives nearby; do you know her?'

'Mrs Haynes? Only slightly. Your mother has often mentioned her though; they used to belong to the same flower club.'

'I understand Mother resigned from the club. Have you any idea why?'

'She said Frank thought it was a waste of time. He said she knew more about flower arranging than all the others put together.'

'Why would he say that? How would he have known?'

'It was after the club organised a flower festival at the church a few months ago. As churchwarden he was naturally involved with all the arrangements and I remember having a feeling he wasn't all that impressed with what they did. Of course he was a man with very high standards, a perfectionist, you could say.'

'I see. Well, that's something to think about. Perhaps Mrs Haynes will be able to fill in a few more details.'

'She might be, I suppose,' Mrs Menzies agreed, a trifle grudgingly. 'Well, I must be off — it's almost time for church.' A look of dismay clouded her stern features. 'People will be asking about your mother — what should I tell them?'

Melissa thought for a moment. 'I suppose you might as well tell them the truth,' she said resignedly. 'Or speak to the vicar and ask him to mention it to anyone he thinks ought to know. Anyway, the news will soon get around, once the press get hold of it.'

Mrs Menzies shuddered at the word 'press', then said, with a touch of her earlier sarcasm, 'I imagine you'll know how to deal with them, with all your experience. What puzzles me,' she went on accusingly, 'is why you should have cut yourself off for all this time from such wonderful parents.'

'One day, perhaps, you'll learn the full story,' said Melissa quietly.

On the way back to the police station, Melissa said, 'I wish I knew the real reason behind Father's insistence on Mother's packing up the flower club.'

'You don't accept Mrs Menzies' explanation?'

'Oh, I'm sure that's what Mother told her and she obviously believes it, but you heard what Mother said to me – he never gave a reason. Even if she'd told me the same tale she told Mrs Menzies I'd have had my doubts because it was never Father's style to be lavish in his praise.' Melissa's mind travelled back across the years. 'Even when I brought home a really good school report, the most he would say was something like, "Yes, not bad. Try and do even better next term."'

'You think he gave your mother a different reason that she doesn't want anyone – even you – to know about?'

'Or he had a different reason that *he* didn't want *her* to know about.'

'Would it have anything to do with money? The high price of flowers, or the cost of the subscription?'

'I hardly think so. He was careful with money, but I never thought of him as mean. In any case, I've always been under the impression that Mother had some money of her own. No, I've a hunch there's something else behind it.'

They had reached the station. Joe parked the car and switched off the engine before saying, 'You surely don't imagine it's got anything to do with his death, do you?'

'Probably not, but it might be interesting to find out what Lottie Haynes thinks about it. I'd like to have a chat with some of the other members of the flower club as well.'

'I take it you found the address book?'

'In here.' Melissa patted her handbag.

'Then we'll go and pay Lottie a visit as soon as we've finished here.'

Chapter Eight

'Hallo. Am I speaking to Miss Haynes?'

'This is Lottie Haynes, yes; who's calling, please?'

'My name's Melissa Craig. I'm Sylvia Ross's daughter.'

'Oh?' The rising intonation conveyed consternation rather than surprise. 'Is something wrong? Is your mother ill?'

'Not ill, but she's in a serious state of shock. Something dreadful has happened; my father is dead.'

'Oh, my goodness! I'll come round to see her straight away.'

'No, wait; there are ... complications. She isn't at home just at present. Would it be convenient if I came to see you?'

'What do you mean by complications?' A hint of suspicion crept into Lottie's soft, slightly husky voice. 'What happened – has there been an accident?'

'No, it wasn't an accident.'

'Then what——?'

'Miss Haynes, if you don't mind I'd rather not go into details on the phone. If you could just spare us half an hour, there's something important I'd like to ask you.'

'You have someone with you?'

'My agent, Mr Martin. He drove me up from Gloucestershire yesterday, as soon as I got the news. Look, if you're unhappy about having strangers call at your house, we'll be happy to meet you somewhere else. We're staying at the Beverley Court, we could——'

'No, no, that's quite all right. You took me by surprise, that's all. Yes, by all means come round; do you know how to find the house?'

'Not exactly. Perhaps you could give me directions.'

Lottie's directions were clear and precise. Ten minutes later Joe pulled up outside a detached, whitewashed cottage with a slate roof tucked away at the end of a cul-de-sac. Set back from the road in a compact, beautifully tended garden enclosed by a variety of shrubs and flowering trees, it looked at least a hundred years older than its neighbours, all of which had the aggressively modern appearance of recently constructed dwellings that have not yet mellowed and whose gardens have still to mature.

'It looks like what the Americans call a "hold-out",' commented Joe as he unlatched the white-painted wicket gate and stood aside for Melissa to enter. 'The site on its own must be worth a fortune.'

Melissa shrugged. 'Maybe the developers couldn't get planning consent – the cottage is probably listed.'

'I wonder what was on the rest of the land before the other houses were built? Maybe Lottie can tell us.'

'I'm more interested in what she has to tell us about Mother.'

The front door was opened almost as soon as Melissa touched the bell, revealing a slender woman whom she guessed to be in her mid sixties. She had finely chiselled features, glossy white hair falling straight from a centre parting into a soft, page-boy roll just below her ears, clear blue-green eyes and a firm skin innocent of make-up. She was wearing a hip-length light-grey tunic over a black ankle-length skirt, a long silver chain round her neck and silver ornaments dangling from her wrists and ears.

'Mrs Craig . . . Mr Martin? Please come in.' She sounded a trifle breathless and her expression was anxious as she stood aside to admit them. 'I'm afraid the place is a bit untidy,' she apologised as she closed the door behind them before leading the way along a narrow, wood-panelled hall to a small, cluttered room at the back of the house. 'I only got back from my holiday yesterday and I haven't finished unpacking,' she went on as she swept a heap of books, a bulging canvas airline bag and a travel rug from a couch and dumped them on the floor. Her movements had a grace and suppleness that suggested she might once have been a dancer. 'Please sit down. Would you like some coffee . . . or perhaps a glass of sherry?' Her voice held a slight tremor and her gaze darted nervously from one to the other, as if she was torn between a desire to know what Melissa had to tell her and a dread of what it might be.

'Thank you, we've not long had coffee,' said Melissa. The three of them sat down, Melissa and Joe on the couch and their hostess in a battered leather armchair facing them. There was a moment's awkward silence before Melissa began, 'Miss Haynes—'

'Oh please, do call me Lottie.'

'Thank you, Lottie. We're Melissa and Joe.'

'I'd like to call you Mel, if I may, that's how I think of you after reading your books. I really enjoy them, you know.' Again, there was a hint of shying away, of a dread of having to face something worse than the mere fact that her friend had suffered a bereavement.

'Thank you,' Melissa said with mechanical politeness. She was beginning to feel affected by the other's nervousness and it suddenly became necessary to clear her throat and swallow before she was able to go on. 'Lottie, I'm afraid this is going to come as a shock and there's no way of softening it,' she said slowly. 'You see, my father was murdered.'

Lottie drew a sharp breath, her eyes dilated and she put a hand to her mouth. For a few seconds she appeared too stunned to speak; when at last she found a voice she could only repeat Melissa's final word, 'Murdered . . . murdered . . . oh, no!' Her voice sank to a barely audible whisper. 'How did it happen?'

'He was struck on the head with an axe. And I'm afraid

there's worse to come. My mother's been arrested on suspicion of having killed him.'

'Oh, dear God!' Lottie covered her eyes with both hands and began mumbling under her breath, so softly that Melissa could only catch the occasional word: '. . . desperate . . . never said, but I guessed there was something.'

'Lottie, what are you saying?' Melissa had expected some display of horror and astonishment, but hardly such an emotional reaction as this. She jumped up and knelt beside the stricken woman. 'Do you mean you were expecting something like this to happen?'

Lottie lowered her hands, but did not raise her head. Staring down at her lap she said, 'I just had the feeling that she was near breaking point. Once or twice it occurred to me that she might do something desperate, but not this . . . I never thought she'd actually—' The final words were drowned in a dry, thick sob.

Melissa put her hands on Lottie's shoulders and gave her a gentle shake. 'You mustn't think like that; please, don't think like that!' she said urgently. 'Things look bad for her at the moment, but she swears she's innocent and I desperately want to believe her.' Moved by the other's distress, she felt her own voice beginning to crack. 'She's asked me to try and find out who really killed him. That's why we're here – we're hoping you might be able to help.'

'I?' Lottie raised her head and looked at Melissa, her large eyes bathed in unshed tears. 'What can I do? I've been away for the past fortnight. I was a bit unhappy about going because I knew she had no one else she could confide in, but she insisted she'd be all right.'

'How much did she confide in you?'

Lottie dried her eyes with a paper tissue from a box lying on top of a heap of guidebooks. 'Well, not a great deal really, except some time ago she showed me this article she'd found in a magazine about Mel Craig, the writer of the Nathan Latimer detective stories, and she said she was sure it was her daughter.'

'You knew she had a daughter, then?'

'She'd let something drop one day a few weeks previously – I think she said it was your birthday and she was feeling down in the dumps.'

Melissa nodded. 'Yes, that's what she told me.'

'She spoke rather sadly, which made me wonder if maybe you'd died. She didn't say any more and I didn't like to ask.'

'That's understandable.'

'And then this article. I think it was in a colour supplement; your photo was on the cover.'

'That was the interview you gave after being short-listed for the Booker, Mel,' said Joe. It was the first time he had spoken and there was a touch of affectionate pride in his voice.

'That was it,' said Lottie. 'It was really touching; she was so proud of your success, but she told me that when she showed it to Frank – to your father, I mean – he flew into a terrible rage and forbade her to refer to it again or even to read any of Mel Craig's – your – books. I got the impression there was some kind of family feud and I thought it might help her to talk about it, but she suddenly got very nervous and begged me never to refer to it again, or to breathe a word to anyone else.'

'It all ties in with what she told me,' Melissa said reflectively. 'She says you've been getting my books from the library for her.'

'That's right, she doesn't dare take them home. She comes to my house to read them while Frank's at the office.' Lottie twisted the tissue between her fingers, slender and delicate like her features. She smiled a little wistfully as she added, 'She was really wound up with excitement over that article, but I could tell there was grief and a lot of pent-up emotion behind it, which seemed natural when she blurted out that she hadn't seen you or had any contact with you for nearly thirty years.'

'And she didn't tell you why we'd lost contact?'

'No — and of course, I wouldn't have dreamed of asking. As I said, she suddenly backtracked. She seemed terrified that Frank would find out she'd spoken to me. It was after that I began to notice little things: something in her voice and in her eyes when she mentioned him. She'd always spoken of him with such . . . respect, I suppose you'd call it, but once or twice I had the impression that secretly she nursed some kind of grudge against him. That's why when you first told me about the murder and Sylvia being arrested, I thought—' Lottie broke off abruptly, stuffed the crumpled tissue into the pocket of her skirt and reached for another. 'Oh, I do so hope it's all a mistake. Do you really think you can do anything to find out the truth?'

'I'm going to do my best, but I'll need all the help I can get.'

'Well, you can count on me,' Lottie promised. 'Look, are you sure you wouldn't like a glass of sherry?' It was more of an appeal than a polite offer. 'I . . . it's been rather upsetting.'

'Of course it has.' Melissa felt a twinge of guilt at having plied this gentle stranger with questions without a thought of the distress she might be causing. 'Forgive me, I wasn't thinking. Yes, a sherry would be very nice, wouldn't it, Joe?'

'If it's no trouble.'

'No trouble at all.' Lottie rose from her chair with another swift, graceful movement and took a decanter and glasses from an antique corner cupboard. While she was pouring the drinks, Melissa took a quick glance round the room. Three walls were lined with shelves, some of which were crammed with books and others with an assortment of knick-knacks which seemed to have come from every corner of the globe: a gondola in Venetian glass, a boomerang, a miniature African drum, a bunch of brightly painted wooden bananas, pieces of carved jade, decorated pottery dishes and plates, a set of Russian dolls. Lottie Haynes, it seemed, had either travelled widely or had friends who brought her souvenirs from their travels. Melissa guessed it was the former.

Lottie had evidently noticed her interest; as she handed

round the drinks she remarked, 'I'm afraid I'm a bit of a magpie, but I do like to have something to remind me of my various trips.'

'You travel a lot?'

'Quite a bit.' Lottie sat down again and stared reflectively into her sherry glass before raising it to her lips. 'It doesn't seem quite right to say "Cheers!" does it?' she said sadly. She drank in a succession of quick sips, tilting her head back slightly after each one like a bird. After a few moments, she said, 'Tell me how you think I can help you.'

'As I told you, Mother has asked me to try and find out who really killed my father. I promised I'd do my best — I couldn't really do otherwise.'

'Of course not — but how in the world do you propose to set about it? Won't the police raise objections if you go round asking questions?'

'It's a free country — I can question who I like. The problem is, I don't know where to start. I know virtually nothing about my parents' life or the circles they moved in, Father's business contacts and so on. I've met the vicar, and Mrs Menzies—'

'That old bossy-boots!' Lottie interrupted. 'I imagine she's practically taken charge. Poor Sylvia!'

'She's certainly taken Mother under her wing in a pretty forthright sort of way. Both she and the vicar have made it clear they don't approve of me, but at least she's promised to help me if she can.'

'Why don't they approve of you?'

'I imagine it's because they think I walked out after a row with my parents and never so much as sent them a Christmas card since. It wasn't like that at all, but I've told her to let them go on thinking that for the time being.'

Lottie raised an eyebrow, but all she said was, 'I don't really see what I can do — I don't know any of Sylvia's friends. Our only contact was at the flower club.'

'Did she have many friends among the other members?'

'Not so far as I know. There wasn't a lot of chat during the meetings. We listened to the tutor, watched her demonstration and then got on with our own arrangements. I remember noticing that she never hung around to gossip at the end, but then neither did I.'

'So how come you and she became friends?'

'It was one day when she forgot to bring her scissors and I lent her mine. Then, when it was time to go home, it had started to rain and she didn't have an umbrella so I gave her a lift. She asked me in for a cup of tea and . . . well, you know how it is, we got chatting about this and that. I sensed at the time that there was an underlying sadness about her—' Lottie broke off and stared reflectively into her empty glass. 'And then, of course, she stopped coming to the meetings.'

'Yes, I was going to ask you about that. Have you any idea why?'

'I had the impression it was because Frank disapproved for some reason, but she never actually said so.'

'Do you remember when it was?'

'Oh yes, it was not long after the flower festival at the

church. We – the members of the flower club – did all the arrangements. Incidentally, that was the only occasion when I actually met your father, although I knew him by reputation. He was involved in all sorts of community activities and his name often cropped up in the local paper.'

Melissa noticed that, unlike her mother, Lottie had no difficulty in consigning Frank Ross to the past. On impulse, she asked, 'What was your impression of him?'

Lottie thought for a moment before saying slowly, 'I think I found him a little . . . awe-inspiring, rather like a strict, slightly humourless schoolmaster. I only exchanged a few words with him – he popped into the church once or twice while we were working to see how we were getting on and he always seemed to be taking everything terribly seriously. Now I come to think of it, though, he couldn't have been totally humourless; I noticed him once chatting to Jessica Round and he was smiling and seemed almost animated. But of course, Jessica has that effect on people; she's so charming it's difficult not to respond. Men seem to find her particularly attractive.'

The final comment was made without any hint of rancour or feminine spite. It crossed Melissa's mind that had it been spoken by Mrs Menzies, the tone would have been very different. Aloud, she said casually, 'Is Jessica Round one of your flower club members?'

'She's the president, actually.'

'I think it might be interesting to have a word with her.

Perhaps she can tell me why Mother gave up the flower club.'

Lottie looked faintly surprised at the suggestion. 'You think that's important?'

'I have a hunch it might be. Do you have her phone number?'

'Yes, of course.'

Chapter Nine

'Jessica Round here. Who's calling, please?' The voice was brisk, cultured, with an underlying hint of impatience suggesting a subtext of, 'I haven't got all day, so please don't waste any of my valuable time.'

'Mrs Round, my name's Melissa Craig. I apologise for disturbing you on a Sunday morning, but—'

Impatience became exasperation. 'Oh, for goodness' sake, what are you selling this time? I keep telling you people—'

'This isn't a sales call, it's personal and—'

'Do I know you?'

'No, but I believe you know my mother. She's a former member of your flower club – her name's Sylvia Ross.'

A slight gasp came over the wire and there was a noticeable pause before Jessica Round said, hesitantly and with a marked change of tone, 'You are Sylvia Ross's daughter?' Another pause. 'Is there something wrong?'

'I'm afraid there is. My mother is in serious trouble.'

'What sort of trouble?'

'I'd prefer not to give any details over the telephone.'

'Why can't Sylvia call me herself?'

'That's something else I'd rather not go into over the phone. It's a very delicate situation and it's just possible you may be able to help. Would it be convenient if I were to come and see you? I won't take up too much of your time—'

'You mean, now?'

'If you wouldn't mind.'

'How do I know you're who you say you are?'

'That's a good question. I don't suppose the name Mel Craig means anything to you?'

There was another pause before Mrs Round said, in a tone of mingled enlightenment and astonishment, 'The writer of the Nathan Latimer stories?'

'That's right.'

'*You* are Mel Craig?'

'I am.'

'But how extraordinary! I do so enjoy your books – and the TV programmes. How very odd,' she went on in a slightly puzzled tone. 'I wonder why he never— I mean, who would have thought . . . yes, by all means pop round, I'd be thrilled to meet you. Do you know where to find me?'

'I have your address, but we need some directions. We're in Shepton Close at the moment.'

'You have someone with you?'

'My agent, Mr Martin. He's a personal friend as well, but if you'd rather he stayed in the car . . .'

'Oh no, I'd be fascinated to meet him too.' In her excitement at the prospect of a face-to-face encounter with Nathan Latimer's creator, Jessica Round appeared to have momentarily forgotten that there was a potentially ominous reason for Melissa's request. 'I know Shepton Close — another of our members lives there,' she went on in her normal voice. 'Turn right into Mallory Road and go straight on as far as the second set of lights . . .' Evidently, it was a route she knew well; while Melissa scribbled frantically on the back of an envelope she rattled off directions like a schoolteacher instructing a class in fire drill, breaking off once or twice to say, 'Got that?' before finishing with the assurance that, 'It'll only take you ten minutes or so if you're lucky with the traffic.'

Melissa switched off her mobile phone and said, 'She sounds a bit of a battle-axe. I'll bet tele-sales people get short shrift when they call her.'

Joe chuckled. 'I assume she's agreed to see us?'

'She can't wait to meet the creator of Nathan Latimer.'

'Right, let's go.' He glanced at the dashboard clock as he reached for the ignition. 'When we've had our chat with her it'll be time for some lunch.'

As they waited at the first set of lights, Melissa said thoughtfully, 'One thing she said struck me as a bit odd.'

'Oh?'

'She didn't just sound surprised, she seemed almost

shocked when I told her I was Sylvia Ross's daughter. She was a bit suspicious at first – understandably I suppose – but when I explained I was Mel Craig, the creator of Nathan Latimer, she got quite excited and went on about how much she enjoyed the books. Then – and it was almost as if she was talking to herself for a moment – she said, "I wonder why he never—" and broke off and sort of rephrased what she was going to say.'

'You're sure she said "he"?'

'Oh yes, she's got a very clear voice.'

'Yes, I caught some of what she said from here,' said Joe with a grin. 'I noticed she went a lot quieter once you'd introduced yourself, though. I take your point,' he went on thoughtfully. 'You'd have expected her to say, "I wonder why *she* never said," wouldn't you?'

'Exactly. This could be a very interesting meeting.'

The lights changed and the line of traffic moved ahead. The roads were quiet, the remaining lights were green and within ten minutes they had reached their destination, a modern, purpose-built block of flats, the entrance controlled by an electronic security system. Melissa pressed the button bearing the number of Jessica Round's second-floor flat. It was several moments before she heard the click that indicated the signal had been received and there was a further interval before there was a crackle from the control panel and a woman's voice, barely recognisable as the one Melissa had listened to earlier, asked hesitantly, 'Is that Melissa Craig?'

'That's right. May we come in?'

'I'm sorry, I can't see you just now . . .' The voice tailed off as if the speaker was struggling with emotion.

'But you agreed not fifteen minutes ago—' Melissa began, but she was quickly interrupted.

'I'm afraid our talk will have to wait for another time. I—' There was the sound of a stifled sob, quickly controlled. 'I've just had some very bad news. I can't see anyone today. Please excuse me.'

'I'm so sorry.' Melissa was careful to avoid betraying any hint of the dawning suspicion this unexpected development, coming so soon after Jessica's earlier slip of the tongue, aroused in her mind. 'I quite understand. I wouldn't dream of inflicting my problems on you while you're so upset,' she went on, doing her best to sound genuinely sympathetic but inwardly seething with frustration. 'Maybe we could meet some other time?'

'Yes, of course.' Jessica's voice became steadier as she continued, 'I'd really like to meet you. It would be nice to have a talk with' — there was a brief pause before she continued, 'with Sylvia's daughter.'

'Shall I give you a ring in a day or two?'

This time the pause was longer. At last Jessica said hesitantly, 'Perhaps I could call you?'

'Of course. You can reach me any time on my mobile.' Melissa dictated the number and heard Jessica repeat it before the connection abruptly went dead. She turned to Joe. 'Are you thinking what I'm thinking?' she said.

'I certainly am. Let's go back and have another word with Lottie Haynes.'

Ten minutes later they were back in the cottage in Shepton Close. Lottie showed no surprise at their re-appearance.

'She rang almost immediately after you left,' she said in response to Melissa's question. 'She guessed you'd been to see me because you'd asked for directions from here and she was curious to know what it was all about. Perhaps I shouldn't have said anything about the murder, but you didn't say it was in confidence.' She looked appealingly at Melissa as if asking forgiveness for a breach of trust. 'I didn't think . . .'

'That's quite all right,' Melissa assured her. 'Can you tell me how she took the news, what she said when you told her?'

'I remember the exact words. She said, "Frank . . . murdered . . . oh no!" She sounded really upset. I thought for a moment she was going to cry, but she controlled herself and asked why I thought you wanted to see her. I said it was probably because Sylvia was being questioned by the police and had asked you to . . . Oh dear, I hope I haven't—'

'It's all right, you weren't to know,' Melissa said as Lottie broke off in embarrassment at what she obviously felt to have been a serious blunder on her part. 'What else did she say?'

'She asked me how it happened and I made out you hadn't given me any details. To my surprise, she didn't argue any more, she just hung up, which was a great relief. By that time I was beginning to wish I hadn't told her anything, but her call found me completely unprepared.' Lottie looked helplessly at Melissa. 'I think, if it had been almost anyone else, I'd have made her wait until you arrived so you could tell her yourself, but she insisted on knowing then and there. She's a very determined woman – it's difficult to say "no" to her.'

'I can imagine,' Melissa agreed wryly. 'Don't worry, Lottie, there's no harm done. No doubt she'd have reacted the same way if she'd had the news from me.'

'Except that she'd have had to explain why the death of someone who so far as we know was little more than an acquaintance should have affected her so badly,' Joe observed as the two women fell momentarily silent.

'That's a point,' Melissa agreed. 'Lottie, you mentioned you saw her chatting and laughing with my father over the church flowers; did you get the impression that they already knew one another?'

Lottie's smooth brow furrowed, as if she was trying to visualise the scene.

'I don't think so,' she said after a moment's thought. 'He just came into the church and introduced himself. He obviously already knew some of the members, the ones who attend the services, but I'm pretty sure Jessica wasn't one of them.'

'So Jessica isn't a churchgoer, then?'

'She might be; she lives in a different parish, but I've really no idea.' A faint smile flickered across Lottie's face. 'She doesn't strike me as the religious type, but you never know.'

'Was my mother there on that occasion?'

'I imagine she was, yes. She'd have been working on the flowers like the rest of us; it was before she dropped out of the club.'

'Well, I guess we'll have to leave it at that for the time being. Jessica did say she'd like to talk to me later, once she'd got over the shock of the bad news she'd just had.'

'It'll be interesting to hear what explanation she gives for being so upset,' Melissa said as, having taken their leave of Lottie for the second time, they returned to the car.

'She might try to bluff it out,' Joe suggested.

'How do you mean?'

'When you do get around to seeing her she might pretend that the "bad news" she was on about had nothing to do with the death of your father. She'll have had time to pull herself together and concoct a convincing story; my impression is that she's a tough character, the sort who could carry it off.'

'What about Lottie's comment that she sounded distressed when she heard about the murder?'

Joe shrugged. 'That could be a problem, but she'll have had time to dream up an excuse.'

Melissa sighed. 'It's a pity Lottie had to be so communicative, but we can't do anything about that now.' She settled in her seat, clipped on her seat belt and glanced at her watch. 'It's just after twelve. I wonder how things are with Mother?'

As if on cue, her mobile phone rang. A man's voice, brisk and impersonal, said, 'Mrs Craig? This is Arnold Fenton, duty solicitor. I'm representing your mother, Mrs Ross.'

'Mr Fenton, how good of you to—'

'I've arranged for my client to be released pending further enquiries. Perhaps you'd like to collect her from the police station.'

'How wonderful!' Melissa gave a thumbs-up signal. 'We'll come at once, thank you so—'

'I should perhaps mention that I'm a little anxious about my client's health. She's had a very severe shock and I think she'd be well advised to see her doctor as soon as possible.'

'As a matter of fact, the same thought—'

'I'll leave that in your hands. The main thing is that I soon managed to convince the investigating officer that she didn't have nearly enough evidence to charge my client.' A hint of satisfaction crept into the solicitor's voice as he added, 'Some of these newly promoted officers get too big for their boots.'

'That's excellent news, thank you very much.' For the first time, Melissa was given the opportunity to utter a complete sentence. 'We'll come and fetch her straight away.'

'Yes, do that. I'm going home for my lunch.'

The line went dead; Melissa put the phone back in her handbag and relayed the news to Joe. He chuckled at the reference to newly promoted officers and said, 'I suppose he was referring to DI Adair. She struck me as being a bit over-confident. Right, what are we waiting for?' He started the engine and drove back to the police station.

Sylvia was sitting in reception; the moment they appeared she got to her feet, saying, 'I've a good mind to sue them for wrongful arrest! That Adair woman — I wish you could have seen her face when Mr Fenton told her that all her so-called evidence was purely circumstantial and the CPS — what does that mean, dear? — anyway, whoever they are, they'd refuse even to consider bringing such a flimsy case to court.' Throughout this speech, delivered with no attempt to lower her voice, Sylvia shot several triumphant glances in the direction of the desk. Melissa could not be certain, but she thought she detected a trace of a smirk on the face of the duty officer, who was making a great show of being absorbed in paperwork.

'How about some lunch?' suggested Joe. 'We stayed at the Beverley Court last night — it has a very good restaurant.'

'What a lovely idea!' exclaimed Sylvia. 'I haven't had lunch in a restaurant for ages.'

She appeared as excited as a schoolgirl being taken on a treat and Melissa experienced a pang at the thought of how restricted her life must have been. Her own pleasure at the turn of events was tempered by nagging doubts that prompted her to whisper, a little uneasily, 'Mother dear, it might be an idea not to appear too full of the joys of spring; don't forget, your husband was brutally murdered a couple of days ago.'

'Yes, of course, although I don't suppose there'll be anyone there who knows me,' said Sylvia cheerfully. She glanced down at her plain cotton dress and jacket and asked, 'Are these things all right or d'you think I ought to go home and change?'

'You look fine,' Melissa assured her.

'Just splendid,' agreed Joe.

Sylvia beamed at them. 'If you say so. Shall we go, then? Bye-bye, officer!' She gave the desk sergeant a jaunty wave and headed for the exit, leaving the others to follow in her wake. Outside, as they made their way to the car park, she tucked her arm into Melissa's and said, 'Tell me what you've been doing this morning, dear. Have you made any progress in finding the real murderer?'

'Oh, Mother, give me a chance.'

'But you must have done something?' Sylvia insisted. 'Thank you so much, Mr Martin,' she went on as Joe opened the car door and assisted her into the rear seat while Melissa got in beside her.

'Please, call me Joe.'

'Joe,' she repeated. 'Such a nice, *dependable*-sounding name!' She settled back in her seat with a little sigh of pleasure. 'What a lovely comfortable car this is! Lissie dear,' she went on persuasively, 'you haven't answered my question.'

'We went to see your friend Lottie Haynes—' Melissa began.

'Ah yes, dear Lottie. She must have been very shocked when she heard the news about your father.'

'She was indeed, she—'

'But that isn't what I meant. Haven't you been doing any detective work?'

'In a way, that was detective work,' Melissa said patiently. 'I'm trying to build up a picture of your everyday life, the people you and Father mix with, that sort of thing. Tomorrow I'll get in touch with the company solicitor – I think you said his name was Mr Bell? I'll have to talk to Father's colleagues, of course, and I'm hoping to have a chat with the president of your flower club in a day or two.' Melissa had already decided not to mention Jessica Round's about-face or her own suspicions as to its cause.

Her mother's reaction increased her latent sense of unease. 'What on earth do you want to talk to that woman for?' she demanded. Her tone was sharp, hostile. 'Such an overbearing, flashy creature. I'm surprised more people don't leave her silly club.'

'Are you saying you left because of her? I thought you said Father had forbidden you to go any more?'

'Oh well, yes, I suppose he did, but . . . oh look, here we are. What a pretty hotel!' Joe had barely brought the car to a stop before she opened her door and began to scramble out. 'I'm so looking forward to my lunch.'

It was all too clear that she was thankful for the excuse

to avoid further reference to Jessica Round. She was, however, noticeably more subdued throughout the meal; taken along with the other events of the morning, the change of attitude did nothing to allay Melissa's sense of foreboding.

Chapter Ten

On their return to the house after lunch, Sylvia shivered a little as they stepped into the hall. 'Ooh, doesn't it feel chilly?' she remarked. 'Of course, the central heating hasn't been on since yesterday morning – I'll put it on right away.' She bustled off, returning after a moment with a little smile of triumph lighting up her pale features. 'You know, it's such a treat to be able to switch that boiler on and off whenever I feel like it. Shall I make a cup of tea?'

'Maybe later – it's a bit soon after lunch, isn't it?' said Melissa.

'Yes, perhaps it is. I tell you what, I'll just put these things in the utility room. I'll be doing a load of washing tomorrow.' Sylvia vanished into the kitchen with the plastic bag containing the previous day's discarded garments; when she returned she said brightly, 'Now, if you two will excuse me, I'd like to go and freshen up. Why don't you go in the sitting-room and make yourselves comfortable? I shan't be long.' Without waiting for a reply she left them standing in the hall exchanging bemused glances as she almost ran upstairs, humming a tune.

'Oh dear,' sighed Melissa as she sank on to the couch where, a little over twenty-four hours earlier, Sylvia had collapsed sobbing in her arms. 'She really will have to try and curb her relief at Father's death, or at least not make it so obvious.' She turned a little helplessly to Joe as he sat down beside her. 'I simply don't know what to make of her. What do you think?'

'I think she's in a pretty unstable condition emotionally,' he said. 'If I were you, I'd try and get her to take the solicitor's advice and see her doctor as soon as possible.'

'Oh, I'll certainly do that. What worries me is how much of what she says can I believe?'

'That may become clearer when the two of you have a chance for some quiet talk. I've been thinking, it might be better if you stayed here with her tonight.'

'She did say something over lunch about asking Mrs Menzies to stay.'

'That was when you mentioned we'd booked one more night at the hotel.'

'Yes, she was quite coy about that, wasn't she? She probably suspects us of having a torrid affair!'

'I'm sure you'll soon disabuse her of that idea.' There was a rueful quality in the half-smile that flickered across Joe's face. To avoid the need to reply, Melissa got up and went to the window where she stood silently gazing out at the meticulously tended garden: the immaculate lawn with its carefully trimmed edges and the lily pond in the middle; the neat, weedless flower-beds. Beyond lay the kitchen garden where the shoots of early potatoes were already thrusting their way through the earth and brightly coloured labels marked the rows where seeds for the new season's crop of vegetables had been sown. She found herself wondering whether they would ever be harvested and felt her eyes misting over. She covered them with her hands and whispered under her breath, 'Oh Father, why did it have to be like this?'

Joe was beside her in a moment, his arms round her. 'Mel, darling, what is it?'

'I . . . it was just looking at his garden. He loved it so much and he often tried to interest me in it, but I never really took to it.'

'You love your garden at Hawthorn Cottage.'

'Yes I know – that was Iris's influence. Ironic, isn't it?' She gave a deep sigh. 'I'm afraid I was a disappointment to him in so many ways.'

'He made you pay pretty dearly for it, didn't he? Anyway, it's no use brooding over it now.'

'That's true.' Melissa fished a handkerchief from her pocket and blew her nose. 'Joe, I've been thinking . . . if Mother really didn't kill Father, obviously someone else did. According to her statement, he went to his workshop before she went out shopping and we've been assuming he was there all the time until he was attacked. If someone came to the house and rang the bell, would he have heard? If not, how did they get in?'

'Through the side gate?' suggested Joe.

'It would almost certainly have been locked; he was always very hot on security.'

'Yes, I noticed the Neighbourhood Watch sticker on the front door.' Joe thought for a moment, frowning slightly, then said, 'I suppose it's possible he was expecting someone.'

'Someone he'd invited round, knowing that Mother would be out?'

'Or someone who telephoned after she left, asking to see him?'

'Would he have heard the phone while he was out there?'

'These are questions we'll have to ask your mother.'

'What questions?' said a voice behind them. Sylvia had entered the room without their noticing. She had changed into a white blouse and a navy-blue cotton skirt. Her hair was brushed smoothly back from her face and there was a faint flush in her cheeks and a sparkle in her eyes. 'I'd have liked a shower, but there's no hot water so I had a little splash under the cold tap,' she explained. 'Do come and sit down.' She settled into an armchair and Melissa and Joe obediently returned to the couch. 'Now, what is it you want to know?'

'There was no sign of a break-in so we have to assume Father knew his killer,' Melissa began. 'If someone arrived unexpectedly at the house while he was in the workshop, would he have heard the front doorbell?'

'Oh no, I don't think so.'

'What about the phone?'

'He wouldn't have heard the one in the house, but he'd have had his mobile phone with him.'

'He had a mobile?' asked Melissa in surprise. 'As I remember, he was always deeply suspicious of what he called "new-fangled gadgets". Have you any idea who knew the number?'

'People at the office, I suppose. That's why he had it, he liked to make sure he was in touch on the days when he didn't go in. Now and again his secretary or someone would ring him with a query, although not so often as he'd have liked.' Sylvia gave a giggle that held a hint of malicious glee. 'He thought they couldn't manage without him, but of course they could, they probably looked forward to his days off.'

'Did he have regular days off?'

'He never went in on Mondays or Fridays.'

'And he was killed on Friday afternoon. Let's assume that some time after you went out, someone rang him on his mobile with a query that couldn't be dealt with on the phone. I assume he kept papers about company matters at home — I noticed the small bedroom has a desk and a filing cabinet.'

'That's right, he called it his office.'

'If whoever it was rang on company business, you'd expect him to have received them in the house,' said Melissa.

'I suppose so.' Sylvia looked puzzled. 'What difference does it make?'

'We don't know yet, we're simply trying to figure out what might have happened between the time you left the house and the time he was killed.'

There was a short silence before Joe glanced at Melissa with raised eyebrows as if seeking permission to ask her mother a question. Receiving a nod of agreement, he said, 'Mrs Ross, do you know if your husband had any enemies? Anyone at the office, say, who would profit by his death?'

Sylvia appeared bemused by the question. 'Profit?' she repeated. 'Are you suggesting he might have left money to someone who wanted it so badly they killed him?'

Joe shook his head. 'I wasn't thinking of money, I was thinking maybe a rival, a person with ambition who might have wanted him out of the way so he – or possibly she – could have more influence on company policy. I get the feeling that your late husband was the kind of man who would run a very tight ship. Could there be someone else, one of his fellow directors perhaps, who wanted to make changes that he wouldn't allow?'

'I've really no idea.' Sylvia looked perplexed; plainly she was completely out of her depth. 'I didn't have anything to do with his business affairs at all.'

'He never discussed them with you?'

'No, never.' Sylvia gave a resentful pout. 'I suppose he thought I wouldn't understand.'

'But you must know some of the people who work for the company. His secretary, for example, and the senior management. Didn't you ever meet them?'

'Oh yes, now and again. At the Christmas party, for example.'

'We'll have to talk to some of them,' said Melissa. Her mind had been racing ahead while Joe was speaking. 'I've just had a thought. He wasn't expected at the office on the day he was killed and then it was the weekend, so presumably no one there knows he's dead. You mentioned the company solicitor yesterday. I think perhaps he should be told. Do you have his home telephone number?'

'Mr Bell? I don't even know where he lives. I think Father kept an address book in his desk upstairs – it might be in that. Shall I go and look?'

'Good idea. If you find it, will you bring it down? There may be other useful numbers in it.'

With an almost childlike eagerness, Sylvia got to her feet and hurried from the room. Moments later they heard the sound of drawers being opened and closed; then she was back carrying a small leather-bound book which she thrust into Melissa's hands. 'Here,' she said breathlessly. She sank back into her chair and closed her eyes for a moment. 'I feel quite . . . *naughty!*' she said with another little giggle. 'Do you know, that's the first time I've set foot in that room without his permission. It was almost' – her smile vanished and she gave a little shudder – 'as if his ghost was watching me.'

'I can imagine,' said Melissa, recalling with a twinge of gooseflesh her own sensation of being under her father's disapproving gaze on entering her parents' bedroom. She was scanning the pages of the book while she spoke and gave a little 'Ah!' of satisfaction as she found what she was seeking. 'Here we are: Bell, Marcus — would that be him?'

'I expect so. Yes, I've heard Frank address someone on the phone as Marcus.'

'His home and office numbers are both here. I'll give him a ring right away.'

'Perhaps you'd like to make the call from the office while I make that cup of tea.'

'I'll come and help,' said Joe gallantly.

The offer was received with a smile of dazzling sweetness and a bright, 'Thank you, that's really very kind of you.' Sylvia led the way into the kitchen while Melissa hurried upstairs. Her hand shook a little as she sat down at her late father's desk, picked up his phone and dialled the number.

After only a couple of rings a man's voice said, 'Good afternoon.'

'Mr Bell?'

'Speaking.'

'My name's Melissa Craig and I'm speaking on behalf of Mrs Sylvia Ross.'

'Frank Ross's wife?'

'That's right.'

'What can I do for you, Mrs Craig?'

'I'm afraid I have some very serious news. Frank Ross has been murdered.'

'Good heavens!' Bell's voice, which until then had conveyed nothing but a polite, impersonal interest, momentarily registered a shocked surprise, instantly controlled as he went on, 'Do I take it you're a friend of Mrs Ross?'

'I'm her daughter. Frank Ross was my father.'

'I see.' His tone gave no hint as to whether the revelation came as a surprise or not. 'When did this happen?'

'On Friday afternoon.'

'Do the police have any idea who killed him?'

'They've been questioning my mother.' Briefly, Melissa outlined the train of events culminating in Sylvia's release from custody. 'I . . . we thought that as the firm's solicitor you should be informed as soon as possible.'

'Most considerate. Perhaps you are not aware that I am also a director of the company?' By his tone, Bell managed to convey the impression that he considered her ignorance on this point, if not inexcusable, at least deserving an apology.

'No, Mother didn't mention that. As a matter of fact, she is still in a state of considerable shock.'

'I see.' Again, there was no hint of human feeling behind the words. 'Please inform her that I will take all the necessary steps to deal with the situation,' Bell continued. 'May I have a number where you may be contacted?'

'I'm making this call from my parents' home and I'll be staying here with my mother for the next few days. When I'm not here you can reach me on my mobile.'

He repeated the number as Melissa dictated it and then said, 'Thank you, Mrs Craig. Please convey my condolences to Mrs Ross and tell her I'll be in touch with her very soon.' There was a momentary hesitation before he added, 'My condolences to yourself as well, naturally.'

'Thank you. Mr Bell, if you could spare a few more minutes—'

'It is Sunday,' he pointed out.

'Yes, I know, but the circumstances are a little unusual. It's quite obvious the officer leading the enquiry is convinced my mother is guilty, but she insists she's innocent and – this may sound slightly bizarre to you – she's asked me to try to find the real killer.'

'Do I understand you are some kind of detective?'

'I . . . have had some experience of private investigation – and some success.' Nettled by the hint of scepticism that had crept into the man's voice, Melissa was on the point of going on to reveal her professional identity, but her instinct told her that the information would be greeted with even more thinly-veiled disdain. 'The point is,' she said, keeping her voice even with an effort, 'my mother has asked for my help and I've promised to do what I can. I should very much appreciate your assistance.'

'What do you want to know?'

'Can you, from your knowledge of the company's affairs, think of anyone who will gain any advantage from my father's death?'

'That's something I'm not prepared to comment on to a perfect stranger.'

'But I'm not a stranger, I'm his daughter, and—'

'And if you're seeking information about the terms of his will,' Bell interrupted, 'I'm not prepared to discuss that with you either, except to inform you that you are not mentioned in it.'

'That's the last thing I had in mind,' Melissa snapped. 'And I apologise for disturbing your Sabbath peace. Perhaps we can continue our talk at a more convenient time.'

'If you think it will serve any useful purpose.' He sounded totally unaffected by her undisguised sarcasm. 'My office hours are from nine to five thirty, Monday to Friday.'

'I'll make a note of it. Goodbye, Mr Bell. *And thanks for nothing,*' she muttered as she slammed down the phone. She sat there seething with resentment for a moment or two; then, acting on a sudden hunch, turned to another page in the address book. There were several entries under R but the one that caught her eye read simply, 'J'. There was no address, but when Melissa checked the number with the one Lottie Haynes had given her it came as no surprise to find that it belonged to Jessica Round.

She went downstairs just as Joe emerged from the kitchen carrying a tray. He followed her into the sitting-room and set it down. 'Did you get through to Mr Bell?' he asked.

'I did, and he was totally unforthcoming.' Melissa relayed the gist of the conversation while setting out cups and saucers. 'Apart from the fact that for a split second he registered mild shock on hearing of Father's murder, and an almost audible curl of the lip when I told him Mother had asked me to do some detective work, he sounded totally detached. It was rather like talking to an android.'

'It was probably just professional caution.'

'I suppose so. Never mind that now. I came across something—' She broke off as her mother entered the room bearing the teapot.

'I'm sorry, there's no cake, only biscuits,' she apologised. She poured out the tea, handed round the cups and offered chocolate fingers, which Joe and Melissa politely declined. When they were all settled she said, 'So Mr Bell sends his condolences and will be in touch soon.' Plainly, she had been hovering within earshot while waiting for the kettle to boil. She turned to Melissa. 'And what was the something you came across that you were about to mention as I came in?'

'It's a bit, well, personal,' Melissa began. 'I mean, you might prefer—'

'Oh, I'm sure there's no harm in Joe hearing it.' The smile that Sylvia directed at him made it clear that he had completely won her over. 'In any case, you were going to tell him just now, weren't you?'

'Well, yes.' Melissa took a sip from her tea and then set her cup carefully back on the saucer before replying. 'First of all, I'd like to ask you a question.'

'Yes, dear?'

'When I mentioned Jessica Round's name earlier, you made it clear that you don't like her very much. What have you got against her?'

'Why, nothing really. I don't dislike her, I just find her

rather irritating. She tends to throw her weight around and she uses too much make-up and wears unsuitable clothes for a woman of her age.' Sylvia gave a thin, slightly artificial laugh. 'Why on earth do you want to talk about her?'

'Because I found her telephone number in Father's address book and I wondered what reason he would have for wanting it.'

Sylvia's eyes narrowed and she ran her tongue over her lips. 'Well, I suppose . . . I mean, she . . . I know!' From appearing seriously disconcerted, she suddenly beamed as if she had hit on the answer to a riddle. 'Of course, it must have been about the flower festival last year; yes, that must be it. She was in charge of all the arrangements. He would have had to know how to get in touch with her, that's all it was. More tea, anyone?'

'Never mind the tea for the moment,' said Melissa. 'There are a couple more things I'm puzzled about. First, the entry in Father's address book doesn't give Mrs Round's name, just the letter J – for Jessica, I assume.'

'So how do you know it's her number?' Sylvia's voice became noticeably quieter and she sat very still in her chair, staring at Melissa as if mesmerised.

'Because I compared it with the one Lottie Haynes gave me.'

'Maybe you wrote it down wrong.'

'I'm afraid not. You see, I rang Jessica and asked if Joe and I could call and see her. She agreed, but by the time we got there she'd spoken to Lottie and learned about

Father's death. She wouldn't let us in and she sounded pretty distraught. Can you think of a reason why she should be so upset, if her only contact with him was over the church flower festival?'

'I haven't the slightest idea.'

'Mother, I hate to have to ask this, but did you ever suspect that Father might have been having an affair with her?'

Sylvia jumped as if she had been stung and her eyes saucered in outrage.

'Lissie! How could you make such a monstrous suggestion? Your father was an absolute pillar of virtue! If this is the sort of horrid way you're going to go about things, you'll make me wish I'd never asked for your help. In fact, I want you to stop your investigations right away, do you hear me?'

Chapter Eleven

The stunned silence that greeted Sylvia's outburst was broken by a sharp ring at the front door.

Joe half rose with a murmured, 'Shall I——?' but Sylvia waved him back into his chair with an imperious gesture.

'I'm quite capable of answering my own doorbell, thank you very much,' she said curtly.

Melissa turned to Joe in consternation. 'I don't like this at all,' she muttered. 'I'm afraid there's a very nasty can of worms waiting to be opened.'

'Then why not leave it unopened?' he suggested. 'You heard what your mother said; she's given you a cast-iron reason for dropping your investigation.'

'On the contrary, she's made me more determined to find out the truth.'

'But supposing——' he began, but broke off at the sound of women's voices as Sylvia opened the front door and greeted her visitor.

'Mrs Menzies, how sweet of you to call!' The heightened tone was obviously intended to reach the sitting-room. 'Yes, everything's fine . . . do come in . . . my daughter and her friend are here, but I expect they'll soon be going.'

'There's no need to leave on my account,' Mrs Menzies assured Melissa and Joe as she followed Sylvia into the room and sat down in the remaining armchair. 'I just popped round to find out how things were. I saw the car outside and I wondered—'

'Oh, I found such a nice man who told that stupid woman she'd only look foolish if she kept me locked up any longer,' said Sylvia complacently.

'The duty solicitor,' Melissa explained in response to a questioning glance from Mrs Menzies, who nodded approval.

'I'm so glad you managed to persuade your mother—' she began.

'Yes, that's what he called himself, the duty solicitor,' Sylvia interrupted. 'I thought it over and decided I needed professional advice.' She took the lid off the teapot as she spoke and peered inside. 'Would you care for a cup of tea? This is still hot.'

'No thank you, I won't stay long. I'm delighted to see you back at home. Have you quite recovered?'

'Recovered? I haven't been ill.'

'I thought you spent last night in hospital.'

'Did I?' Sylvia puckered her brow in apparent surprise. 'Oh yes, so I did.'

'Well, I must say you look all right now.'

'Oh yes, I'm fine. We've had a lovely day. Melissa and Joe took me out to lunch.'

'That was nice. Tell me, what happens now?'

'Oh, Mr . . . what did he say his name was?' Sylvia frowned again and put a hand to her brow; the question was plainly addressed to herself.

'Mr Fenton,' said Melissa quietly.

Her mother shot her a suspicious glance and said, 'How did you know?'

'He phoned me to say he'd arranged for your release and asked me to fetch you.'

'There was no need for that. I could have taken a taxi.'

'How would you have got into the house? I have the keys, remember?'

'So you have. You might as well let me have them back now.' Sylvia thrust out her hand, like a shop assistant waiting for money. Melissa hesitated for a moment, then took the keys from her bag and silently handed them over. 'I expect you're anxious to be on your way,' Sylvia went on. There was no mistaking her meaning.

'Are you sure you'll be all right?'

'Of course I will.'

'Don't worry, I'll be here to keep an eye on her.' Mrs Menzies gave a reassuring nod as she caught Melissa's anxious look. 'She can stay at my house again tonight if she likes.'

'There you are, you see!' Sylvia looked at Melissa with a smug little smile, like a child that has managed to get its own way in the face of parental opposition. 'Now, if no one wants any more tea, I'll just take these things into the kitchen.' She loaded the cups and saucers on to the tray and went out of the room.

Melissa turned to Mrs Menzies and said in a low voice, 'She's been acting a little strangely and I'm rather concerned about her. I think she should see her doctor.'

Mrs Menzies gave a quick nod of understanding. 'I'll see if I can arrange an appointment for her in the morning. Try not to worry – she's probably still feeling the strain of it all. And if you want a word in private, my number's in the book.'

'You're very kind. Thank you for looking after her.'

'What else are friends for?'

Sylvia came bustling back. 'Right, that's that little job done. Now you two, just run along and enjoy your evening. As you can see, I'm perfectly all right.'

Recognising that in her present mood there was no point in prolonging the visit, Melissa got to her feet and Joe followed suit. 'Yes, we'll be getting back to our hotel now,' she said calmly. 'I'll give you a call in the morning.'

'Yes, do that, dear.'

As they parted at the front door Melissa kissed her mother on the cheek, prepared for a rebuff but determined to part on the best possible terms. She received a brief hug in return, accompanied by an urgently whispered, 'You will remember what I said, won't you? No more investigations. Mr Fenton will take care of things now.'

'I'll remember. I'll see you again very soon.'

As soon as they were back in the car, Melissa said wearily, 'What d'you make of all that?'

Joe was silent for a minute or two. Eventually he said, 'I'm afraid the indications are that your father and Jessica Round were lovers — or at least had a fairly intimate relationship — and that your mother had her suspicions even if she didn't know for certain.'

'That much is obvious. What's troubling me is, do I put her insistence that I call off my enquiries down to her fear of possible scandal, or . . .' She could not bring herself to voice the alternative.

'Or she had a very strong motive for murder,' Joe finished quietly. They had stopped at traffic lights and he took one hand from the wheel and reached for hers. 'Look, Mel, if you want my advice, I suggest you do as she says, back off and let things take their course.'

'I can't do that.' Melissa gripped his hand tightly for a moment, then released it as the lights turned green. 'I can't bear to think of my mother as a murderess, but I have to be sure. The police aren't going to drop their enquiries just because they haven't enough evidence yet to bring charges. If there's dirt to be dug up, they'll find it and if it points back to her they won't look any further. No, whether she likes it or not, I'm going to go on ferreting around.'

'Which, knowing you, comes as no surprise!' he said with a sigh of resignation. 'Well, I've said my piece and you've said yours. I suppose the next thing is to figure out a plan of campaign.'

*   *   *

Back at the police station, Detective Inspector Mollie Adair sat chewing the end of a ballpoint pen and scowling across her desk at Detective Constable Carole Sharwood, who sat with her hands folded in her lap, waiting for her superior officer to speak.

The DI took the pen from her mouth and stabbed the air with it. 'Sod Fenton!' she exclaimed viciously. 'Just our bloody luck. If we'd had almost anyone else we'd have been able to continue our questioning for at least another hour or so. I'm positive the old bat would have cracked by then. As it is—' She broke off and began doodling on a notepad.

After a moment, the DC ventured to ask, 'So what's our next move going to be, Guv?'

'We'll have to start probing more deeply into the background, try and dig up some evidence of hostility between Sylvia Ross and her late husband. That means further, in-depth interviews with friends, neighbours, acquaintances, the postman—'

'What about business associates?'

'We know Ross owned a local manufacturing company. I suppose we'll have to talk to some of the people there.' Her tone made it clear that she did not consider that a particularly fruitful line of enquiry. 'Anyway, Sylvia Ross is the killer, I'm sure of it. If only Fenton—' The inspector threw down the pen in a peevish gesture. 'Sod him!' she repeated.

'D'you think perhaps some sort of business rivalry . . .' Carole suggested tentatively, but the suggestion was greeted with a dismissive sniff.

'A business rival would hardly choose to brain his victim in his own home, would he? No, this is a domestic, I'll stake my pension on it. It's going to mean a lot of legwork for you. I'll try and get you some help, but you know how things are at the moment.'

'There's the daughter, Mrs Craig.'

'What about her?'

'Mrs Ross boasted as she was leaving the hospital that her daughter was going to "help us find the killer", as she put it.' Just in time, Carole checked herself from adding, 'Don't you remember me telling you?' In her experience, DI Adair did not like to hear it so much as hinted that she might have missed something.

Mollie Adair made a dismissive gesture. 'I don't think we need take that threat seriously,' she said scornfully.

Carole was on the verge of pointing out that Mrs Ross's daughter was the well-known crime writer and amateur sleuth Mel Craig, but decided to keep that information to herself for the time being. It would only have made the DI even more irritable. 'You're probably right, Guv,' she agreed meekly.

'Of course I am. You can forget all about her.'

That evening, after a relaxing hot bath and a change of clothes, Melissa joined Joe in the bar of the Beverley Court Hotel. He set their drinks on a corner table, sat down beside her and pulled his chair closer to hers. 'Have you had any thoughts about what to do next?' he asked quietly.

'A few – all of them negative, I'm afraid.' She picked up her glass of gin and tonic, took a mouthful and put it down again. There were only a handful of people in the bar and none sitting close to them, but despite the inescapable background of piped music that partially masked their voices she lowered hers almost to a whisper as she went on, 'I've been trying to think of a way of approaching some of the people at Father's firm. I need to know how he got on with his colleagues – and his employees, of course – and what they thought of him. The problem is, where do I start? My only contact so far has been with Mr Bell and it's quite obvious he isn't going to be much help. He might even advise people against talking to me. In any case, how do I prove I'm Frank Ross's daughter? Until this afternoon, I could have relied on Mother to vouch for me, but given her present state of mind, I'm even beginning to have doubts about that.'

'She can hardly deny it.' Joe took a long pull from his tankard of beer before adding, with a mischievous grin, 'You can always prove you're Mel Craig, of course!'

'I'm not sure that would work – people might think I'm researching a plot.' For a moment she felt the tension lift; then it returned as she said gloomily, 'I have the same sort of feeling as I get when I come up against a really knotty problem in a book – it's as if I've run into the sand.'

'You always dig yourself out very successfully.'

'This is a bit different, isn't it? I can't manipulate people in real life the way I do my characters.'

'There's still time to abandon the idea.'

Melissa shook her head. 'That's not an option,' she said firmly.

'Then all I can suggest is that you ring your father's office tomorrow and ask to speak to his secretary. If she's been with him for any length of time, she's the one who can best tell you the things you want to know. If you can gain her confidence she may drop a few hints about the general atmosphere in the company — inter-departmental relations, rumours of boardroom spats, that sort of thing. How big an outfit is it, by the way?'

'I've no idea how big it is now. All I know is that up till the time I left home it made door and window fittings and employed about a dozen people. That was thirty years ago and there could have been all sorts of changes. Not that Father would have encouraged them,' she added, staring reflectively into her glass. 'I remember once hearing him talk about diversification — I think someone at the firm was trying to persuade him to widen the product range — and he said very dogmatically that "a cobbler should stick to his last".'

'There's nothing unusual about that — plenty of folk are resistant to change,' Joe observed. 'I suppose,' he went on after a moment's thought, 'if he was still clinging to that sort of attitude, there might well be someone with ideas for expansion — a fellow director, maybe — who saw him as standing in the way of progress.'

'That's hardly a motive for murder, is it?'

'You never know what's involved financially. I'm sure

your best bet, if you really are set on going ahead, is to try and get in with the secretary.' He drained his tankard, put it down and reached for the bar menu. 'Now, I know we had a pretty substantial lunch, but how about a spot of supper?'

'Order me a sandwich, will you? I'm going to call Mrs Menzies and find out how Mother is now.'

'Good idea. I noticed the old dragon seemed a lot less prickly this afternoon.'

'I thought so too.'

When Mrs Menzies answered, Melissa said quietly, 'Is my mother within earshot?'

'No. What do you want?' The curt, almost rude response, after the apparent softening in attitude that had been so noticeable earlier, came as a shock.

'I'm sorry if I've called at an inconvenient time. I just wanted to know how she is.'

'What do you expect?' Mrs Menzies snapped. 'She's very upset at the way you've let her down.'

'Whatever do you mean? How have I let her down, as you put it?'

'By telling her you've decided to drop your enquiries.'

Melissa could hardly believe her ears. 'Is that what she told you?'

'Isn't that the case?'

'It most certainly is not; on the contrary, she was very insistent that I abandon the whole idea.'

It was Mrs Menzies' turn to sound taken aback. 'I don't understand. She seemed quite sure—'

'What exactly did she say?'

'She said she supposed you'd decided you didn't want to bother now that she has this Mr Fenton to take care of her.'

'Oh dear, she really has got things confused. The truth of the matter is that I let her think I was going to do as she says, but I've made up my mind just the same to try and find out who killed my father. Perhaps the best thing for the moment is to let her believe her own version.'

'I don't understand,' Mrs Menzies repeated.

'Neither do I,' Melissa agreed with a sigh, 'but I suppose it must have something to do with the trauma of the past couple of days. If you could manage to get her to the doctor tomorrow, I'd be so grateful.'

'Leave it to me.'

'Thank you very much. By the way, I suggest you don't mention this call to her.'

'If you say so.'

Melissa went back to the bar and relayed the gist of the conversation to Joe. 'I can't for the life of me figure out what's got into her,' she said despondently.

He hesitated for a moment before saying, 'She could be in the state therapists refer to as "in denial".'

'You mean, she's deliberately deceiving herself, refusing to face the truth?'

'Something like that.'

'It's possible, I suppose, but—' Melissa shivered; despite the warmth of the room she felt suddenly cold. 'First she begs me to find out who really killed Father and then, when I say I'm planning to talk to a woman who apparently knew him very well, she insists that I drop the case. Next, she cooks up a tale for Mrs Menzies, who knew what was being planned and was bound to ask if I'd made any progress.'

'And she wouldn't want her to know the true position, for the same reason that she warned you off.'

'And we've already thought of two possible reasons, both pretty compelling from her point of view, as to why she—' Melissa turned to Joe, her spirits at zero as she forced herself yet again to admit to the awful possibility. 'Is it because she's "in denial" as you put it that she started this whole bizarre pantomime? In other words, is she guilty after all?'

Chapter Twelve

Joe picked up his empty tankard and got to his feet. 'I think I need a refill,' he muttered. 'How about you?'

'I haven't finished this one yet.'

'Mind if I . . .?'

'Go ahead.'

By this time a few more people had drifted in and were ordering drinks and food. Melissa, struggling to come to terms with the hideous prospect opened up by the two simple words 'in denial', paid scant attention to the newcomers or to the waiter who put two plates of sandwiches and two sets of cutlery wrapped in dark-blue paper napkins on the table in front of her. Neither did she notice that Joe, who while waiting to be served had been idly scanning a newspaper lying on an adjacent table, suddenly picked it up and began studying it with such fixed attention that the man behind the bar had to speak to him twice to ask what he wanted.

Even when he returned and handed her the paper with the terse question, 'What do you make of that?' she gave only a perfunctory glance at the headline that he indicated. Not until she had read the brief passage twice did its significance fully dawn on her.

LOCAL FIRM SUBJECT OF TAKEOVER BID

An offer has been made by Metal Furniture plc for Frank Ross and Company, manufacturers of door and window fittings. A spokesperson for Ross said the offer is being considered by the directors, who are the sole shareholders, and an announcement will be made shortly.

'This is Friday's edition of the local weekly,' Joe pointed out. 'Obviously, it went to press well before your father's death. It would be interesting to know how long ago the offer was made, wouldn't it? And what the boardroom reaction was – and what effect his death will have.'

'I can guess Father's reaction,' said Melissa. 'He'd have said "No" almost without thinking.'

'And presumably he had a majority holding so no matter how attractive the offer or how much his fellow directors wanted to accept, there would have been nothing they could do if they failed to talk him round?'

'Probably not.' Melissa sipped at the remains of her drink as, her interest now thoroughly aroused, she considered the possible ramifications. 'What happens now will depend on what happens to his shares. Mr Bell will know the answer to that one, but he's already made it clear he's not going to tell me anything if he can help it.' Her mind slipped into overdrive, her anxiety over her mother swept aside by the abruptly altered scenario. 'Let's assume for the moment that with Father out of the way, the remaining directors are now free to decide whether or not to accept the offer.'

'And possibly enjoy better conditions than they've had under the old regime,' Joe pointed out. 'All sorts of wheeling and dealing might have been going on already; maybe they've even been negotiating with Metal Furniture behind your father's back, perhaps been promised some extra sweeteners to get him to change his mind.'

'We don't know how badly Metal Furniture want the company.'

'Or what terms they're offering.'

Their eyes met as the questions surged into their minds like bargain-hunters into a store on the first day of a sale. 'We could be into a whole new ball game, couldn't we?' said Melissa. 'There might be several people whose interests have been served by Father's death.' She began to tackle her chicken sandwiches and salad with a suddenly reawakened appetite. Then a thought struck her. 'Joe, you've got your own business to run. I can't expect you to stick around playing detectives indefinitely.'

'Funny you should say that. I do have a couple of important meetings during the next few days and I've been wondering – I mean, I hate to leave you to cope with all this on your own, but—'

'Don't you worry about me,' she said firmly. 'This is going to give me plenty to keep me occupied.'

'You know where to find me if you need me.'

'Thank you.' She gave him a grateful smile, touched as ever by his unfailing support. 'You're such a rock, Joe. What would I do without you?'

'You don't have to.' A casual listener would have detected no hint of emotion in the lightly spoken words, but for a moment his eyes betrayed the sentiment that lay behind them. Then, as if consciously retreating from a potential danger zone, he reached for his last remaining sandwich and remarked, 'You'll need a car.'

'I'll see about hiring one first thing in the morning.' She paused with a forkful of salad halfway to her mouth as another question occurred to her. 'I wonder if Mother knows anything about the takeover bid?'

'Probably not — wouldn't she have said?'

'I suppose so.' Melissa thought for a moment before coming to a decision. 'I'll tackle her about it tomorrow and suggest there could be a connection with Father's murder. She might be happy for me to carry on ferreting around once she understands it's people in the company I'll be investigating and not Jessica Round.'

'It would be nice to think so.'

For a moment, the hint of doubt in Joe's voice cast a shadow across Melissa's newly found optimism. Resolutely, she thrust it aside. 'I'm sure of it,' she asserted.

In an obvious move to change the subject, he said, 'I

wonder if DI Adair knows? Do you think you ought to give her a call tomorrow and tell her?'

'Not likely. Thanks to Mother's little boast, she'll probably be on the watch for any sign that I've been poking my nose into her case. She's already been given a flea in her ear by Mr Fenton and I'm sure it would give her great pleasure to be able to take her frustrations out on me. Anyway, she'll almost certainly hear about the take-over bid before long – or one of her minions will point it out to her. Meanwhile, let her grub around looking for evidence against Mother for a while.'

'Mel, I don't want to put a damper on things,' Joe said hesitantly, 'but there's always the chance she might find some. You've admitted yourself—'

'I know, and I can't dismiss the possibility out of hand, but mightn't my father have been killed by someone who either works for or is closely connected with Frank Ross and Company?'

'I suppose so.' Joe sounded unconvinced. 'So what's your next move going to be?'

'To take your earlier advice and make contact with his secretary. What about you?'

Joe glanced at his watch. 'I think, if you're sure you can cope without me, I'd like to get back to London this evening rather than face the Monday morning rush-hour traffic.'

'That makes sense.'

Less than an hour later he was gone. He had given her a brief hug and kissed her on the cheek before climbing into his car and driving away. She stood watching his tail lights fade in the gathering dusk and felt an unexpected sense of desolation. Then she told herself not to be so wimpish, went to her room and settled down with notebook and pen to plan her moves for the following day.

Melissa parked her rented Fiesta and punched out a number on her mobile phone.

'Good morning, Frank Ross and Company Limited.' The voice, youthful-sounding and cheerful, conveyed no hint of awareness that her employer had met with a violent end a mere three days ago. Perhaps the news had still not reached the junior staff.

'Good morning. Would it be possible to speak to Mr Frank Ross's secretary?'

'Miss Lester? I'll put you through.'

'Thank you.' How obliging of the girl, Melissa thought, not only to reveal the name but to connect her without asking who she was. The thought flashed into her mind that, had her father been listening, the girl would undoubtedly have received a stern rebuke for such an unbusinesslike response.

There were several bursts of ringing tone before a woman said, 'Eunice Lester.' The voice, more mature this time, held a sharp, authoritative edge.

'Am I speaking to Mr Ross's secretary?'

'His personal assistant. Who's calling, please?'

'My name's Melissa Craig.'

'Of what company?'

'No company, this is a private matter. I realise this may not be the best of times to call—'

'It certainly is not.' The tone was impatient almost to the point of rudeness. 'Will you please state your business as quickly as possible?'

It had been Melissa's intention to reveal her identity straight away, but fearing from the woman's attitude that such a claim would be challenged and her request for an interview refused out of hand, she decided to adopt a less direct approach. 'This may sound an odd question,' she began cautiously, 'but I think it likely that you have received an urgent call this morning from one of your directors, Mr Bell?'

'What if I have?' The voice became harsh with suspicion.

'So you are aware that your employer, Frank Ross, has died in very tragic circumstances?'

'What has that got to do with you? Are you from the press?'

'No. I'm Frank Ross's daughter.'

'His daughter? I didn't know—'

'You and quite a few others,' Melissa interrupted drily. 'Please, could I possibly see you for a few minutes?'

'How do I know you're telling the truth?'

'I promise you I am. I'd rather not say any more on the phone, but if you'll be kind enough to see me I'm sure I can very quickly convince you of my bona fides. If not, you can always have me thrown out.'

'Look, I'm very busy, I have to arrange a meeting of the senior personnel and—'

Sensing that the woman was beginning to waver, Melissa pressed home her advantage. 'That's no problem,' she said. 'What I have to say won't take long and I'm here already, in your car park.'

'All right, you'd better come up, but I warn you—'

'I'll be with you in a couple of minutes.'

The offices and factory of Frank Ross and Company Limited were on a landscaped industrial estate which appeared to have been developed according to an overall plan, since the buildings, although of modern design and each retaining a certain degree of individuality, formed part of a cohesive whole which gave a very pleasing appearance. Melissa was struck by the contrast with the somewhat ramshackle premises she remembered from her early years when she had spent part of her school holidays sharpening pencils, putting letters into envelopes and sticking on stamps moistened with a repulsive-looking rubber sponge under the eagle eye of her father's then secretary, Miss Thorpe. She could not recall ever having entered the factory, but she had vivid recollections of the poky room with sagging leatherette chairs where visitors waited; her father's office with its huge wooden desk and a heavy metal safe containing the company seal and minute book, which she had once been shown with as much ceremony as if they had been part of some national treasure; the dingy outer office, its floor covered with dark linoleum, through which visitors had to pass before being ushered into her father's presence and where Miss Thorpe, a stern woman with rimless glasses, a shining face innocent of make-up and grey hair scraped into a bun, spent her days behind a manual typewriter; the cubby-hole where she brewed tea for herself and her employer, so crammed with rows of box files that there was barely room for the electric kettle.

With such images still vivid in her memory, it came as something of a shock to Melissa when automatic glass doors slid apart to admit her to a bright, carpeted reception area, with a ring of tubular-framed chairs surrounding a glass-topped table spread with neatly arranged trade magazines and a self-service coffee machine installed in one corner. Evidently Frank Ross had at some stage been persuaded to update the company's image to an extent that she found surprising.

The telephone voice that had greeted her call turned out to belong to a jolly, freckle-faced girl with bright ginger hair, who directed her to an office on the first floor. She experienced a momentary pang on seeing a door marked, 'Frank Ross, Chairman', before it opened to reveal a slim, dark-haired, strong-featured woman in her early forties who eyed her up and down and said, 'Ms Craig? I'm Eunice Lester. Come in.' There was no smile or offer of a hand as she stood aside for Melissa to enter, closed the door behind her, sat down behind a modern, limed-oak desk and pointed to a chair facing her with the terse command, 'Please sit down.'

Feeling as if she was about to be interviewed for a job –

and a fairly lowly one at that – Melissa obeyed. She felt her hackles rising, then told herself that the controlled manner was probably a defence mechanism thrown up by the shock of her employer's sudden death. 'I undertook to give you some proof that I am who I say I am,' she began. 'I haven't actually got my birth certificate with me, but—'

'I don't think that will be necessary.' Something that could almost have been mistaken for a smile briefly softened the severe expression. 'You are very like him.'

'I am?' Melissa experienced another flash of memory, of hearing her mother saying proudly to some acquaintance while her thirteen-year-old self squirmed inwardly with embarrassment, *People say she has my eyes, but otherwise she's the image of Frank.* Aloud, she said, 'Have you worked for my father long?'

'Just over ten years.'

'That's quite a long time; long enough to have got to know him pretty well.'

The pale-blue eyes narrowed. 'What are you suggesting?'

'Only that you might have some idea why anyone would want to kill him.'

Eunice gave a start. 'What are you saying?' she demanded suspiciously. 'Mr Bell never—'

'There's no point in beating about the bush,' Melissa said bluntly. 'My father was murdered with a blow to the head from a sharp instrument, probably an axe, and the police suspect my mother of killing him.'

'But that's appalling! Sylvia couldn't possibly . . .'

For the first time, Melissa detected a note of genuine feeling that told her there was a human being behind the façade. She responded by saying in a gentler tone, 'You know my mother?'

'I've met her a number of times at functions, the firms' annual dinner and so on, but I can't say I really knew her. I used to make a point of having a chat with her because she always seemed to be a bit out of things; she didn't appear to have much in common with the other wives and of course FR – your father – was always circulating, doing his chairman thing.' Eunice shook her head in bewilderment. 'She always struck me as a very gentle person, utterly loyal to him. I can't believe she'd want to kill him – but you never can tell, can you?'

'Ms Lester, or may I call you Eunice?'

'Of course, and you are Melissa?'

'That's right. Now, I know you're pushed for time and you'll have a great deal to do and think about in the next few days, so I'll come straight to the point. In spite of some fairly strong circumstantial evidence my mother insists she didn't kill my father. I believe she's telling the truth and that's why I'm here. The police seem in no hurry to widen their enquiries and so I'm doing a bit of detective work on her behalf. I'm hoping you might be able—'

'You want my help in tracking down the real killer?' Eunice broke in. She sounded faintly incredulous. 'Is that what you're saying?'

'In a nutshell, yes. You've worked for the firm for ten

years – you must know everyone here. Have you any idea who might benefit in some way from his death?'

Eunice hesitated for what seemed a long time before saying, 'I can think of several.'

'Are you prepared to give me any names?'

'Not at the moment.'

'What about the takeover bid? Has that caused any dissension?'

'Quite a lot.' Eunice picked up a pen and began doodling on a notepad. 'Look, I can't discuss it now. I'd like a little time to think. Where can I contact you?'

'I'll probably be out and about quite a lot so I'll give you my mobile number.' Melissa wrote it down on a pad which Eunice pushed across the desk. 'I won't take up any more of your time. Thank you so much for seeing me.'

'Not at all.' Eunice extended a slim hand with well-manicured but unvarnished nails. 'I'm sorry if I appeared a little unfriendly at first.'

'No need to apologise. Oh, just one other thing. Did Father ever mention a woman called Jessica Round?'

'Not that I remember. Who is she?'

'She's president of a local flower club. My mother used to be a member but she resigned a few months ago. I have the impression that there was some kind of disagreement and I wondered if Father had mentioned it.'

'He never discussed his private life with me.'

'No, I didn't really think he would have done. One of his favourite sayings used to be "Never mix business with pleasure."'

Eunice pursed her lips, frowning. 'You're surely not suggesting this Mrs Round had anything to do with your father's death?' she said.

'No, of course not,' Melissa replied. 'On the contrary, she sounded very shocked — and very upset — when she heard about it.'

'You've been to see her?'

'Not yet, but I'm hoping to. Not that I really expect her to be able to shed any light, but you never know.'

As it turned out, Melissa's expectations in that direction proved considerably wide of the mark.

Chapter Thirteen

Back in her car, Melissa's first task was to jot down a brief record of her conversation with Eunice Lester. Next, she rang Mrs Menzies. 'How are things this morning?' she asked.

'Oh, Mrs Craig, I'm so glad you called. I've been trying that number you gave me, but—'

'Sorry, I had my mobile switched off while I was in a meeting. Is there a problem?'

'Your mother wants to go home, but she daren't go near the house because it's surrounded by people. I think they're from the newspapers.'

Melissa suppressed an expletive. 'I was afraid of this,' she said. 'In a way, I'm surprised they haven't turned up before.'

'Is there anything you can do to make them go away? They're all over the place, banging on the door, peering through the windows and shouting through the letterbox. Your poor mother's terrified.'

'I'll try, but from past experience I know how persistent reporters can be.'

'Please do. There's quite a crowd collecting, wondering what's going on.'

'I'll be with you in fifteen minutes.'

As Melissa turned into Brimley Road she saw three or four women — presumably the 'crowd' referred to by Mrs Menzies and, since none of them seemed to be wearing outdoor clothes, almost certainly curious neighbours — gathered on the pavement opposite her mother's house. No doubt, she thought as she drove past with no apparent show of interest, others were watching from behind their curtains. She parked the Fiesta further along the road, which enabled her to walk back to Mrs Menzies' house without having to pass her mother's. Through the screen of shrubs separating the two front gardens she spotted a group of people, obviously from the media, one with a camcorder and a furry microphone, clustered at her mother's front door. None of them appeared to notice her as she slipped quietly through Mrs Menzies' gate. The door opened before she had time to press the bell-push and she was ushered inside. In the hall, her mother rushed into her arms.

'Oh, Lissie!' she gasped. 'Thank God you're here! Those dreadful people are after me. I'm sure they think I killed Father. They'll attack me if they find out where I am!'

'Nonsense, Mother, no one's going to hurt you.'

'How did they get here? How do they know?'

'The police will have told them at this morning's briefing.'

'What's a briefing?'

Patiently, Melissa explained. 'There might have been a short statement on Saturday morning that a murder had taken place in this neighbourhood, but without naming the victim or the address. Now the police have obviously released more details and the reporters want a story.'

'But I can't talk to them, I can't.' Tears rolled down Sylvia's pale cheeks.

'Of course you can't, dear,' Mrs Menzies interposed. She turned to Melissa, her face flushed with indignation. 'Isn't it enough that her husband's been brutally murdered and she's been questioned by the police, without having to face those ghouls? They ought to be arrested themselves, the lot of them.'

'They're only doing their job. I'll go and talk to them and give them some sort of statement. Then perhaps they'll go away. I'll have to have some reason for being here so I'll say I've come to collect some things for you, Mother. Will you let me have your keys?'

'Of course, dear, I'll get them.'

Sylvia hurried upstairs and Melissa took the opportunity of saying in a low voice to Mrs Menzies, 'How did she sleep?'

'Quite well, considering. I've spoken to her doctor and he's coming to see her later on today.'

'Thank you so much. I can't tell you—' Melissa broke off as Sylvia came hurrying back downstairs.

'Here you are, dear,' she said, a little breathlessly, handing over the keys. 'I'm so thankful you're here, Lissie. If anyone can persuade those horrid people to leave me alone I'm sure you can.'

'I'll do my best to convince them they'll only be wasting their time if they hang around. I'll come back as soon as I'm sure the coast is clear.'

Let's hope I get lucky, Melissa thought. Her heart was thumping and she felt her knees shaking as she walked through the open gate of her mother's house and was immediately surrounded and bombarded with questions.

'Are you a relative?'

'Can you tell us how the victim died?'

'We understand someone has been questioned; can you give us any details?'

'All right, one at a time please.' It was not the first time she had been cornered by reporters and experience came to her aid now, helping to overcome the nervousness. 'I'm Mr and Mrs Ross's daughter, Mrs Craig,' she announced. 'Can I help you?'

'Do you live locally, Mrs Craig?' asked a pale young woman with an earnest expression.

'No, I live near Gloucester. I came to be with my mother as soon as I heard the dreadful news.' Melissa gave a mental vote of thanks that at least no one appeared to recognise her; the last thing she wanted at this stage was for her professional identity to become public.

'The police said it was a particularly brutal crime. Can you give us a few more details, or say who found the victim?' asked another, older woman holding up a small tape recorder.

'I'm not prepared to give you that kind of information; you'll have to wait until the police make a further statement.'

'Have the police any idea who might have killed your father, or what the motive might be?' the woman persisted.

'You'll have to ask them.'

'Have *you* any idea?'

'None whatsoever at present, I'm afraid.'

'Can we have a word with the widow, or a picture?'

'You can have a picture of me, by all means,' said Melissa with a wry smile, since cameras were already clicking. 'My mother isn't here. She's naturally very shocked by what has happened – in fact, she spent Saturday night in hospital under observation – and she's presently staying with a friend.'

'You don't appear particularly shocked.' The remark came from a middle-aged man with a beer belly and a broken front tooth. He eyed Melissa with his head cocked on one side. 'I've seen you before, haven't I?'

'Not that I remember,' she said warily. 'Now, if there are no further questions . . .'

With a certain reluctance, but appearing to accept that there was nothing to be gained by pressing her further, the group began melting away. Melissa turned, put the key in the front door lock and was about to step into the porch when she felt a tap on her shoulder. It came as no surprise to find herself face to face with the man who had claimed a previous acquaintance. The smell of beer on his breath made him even less attractive at close quarters and it was all she could do to avoid sounding rude as she said, 'I think I made it clear that I've said all I'm going to say.'

'Oh you did, indeed you did, Mrs Craig – or should I say, Mel Craig?' he added with a conspiratorial lowering of his voice. Melissa's heart sank; it was the realisation of her fears. 'Knew I'd seen you somewhere – you were on the *Bookshelf* programme on the telly a few weeks ago, weren't you?' Without waiting for confirmation he added, 'Name's Botting – Denis Botting, freelance journalist.'

'Well, Mr Botting, thank you for not revealing my identity in front of all the others.'

'Wouldn't want to do that, would I? This is my story.'

'Look, I'd be very grateful if you'd—'

'Oh, don't worry, I'm not planning to release this one just yet.' He moved closer and the whiff of beer became almost overwhelming. 'Bearing in mind that your name has been associated with one or two murder enquiries in the past, I assume that you'll be taking a special interest in this one – doing a spot of sleuthing of your own, maybe?'

'I'm sure the police have the matter well in hand,' she protested, desperate to be rid of him yet curious to know what he had to say. 'Now, if you'll be kind enough to explain what this is all about?'

'Don't worry, I don't expect you to answer any more questions – not just yet, anyway.' He took a card from an inside pocket of his anorak and offered it to her. 'I know a lot about what goes on in this town and I could be very useful to you. Likewise, you could be very useful to me.'

Reluctantly, she accepted the card. 'Are you suggesting some kind of a deal?'

'Why not? I give you the lowdown on anyone you might be interested in, you pass on to me anything you turn up in your enquiries – and I'll keep stumm about who you really are.'

'The police already know who I am.'

The journalist appeared taken aback. 'They do?'

'My mother told them. I'm afraid at the same time she rather indiscreetly hinted that I'd be tracking down Father's killer for them. I don't think Detective Inspector Adair is amused.'

He gave a hoarse chuckle. 'She wouldn't be. Thinks the sun shines out of her fanny, that one does. Likes to be one of the boys, makes the lower ranks call her Guv instead of Ma'am. She certainly won't be telling the world she's being helped by a crime novelist. Well,' he went on as Melissa said nothing, 'What do you say?'

'I'm sorry, I can't see where all this is leading. You talk about having a lot of local knowledge, so what makes you think I'll be in a position to help you?'

'Ah!' A crafty expression spread over Botting's fleshy features. 'Local knowledge, yes. Inside knowledge of what goes on in Frank Ross's business, no. The takeover bid?' he suggested as she made no response. 'I imagine you know about that?'

'Of course.' She saw no reason to reveal that she had

learned about it only the previous evening from a news-paper report.

'And your father opposed it?'

'Who told you that?'

'Just a hunch based on what I know of his reputation as one of the old school. The problem is, I haven't been able to get anyone to confirm it. No one at Ross's will tell me anything. I'm what you might call *persona non grata* there.'

'I wonder why that is?'

He gave a slight leer. 'That's another story.'

'So what exactly are you suggesting?'

'You want to know who topped your Dad, I imagine?'

'Of course.'

'And you plan on doing a bit of nosing around. No, don't give me that crap about leaving it to the police,' he went on, sensing that she was about to protest. 'I'm sure you'll be interested to know rumour has it that there have been a number of, shall we say, internal pressures. Frank Ross was not the most liberal-minded of employers. In fact, I heard on the grapevine a while back that after being sacked for alleged bad timekeeping, one of the factory workers was planning to sue for wrongful dismissal.'

'Go on.'

He gave another gravelly chuckle which led to a brief coughing fit. 'Thought that'd get you,' he spluttered from behind a surprisingly clean handkerchief. 'Now in my book, the odds are heavily in favour of the motive for your Dad's death lying somewhere within the company. And you, as his daughter, will surely have every right to talk to the people there. Maybe' — the crafty look returned — 'you've already been to see them.'

'Maybe.'

'Learn anything?'

'Not yet.'

'But you're hoping to.'

'Maybe.'

He gave a satisfied nod, blew his nose and returned the handkerchief to his pocket. 'You give me names, I'll fill you in on individual backgrounds. Do we have a deal?'

Melissa heaved a sigh. 'I suppose so.'

'Great. Where can I contact you?'

Resignedly, she gave him her mobile number. He wrote it down in his notebook and then, to her relief, went back to his elderly fawn Rover — the only car remaining outside the house — and drove away. She went indoors and peered out of an upstairs window for signs of anyone hanging about, but the street was, so far as she could see, deserted. After watching for a few minutes, she called Mrs Menzies. 'I think they've all gone, but it's quite possible one of them is lurking around somewhere, waiting to see where I go when I leave here. Is there any way I can get back to your house without going out into the street?'

'As it happens, there's a gap in the hedge in the back garden where your father took out a dead tree a few days ago. I'll come and point it out to you.'

'Thank you. Ask Mother where she keeps the back door key, will you?'

Minutes later the three women were together in Mrs Menzies' sitting-room. Sylvia's eyes were glowing with pride. 'You're so clever, Lissie!' she exclaimed. 'They were gone in no time – how did you do it?'

'Never mind that now. There are some things I have to ask you, Mother, and I want you to promise to tell me the truth.'

'Of course, dear. Would I lie to my own daughter?' *Yes, if it meant concealing something you don't want her to know,* Melissa thought as Sylvia, assuming a slightly hurt expression, waited expectantly for the first question.

'I found out yesterday that a big company is trying to buy the firm. Do you know anything about it? I know you said Father never discussed business with you, but didn't he even mention a takeover bid?'

'Yes, he did say something about it, but he said he wasn't going to sell, no matter what the others thought.'

'Did he say who he meant by the others?'

'I suppose he meant other people at the firm. He was the boss, so they'd have had to do what he told them.'

'Do you know any of the people he was talking about?'

'I met a few of them, but I don't really know them.'

'Can you tell me their names and what their jobs are?'

Sylvia frowned. 'There's Mr Patmore and Mr Fingle but I don't know exactly what they do. And there's Miss Lester, of course. She's your father's secretary and she's such a nice person. She always made a point of chatting to me—' She broke off, her face clouding. 'She's been with him for several years and she's quite devoted to him. She must be very upset.'

Feeling that in the circumstances a little dissimulation was excusable, Melissa said, 'So you'd have no objection if I went to see her?'

'Why would you want to do that, dear?'

'Because I believe Father could have been killed by someone within the company, or closely connected with it, and she might have some idea who would benefit by his death.'

'Do you really think so?' Sylvia's eyes widened in almost girlish excitement at the suggestion.

'It's just an idea at the moment. Now, I know you changed your mind about wanting me to sleuth around . . .'

Sylvia assumed an expression of total innocence. 'I don't know what gave you that idea, Lissie,' she protested. 'Of course I want you to find your father's killer, just to stop that horrid policewoman arresting me again. You go and talk to Miss Lester — or anyone else at the company you like.'

Melissa gave no sign that she regarded the words 'at the company' as significant. 'Fine,' she said. 'Now, Mrs Menzies said you'd like to go home.'

'Yes, please, if you're sure those dreadful people have gone.'

'It's possible one of them is still keeping an eye on the house in the hope of spotting you, so I advise you to stay indoors for the next couple of hours.'

'But I want to go shopping and buy something for your

supper. You will be staying with me tonight, won't you, Lissie? Please!'

'Yes, of course. I'll stay as long as you need me.' Impulsively, Melissa leaned across and kissed her mother on the cheek. 'Leave the shopping till this afternoon.'

'The doctor's supposed to be coming this afternoon.'

'So he is, I'd almost forgotten. Why don't I stay with you until he's been? Then we can go shopping together.'

'Oh no, dear, you mustn't waste any more time here – you go and start your enquiries.'

'But someone should be with you.'

'That's all right, I'll be here,' Mrs Menzies interposed.

'There you are!' said Sylvia with the same look of childish triumph Melissa had noticed before. 'You run along, Lissie.'

'If you're sure.'

'Quite sure,' said Sylvia firmly.

'All right, I'll go as long as you promise not to leave the house for the rest of the morning, just in case.'

'I promise.'

'Good. I'll go and check out of my hotel and then I'll make some phone calls. I'll keep in touch and I'll see you later on.'

Having handed over her mother's keys and thanked Mrs Menzies for her continued help and support, Melissa made her escape from the house by the same circuitous route as she had reached it. As she fastened her mother's front gate and returned to the Fiesta she glanced up the street. She was not surprised to see a fawn Rover waiting by the kerb a short distance away, nor by the fact that the driver bent down as if reaching for something from the passenger footwell as she drove past and then pulled out to follow her. By accelerating hard to beat an amber light she managed to give it the slip at the first set of traffic lights and could not resist a jaunty wave as Denis Botting was forced to come to a screeching halt on the red.

Chapter Fourteen

Back at the Beverley Court Hotel, Melissa ate a sandwich lunch, packed her bag and checked out. Next, she phoned Jessica Round. The voice that answered had the same peremptory tone as on the previous occasion, but mellowed instantly when she introduced herself.

'Oh, Mrs Craig, I was going to call you. I feel I owe you an apology.'

'Not at all. You'd had bad news and you were upset. I quite understand.'

'I don't think you do. I'd like an opportunity to explain.'

'And I'd welcome the chance of a chat. Would it be convenient if I called round now?'

'Is your friend with you, or . . .?'

'No, he's gone back to London. I'm on my own.'

'In that case yes, please do come.' There was no doubt about the note of relief in the carefully modulated voice. 'I'm here all afternoon.'

'I can be with you in fifteen minutes if that's all right.'

'Fine.'

During the short drive Melissa tried to form a mental picture of the woman whom she suspected of having had, if not an affair, at least a close personal relationship with her father. Her mother had described Jessica as over-bearing and flashy; the former description was certainly consistent with her own early impression, but it was difficult to imagine the austere, fastidious man she recalled from childhood being attracted to anyone possessing even the slightest touch of vulgarity. Remembering his outrage on learning of her own fall from grace, she found it even more difficult to picture him involved in any kind of liaison, however platonic. Then she reflected that, in common with so many men of his generation, he might well have demanded that his own women remain chaste while excusing his own sexual adventures as mere pecca-dillos.

'Elegant' was the first adjective that came into Melissa's mind as the door of the flat was opened by a woman of about her own age. Her beautifully styled head of pale-gold hair was held proudly erect on a long, graceful neck; her fine-boned features were expertly but discreetly made up and the hand she offered Melissa was cool, perfectly manicured and tipped with pearl. She was wearing a simple navy-blue dress that fell in flattering folds round a well-proportioned figure; a bracelet in three different shades of gold on her right wrist was complemented by a matching chain round her neck and small 'lover's knots' in her ears. Her demeanour was poised and confident, yet Melissa sensed an underlying nervousness and there was a strained, tense look in her blue-grey eyes.

She greeted Melissa warmly by name before leading her through a small entrance hall into an L-shaped room. The shorter of the two sides was laid out as a dining area; the longer was furnished with chairs and a sofa upholstered in cream leather facing a picture window overlooking landscaped grounds. Professional designers and craftsmen had clearly been at work; the hand-made furniture, the floor-length curtains with their pelmets and swags, and the thick, discreetly patterned carpet were all of the highest quality, chosen and arranged with skill. The overall effect was a combination of opulence and perfect taste, but this was no expensive showroom designed to impress. Everywhere were indications that it was a well-loved home, with books, pictures and photographs in plenty and several artistic flower arrangements which filled the room with the sweetness of spring.

'Mrs Craig, it's such a pleasure to meet you,' Jessica Round began as she invited her visitor with a gesture to sit on the sofa beside her. 'As you see,' she went on, pointing to a low table on which Melissa was gratified to see hardback copies of several of her novels, 'I am a great fan of Nathan Latimer and I hope you'll do me the honour of signing those for me.'

'I'll be delighted, but please call me Melissa.'

'Thank you Melissa, and you must call me Jessica.' There was a short, slightly embarrassed silence before she said, 'I do apologise for putting you off like that yesterday, but I couldn't face you – or anyone. It was such a dreadful shock; he was a very dear friend . . .'

Her voice failed for a moment and Melissa said quietly, 'You're speaking of the death of my father? Or, to be more precise, of my father's murder?'

At the mention of death, Jessica winced; at the word 'murder' her poise collapsed. She covered her face and began weeping quietly, the tears trickling slowly between her fingers. After a moment she said, in a voice half strangled by grief, 'I don't know what you must think of me.'

'What I think of you isn't important just now. I already know – or rather, I have reason to believe – that you had a very close relationship with my father.'

'Who told you that?' Jessica whispered from behind the shield of her hands.

'No one – not in so many words – but several things made me curious. It appears that my mother left your flower club shortly after the church festival and I've heard conflicting reasons for her resignation. That's what was behind my original call – I wondered if you could tell me exactly what happened. You see, I've been estranged from my parents for many years.'

Having partially regained her self-control, Jessica took out a handkerchief and dried her eyes. 'Yes, I know,' she said quietly.

'I thought you probably did. It didn't occur to me at the time, but I recalled later that unlike one or two other people I've spoken to you expressed no surprise at my existence – although you did sound taken aback when I said I was Mel Craig.'

'That's something he didn't tell me.'

'That was obvious. Anyway, I knew Lottie Haynes was the only person my mother had confided in, so it must have been Father who told you about me. And then, your sudden change of attitude, your refusal to see me after you learned about the murder from Lottie. But the thing that made me wonder if you and my father had' – Melissa hesitated in her search for a diplomatic way of making her point before going on – 'that you and he knew one another rather better than I supposed at first was the way my mother jumped down my throat as soon as your name was mentioned.'

Jessica gave a horrified gasp. 'She knew? Sylvia knew about me and Frank?'

'Knew, or suspected.'

'But how? We were so careful.'

'I've no idea, but she's got eyes and she's not daft.'

'Was it at her suggestion that you contacted me?'

'On the contrary. Look, I'd better put you in the picture from the beginning.' Melissa gave a brief account of the events following her mother's arrest and subsequent release. 'She swears she's innocent and she begged me to make some enquiries, but when I said I'd spoken to you she became very agitated and insisted I forget it. Later, when I said I thought the murder might have something to do with the takeover bid for the company and Father's determination not to accept, she changed her mind again and urged me to carry on ferreting around.'

Jessica's carefully shaped eyebrows lifted. 'Would that include permission to talk to me?' she asked with a touch of irony.

'I'm sure it didn't, but as she didn't specifically exclude you I decided to take it I'd been given *carte blanche* to talk to whoever I thought appropriate.'

As they exchanged faintly conspiratorial smiles, Melissa was conscious of a dawning sympathy for this woman who had evidently played a significant part in the last few months of her father's life. 'Can I ask you a very blunt question?' she said.

'I think I can guess what it is. You want to know if Frank and I were lovers. The answer's yes. It all happened very suddenly – I think it took us both completely by surprise.'

'These things sometimes do.'

'It began when he called here to settle a bill for some flowers and equipment I'd bought for the festival. We'd met before – at the church, of course – while it was all in the planning stage. I think we were both aware from the outset that there was some kind of chemistry between us, but it wasn't until he phoned and said he'd like to bring the cheque to me here that I guessed . . . I *knew* what he had in mind and what was likely to happen. I'd always had this feeling, you see, that behind that reserved, rather cold manner was a deeply unhappy man and I wanted to—' Jessica broke off, her face working as she fought once more to contain her emotion.

'I think he must have confided in you quite a lot,' said Melissa gently. 'Did he tell you what happened to me, why I left home?'

'Oh yes, and it nearly broke his heart. You were his pride and joy, his untarnished angel—'

'And he couldn't forgive my fall,' Melissa interrupted, suddenly and painfully aware that the uncontrollable tremor in her voice was caused not only by bitterness but also by sorrow for the insight that had come too late. 'At the time, I could think only of myself and how ill-used I felt. It never entered my head that he was suffering too.'

'You were very young – you mustn't feel guilty.'

'It's not guilt so much as regret that I feel now. We were both proud and stubborn.'

'Believe me, he had his regrets as well.' Jessica reached out and touched Melissa lightly on the arm; the warmth of her compassion and understanding was almost palpable. 'I can't be certain, of course, but I believe that if this terrible thing hadn't happened, he would in time have been able to swallow his pride and do something to try and heal the breach between you, and to get to know his grandchild, if possible.'

'That's comforting to know,' Melissa said huskily. 'He'd have been so proud of Simon.'

'What about your mother?' Jessica asked after a moment. 'How did she react when your father disowned you?'

'She took his part, like she always did. She claims now

that she had no choice, that she was totally dominated by him.'

'You sound as if you have your doubts about that.'

'I'm not sure what to believe. You've probably been closer to him than anyone these last few months. What's your opinion?'

'He never spoke a disloyal word about your mother, but' – Jessica hesitated in evident embarrassment before continuing – 'he gave me to understand that the physical side of the marriage virtually ended after you left. It's my belief she froze him out; he once said he would never force himself on a wife who didn't want him, however compliant she might be.'

'Perhaps that was her revenge on him for throwing me out.' The pity of it, the bleak tragedy of two people struggling in a web of intolerance and misunderstanding of their own making, had Melissa once more blinking away the tears. 'It was probably the only weapon she was able to use against him. Of course, she'd never speak of anything like that to me, she was always too shy to talk about sex. In any case, she's changed her attitude on several matters in the short time I've been with her and I'm never sure—'

'It's probably due to shock.'

'Yes, that's what I've been telling myself. Her doctor's coming to see her this afternoon.'

'Then I mustn't keep you long – I expect you'll want to get back to her.'

'No, that's all right. Mrs Menzies, her neighbour, is

looking after her. I've been dismissed with instructions to pursue my enquiries. I've had a word with Father's secretary – personal assistant, I should say – and enlisted her help.' As Melissa described her meeting with Eunice Lester a thought struck her. 'Did you know about the takeover bid, by the way? I've been wondering whether there was conflict between Father and any of his colleagues.'

'If there was, he never referred to it; in fact, he never discussed business with me at all.'

'And Eunice told me he never mentioned his private affairs in the office.'

'I'm sure that's true. I think he kept the two sides of his life in entirely separate compartments.'

'So you wouldn't know if there was anyone in the company who might have had a grudge against him?'

Jessica shook her head. 'I'm afraid not,' she said sadly. 'I'd give anything to be able to help find his murderer, but I can't think of a single thing that might be useful.'

'Well, if anything does occur to you, will you get in touch? You have my mobile number. I keep it switched off quite a lot of the time, but you can always leave a message. Now, you wanted me to sign some books?'

'Yes please. Would you like some tea?'

'That would be nice.'

They drank tea and chatted about books and writing for a while before Melissa got up to go. As they parted at the front door, Jessica hesitated for a moment before asking, 'How exactly did he die?'

'A single blow to the head, probably with an axe.'

As she drove away, Melissa reflected that the stricken expression on the face of her father's lover on learning the savage truth would remain with her for quite a while. Subsequent events were to etch it indelibly on her memory.

Chapter Fifteen

On leaving Jessica Round's flat Melissa drove straight back to her mother's house. She parked the Fiesta on the drive and rang the bell. The door was opened by Mrs Menzies who announced, without any preamble, 'She went out. She asked me to stay and let you in, just in case you got back before her.'

The lack of warmth in the woman's manner reminded Melissa of her earlier hostile demeanour towards herself, which had begun to soften over the past forty-eight hours. Wondering what lay behind the change, and making a special effort to sound placatory, she said, 'That was really very kind of you.'

The remark was greeted with an audible sniff and Melissa hesitated for a moment before asking, 'Did she say where she was going?'

'She said something about shopping. I offered to go with her, but she's obviously had enough of my company.'

A hurt note crept into Mrs Menzies' voice. Melissa opened her mouth to say something reassuring, but before she could speak Mrs Menzies added, almost grudgingly, 'She made a phone call before she left.'

'Do you know who she was speaking to?'

'She used the upstairs phone and I'm not in the habit of eavesdropping!'

It was clear that Sylvia had caused grave offence by not having taken Mrs Menzies into her confidence. In a further attempt to soothe wounded pride, Melissa said hastily, 'It never occurred to me for a moment that you were. I just wondered if Mother happened to mention—'

'Well, she didn't.'

'I'm sure she'd have told you if it was anything important. Did the doctor come, by the way?'

'He did.'

'What did he say?'

'I wasn't present while he examined her.'

'I just thought she might have told you—'

'She didn't tell me anything. All I know is what I heard him say as he left: she's to take things quietly and see him again in a week's time.' Resentment at what was clearly considered to be a deliberate withholding of information became more evident by the minute.

'It doesn't sound as if there's anything too serious the matter with her then,' said Melissa. 'Just the same, I think I'll try and have a word with him. Do you know his number?'

'It'll be in the phone book: Doctor Newton. His surgery's in Ravenscroft Road.'

The subtext of the last remark was so plainly, *Look it up for yourself. I see no reason to go out of my way to be helpful after the way I've been treated*, that Melissa hesitated a second time before asking diffidently, 'Do you happen to remember what time she went out?'

'About ten to three, to catch the three o'clock bus.'

'Did she say what time she'd be back?'

'She said by five at the latest.' Mrs Menzies sounded almost reluctant to part with the one scrap of information she had been privy to.

'I see.' Melissa glanced at her watch. 'It's four fifteen now; she shouldn't be long.' In a final effort to thaw the chilly atmosphere she said, 'Would you like a cup of tea? I'm sure I can—'

'Not for me. I'll be going now.'

'Well, thank you once again for all your help – it's greatly appreciated.'

There was no response to this remark and a move to accompany the stony-faced visitor to the front door was forestalled by a gesture and a curt, 'I can let myself out.'

'Oh dear!' Melissa said aloud as the front door slammed shut. 'There are some fences to be mended there. Now, where's that phone book.' She dialled the number of Doctor Newton's surgery with one ear cocked, in the hope that not only would he be in, but that he would be prepared to answer her questions and that the call could be completed before her mother's return.

She was in luck on all counts. 'I'm very glad of this opportunity to have a word with you,' said Doctor Newton after she had introduced herself. He sounded young and friendly. 'It's quite obvious that your mother is still suffering from shock after her terrible experience. That's only natural and probably explains a certain amount of confusion which I'm hoping will right itself once she's recovered from the trauma. Will you be staying with her for a while?'

'Until she's well enough to be left on her own, yes.'

'In that case, I suggest you keep a close eye on her and let me know if she shows any further symptoms.'

'What sort of symptoms?'

'It's hard to say, but she did make one or two contradictory statements and when I pressed her to say which was correct she became agitated and brushed my questions aside. She said several times that she was quite all right and couldn't understand why I'd been called.'

'I presume she told you about being taken to the police station on Saturday . . . and how she passed out and spent the night in hospital?'

'The lady who called my surgery outlined the situation, yes. Your mother was at pains to assure me that her arrest was what she called "just another example of police stupidity".'

'I'm inclined to agree with her there. The duty solicitor soon convinced them they didn't have enough evidence to detain her.'

'Well, as I say, the whole experience has obviously

traumatised her, so don't hesitate to call me again if things don't improve. I've given her a prescription for a mild sedative which should help settle her down.'

'Thank you, Doctor. I'll keep in touch.'

Melissa put down the phone and went into the sitting-room to wait. Thinking that Eunice Lester might have been trying to contact her, she checked her mobile for messages. There was no word from Eunice, but to her surprise Jessica Round had called shortly after she left the flat. There was a hint of bewilderment, almost of anxiety in the recorded voice. 'Melissa, this is to let you know your mother has just phoned. She sounded a little strange; she wants to come and see me, but she wouldn't say what it's about. I thought I'd better let you know in case you're wondering where she is.' After a brief pause, Jessica added, 'I did so enjoy our chat. Perhaps we'll meet again some time.'

Melissa barely had time to register this unexpected turn of events when she heard a key in the front door. The next minute Sylvia's voice hailed her from the hall. 'Are you there, Lissie? I'm home!' She came into the room beaming and gave Melissa a hug. 'I'm sorry I wasn't in when you got here, but I wanted to get something really nice for your supper.'

As Melissa returned her embrace she could feel the slender body shaking slightly. 'Are you all right, Mother?' she asked anxiously.

'Perfectly all right, dear. Why do you ask?'

'You're trembling, and you're out of breath.'

'That's because I've been hurrying from the bus stop – I thought it looked like rain. I'm a little puffed, but I'm perfectly all right. Now, have you had a cup of tea?'

'Not yet. I offered to make one for Mrs Menzies, but she wouldn't stay. I'm afraid she went off in a bit of a huff.'

'Oh dear, why do you think that was?'

'I think it was because you wouldn't tell her what the doctor said, or—' On the point of adding, 'or who you phoned before you went out,' Melissa decided instead to wait and see what information would be volunteered.

'Oh, she's such a nosy old thing!' said Sylvia impatiently. The possibility that she had offended a loyal and supportive friend did not appear to cause her undue concern. 'Let's go into the kitchen. You put the kettle on while I unpack the shopping. I'm going to do lamb chops with mushrooms and tomatoes and mashed potatoes – I hope that's all right. It used to be your favourite meal, do you remember?'

Melissa's throat tightened momentarily. 'I remember,' she said softly. She filled the kettle at the sink while her mother bustled about putting her purchases away. 'Did you meet anyone you know while you were out?' she asked casually.

'No dear. Would you like a piece of cake with your tea? I bought a chocolate sponge. The cups and saucers are in that cupboard.'

It was plain that she had no intention of mentioning her telephone call to Jessica Round or of saying whether the proposed visit had taken place. Melissa was conscious of a vague sense of disquiet, but since she could hardly refer to the matter herself without revealing the source of her knowledge and risking an indignant outburst she decided not to pursue it for the time being. Instead, she asked, 'What did the doctor say?'

'Oh, nothing much – just to take things quietly and see him again next week if I was worried about anything.'

Not much to be learned there either, thought Melissa as they settled down to their tea and cake. There was, she felt, an unreal quality about the situation. Outwardly it was perfectly normal – a mother and daughter enjoying a quiet chat before beginning preparations for their evening meal – but beneath the surface lay the shared knowledge of a terrible deed, the truth of which had yet to be revealed, a truth that could either bind them more closely together or tear them apart for the remainder of their lives. Unanswered questions and nagging doubts jostled for attention in Melissa's brain. Covertly, she watched her mother placidly drinking her tea, eating a slice of cake, inspecting the teapot and adding more boiling water before pouring out second cups. She marvelled at her composure . . . and then experienced a rush of apprehension at the thought of what might lie behind that calm, controlled demeanour.

When they had finished their tea Sylvia said, 'I've made up the bed in the spare room – and I've got a little surprise for you. Come along.' She led the way upstairs, opened a door and turned to her daughter with a brilliant smile and a gesture of triumph, like a conjuror producing a rabbit. 'There!' she exclaimed.

It was a simply furnished room with a single bed, a chair, a chest of drawers and a small wardrobe. The rose-sprigged curtains matched the bedspread and there were a few pictures of rural scenes on the white-painted walls, but Melissa noticed none of these. Once again she felt a stab of emotion as her eyes were drawn to the line of soft toys ranged on the pillow: a rabbit with one ear missing, a dog with bald patches on its fur, a china doll, a battered teddy bear with a scarlet bow round its neck. 'Your father put all your toys in a bag for a local charity, but I managed to rescue these and hide them,' said Sylvia. She sounded like a naughty child who had played a trick on her teacher. 'Teddy's bow was falling to pieces so I found that bit of ribbon and made him a new one.'

'That was a very sweet thought,' said Melissa huskily. She put her arms round her mother and held her close for a moment. 'The room's lovely,' she went on. 'I don't recognise any of the furniture though; I suppose Father threw out everything that reminded him of me,' she added, half to herself.

Sylvia's mouth tightened momentarily, but all she said was, 'You unpack your case and have a freshen up while I start preparing the supper. The bathroom's next door.'

Later, when they had eaten their meal, they went into the sitting-room with their cups of coffee and Sylvia switched on the radio. An advertising jingle promoting a mobile phone network was followed by a breezy voice announcing that a round-up of the latest news within the county would follow in a couple of minutes. 'Just time for a quick skip to the loo!' Sylvia said coyly and left the room.

Melissa put down her cup and saucer, sat back in an armchair and closed her eyes. The sense of unreality returned; the relaxed atmosphere and the dawning sense of companionship with her mother seemed to have created a protective bubble, a temporary refuge which had given them an opportunity to take the first tentative steps towards re-establishing the old loving relationship. For the first time since her arrival the death of her father and the need to know who had killed him slid to the back of her mind. There were leads to follow, people to talk to. Tomorrow she would try Eunice Lester again, and there was Mr Bell, who would surely not refuse to speak to her once he knew she had her mother's authority to approach him. And she would have a word with Jessica Round about that telephone call and the request for a visit.

She was tired; she felt herself drifting, then jerked awake as a voice from the radio announced, 'We understand that the body of a woman has been discovered in a flat in Alderley Court. Reports that she was stabbed are unconfirmed, but it is believed that the attack took place some time during this afternoon. The victim has not been named and no further details have been released so far.'

Melissa sat bolt upright in her chair, her heart pounding

in mingled shock and apprehension. At that moment Sylvia re-entered the room, took one look at her and exclaimed, 'Are you all right, dear? You look as if you've seen a ghost.'

For a moment Melissa was speechless; then she said in a voice made hoarse with fear, 'Mother, where did you go this afternoon? You must tell me, please!'

'I told you, dear. I went shopping.'

'Did you pay anyone a visit?'

'No, of course not.' The denial came quickly – too quickly. Sylvia refused to meet Melissa's eye as she asked in a voice that shook slightly, 'Whatever makes you think—'

'Please, Mother, don't lie to me. You went to see Jessica Round, didn't you?'

Sylvia sat down and sent darting glances from side to side. 'It's not nice for a daughter to accuse her mother of lying,' she protested uneasily.

'It isn't nice when a mother lies to her daughter. You did go and see Jessica Round, didn't you?'

'Why would I want to see her?'

'You tell me. You phoned her during the afternoon and asked if you could pay her a visit.'

'However did you know that?' Sylvia's manner switched from evasion to indignation. 'That nosy Mrs Menzies, she told you; she must have listened in—'

'It wasn't Mrs Menzies who told me, it was Jessica.'

'Jessica! You've been talking to her behind my back? Lissie, how dare you interfere in my—'

'Never mind that for the moment. You did go to see her, didn't you?'

Like water draining from a colander, Sylvia's anger subsided as quickly as it had flared and her eyes dropped to her lap. 'Yes,' she admitted in a whisper.

'Why?'

There was a long pause. At last she said, so quietly that Melissa could only just hear the words, 'I wanted to tell her that I've forgiven her.'

'You mean, for having an affair with Father?'

'Yes.' The admission was a barely audible sigh.

'I don't understand; you nearly jumped down my throat when I suggested—'

'I was only trying to protect you, dear.' Sylvia's voice became stronger and she raised her head to meet Melissa's eye. 'I didn't want you to know. I didn't want you to think of him as an adulterer; it wasn't entirely his fault, you see, and ever since he died I've been feeling so guilty, I felt I had to do something to . . .' The voice trailed off again; the brown eyes filled with tears. 'I'll try and explain one day.'

'I think I understand,' said Melissa. 'Now, Mother, I want to ask you a very important question.'

'Yes, dear?'

'Was Jessica all right when you left her?'

'Of course she was. Why do you ask?'

'It's only that—' Melissa broke off at the sound of the doorbell.

Sylvia jumped. 'Whoever can be calling at this time of night?' she said nervously.

'I'll go and see.' With a sense of impending disaster, Melissa went out into the hall and opened the front door. In the porch stood Detective Inspector Mollie Adair and Detective Constable Carole Sharwood.

Chapter Sixteen

'A murder at Alderley Court!' Sylvia stared at Detective Inspector Adair in consternation. 'How terrible! But why have you come to tell me?' Her expression changed suddenly; she put a hand to her mouth and sank back on the couch with the colour draining from her face, staring fearfully at the detectives as if they were angels of doom come to carry her away. 'It's Jessica, isn't it – Jessica Round? She's been killed and you think I did it, don't you? First you accuse me of killing my own husband and now . . .' Her voice rose to a thin, piteous wail. She turned to Melissa and buried her face on her shoulder. 'I didn't kill her; why would I kill her?' she sobbed.

'No one's saying you did,' said Melissa, gently stroking her head and praying that it was true.

'Why are they here, then?'

'Mrs Ross, your daughter is absolutely right – we aren't here because we think you had anything to do with this particular crime.' In marked contrast to their earlier encounters, DI Adair's manner was almost conciliatory. She drew up a chair, sat down and arranged her black calf-length skirt round her shiny black-nyloned legs while DC Sharwood settled on a low, tapestry-covered stool and pulled out her notebook. 'This is just routine,' the inspector explained. 'We're trying to contact everyone who was in or near Alderley Court this afternoon and eliminate them from our enquiries. Now, we under-stand—'

Melissa felt her mother's body stiffen against her own as she said in a muffled voice, 'What makes you think I was there?'

'A Mrs Trew told us that she saw someone she thought was you getting into the lift this afternoon.'

Sylvia sat up and raised her head. 'Mrs Trew?' she said in apparent bewilderment. 'What was she doing there?'

'I understand she's a resident.'

Sylvia looked troubled. 'I didn't know that.'

'But you are acquainted with her?'

'Of course. She's a member of Jessica's flower club – but I didn't see her this afternoon.'

'She said she didn't think you'd noticed her. She thought you seemed a little agitated.'

'I don't know what made her think that.' Making an obvious effort to pull herself together, Sylvia found a handkerchief, dabbed her eyes and blew her nose. 'Why should I be agitated?' she said with a touch of defiance. 'And anyway, what was so strange about my being there? There's nothing unusual in paying a friend a visit.'

'Of course there isn't. I'm just trying to—'

'And I don't have to tell you why I—'

Fearing that her mother was about to blurt out something to arouse suspicion where so far there appeared to be none, Melissa said quickly, 'It's all right, Mother, the inspector's only doing her job. There's no need to get worked up, just answer her questions. Inspector Adair,' she went on, 'I do hope you'll bear in mind that my mother is still severely traumatised by my father's murder and she's already had to undergo a great deal of—' She was on the point of saying 'harassment', but thought better of it. 'She's already been subjected to a great deal of questioning about that tragedy,' she continued. 'As you can see, this news has come as a great shock to her.'

DI Adair turned a far from friendly eye on Melissa and replied coldly, 'Yes, I'm well aware of that, but I hope you'll also bear in mind that I have a duty to interview potential witnesses as soon as possible.' She turned back to Sylvia. 'So Mrs Trew is correct, it was you she saw?'

Sylvia bit her lip and nodded. 'I suppose so,' she muttered sulkily.

'And you were there to call on Mrs Jessica Round?' Another nod. 'What time would that have been?'

'I don't recall exactly; some time after three, I suppose. I'd been doing some shopping.'

'How long did you stay?'

'About an hour, I suppose, maybe less. I'm not sure.'

'When you arrived, did you notice anyone hanging about or anyone acting suspiciously?'

Sylvia shook her head. 'No.'

'What about when you left?'

'No.'

'While you were with Mrs Round, did she happen to mention anything unusual that had happened recently?'

'What sort of thing?'

'Any suspicious telephone calls, maybe someone watching the building from a car or trying to gain access, things like that.'

'We didn't talk about that sort of thing, and I'm not going to tell you—'

'It's all right, I'm not asking you for a detailed account of your visit,' the detective said soothingly. 'All I'm trying to do is to establish the time when the victim was last seen alive.'

Sylvia gave a nervous start. 'Jessica was quite all right when I left. You must believe me!' she pleaded.

'I have no reason at the moment to disbelieve you.' The detective's voice became suddenly neutral, detached. She stood up and nodded at her colleague, who put away her notebook. 'I think that's all for now so we'll leave you in peace. Thank you for your help.'

Melissa stood up. 'It's all right, Mother, I'll see them out,' she said hurriedly, gently pushing Sylvia back into her chair as she too made an attempt to rise. At the door she said, 'Inspector Adair, this is terribly upsetting for her, coming so soon after my father's murder. I do hope there'll be no need to trouble her any further.'

'That depends on how our enquiries proceed.'

'You didn't mention the cause of death.'

'That information hasn't been officially released.'

'Do you have any idea of the time of death?'

A carefully shaped eyebrow edged upwards and the keen blue eyes narrowed slightly. 'I'm sure, with your specialist knowledge, you're aware of how difficult that is to determine precisely.' There was a hint of sarcasm in the deceptively soft voice. 'Are you planning to use the case in one of your plots, or do you have a particular reason for wanting to know?'

'I suppose . . .' Melissa felt suddenly wrong-footed and realised that asking such pointed questions might have been unwise. 'I suppose you could put it down to a crime-writer's natural curiosity,' she said lamely.

The detective's upper lip curled slightly. 'I hope that's all it is. May I suggest that you confine your activities to looking after your mother and leave the investigation to us.' Without giving Melissa a chance to respond she swung round, called 'Goodnight' over her shoulder and strode towards the waiting car. Melissa watched it drive away with a sick sense of foreboding. When the sound of the engine had died she closed and locked the front door before returning to the sitting-room.

She found Sylvia sitting bolt upright like a figure carved in stone. Her hands were locked together on her lap and her eyes appeared fixed on infinity. For one frightening moment Melissa thought shock had brought on some kind of seizure and she knelt in front of her, put her hands on her shoulders and gave her a gentle shake. To her relief, Sylvia gave a start and whispered, 'Have they gone?'

'Yes, Mother, they've gone.'

'Do you think they'll be back?'

'I don't know.'

'Whyever did I . . . how was I to . . . it's so terrible, poor Jessica . . .' Sylvia wrung her hands as the words tumbled out in a confused jumble. 'I only wanted to—'

'Yes, why did you go there? Please, you must tell me the truth.'

'I've already told you, I wanted her to know I've forgiven her.'

'Do you really expect me to believe that?'

'But it's true! I've had such wicked thoughts, ever since I found out about her and Father.'

'How did you find out?'

'I heard him talking on the phone one day. He thought I was out; I had gone out but I found I'd forgotten my shopping list so I popped back. He never heard me come in, he was on the phone and I was just in time to hear him say, 'I'll be with you in ten minutes . . . I love you too, darling,' and then he put the phone down. I couldn't believe it was him speaking, his voice was so different, tender and gentle like it used to be when he spoke to me, years ago—' Sylvia broke off and swallowed hard, her mouth working.

'So what did you do?' Melissa asked.

'I just stood there in the kitchen with my shopping list

in my hand. I thought, if he sees me here he'll realise I must have overheard; but he didn't, he went straight out into the hall and the next thing the front door banged and I heard the garage door go up and the car starting. Part of me wanted to run after him, tell him I knew what was going on, but then I thought, I only had myself to thank because—'

Blood suddenly surged into the colourless face and Melissa, remembering what Jessica had told her, said quietly, 'Because you refused to have sex with him after he told me to leave home, is that it?'

Crimson with embarrassment, Sylvia covered her face with her hands. 'How did you know?' she whispered.

'It was just a guess,' said Melissa hastily. 'Anyway, how did you know it was Jessica he'd been speaking to?'

'I remembered about the button on the phone for redialling the last number, so I pressed it and she answered. I hung up at once of course.'

'What did you do then?' Recalling the conversation afterwards, Melissa could hardly believe how calm and detached she had been throughout, as if it were a scene in one of her novels, one she had yet to write, would never write . . . 'Did you tell Father what you'd found out?' she went on as her mother remained silent.

'Oh no, that would never have done! He was so proud, I think he'd have died of shame if he'd realised I knew. No, I had to let life go on as if nothing had happened, but inside I was full of anger and hatred and bitterness. It was so wrong of me, I'm supposed to be a Christian and yet . . .'

'It's quite understandable. Anyone would have felt the same, having to grapple with so much anger and guilt.' It struck Melissa that she must sound like a therapist helping a patient to rationalise her feelings, but it was a relief to see her mother's face light up at the words.

'How wonderful of you to understand that!' Sylvia gave a little sigh, took one of Melissa's hands in both her own and gazed at her with a look of gratitude. 'That's how I've been ever since: hating them both, hating myself for hating them.'

'At least you have the comfort of knowing that you were able to forgive Jessica before she died.'

'Yes, that's true. Oh Lissie, I'm so thankful you're here.'

'So am I. Now, please listen carefully because there's something important I want to say.'

'Yes, dear?'

'If the police do come again – I'm not saying they will, but they might just want to check something – whatever you do, don't tell them the real reason why you went to see Jessica this afternoon. You can say it was something to do with the flower club.'

'Oh Lissie, what do you take me for?' Sylvia's look of mild reproach was almost childlike. 'Of course I wouldn't tell. Didn't you hear me say—'

'Yes, I heard.' Melissa felt a chill at the recollection. That defiant refusal to give a reason when none had been demanded had doubtless not escaped the detective's notice either. She recalled as well the words 'at the moment' that

DI Adair had used to qualify her response to Sylvia's frantic plea to be believed. It was, she knew, almost certain that door-to-door enquiries would reveal at least one resident at Alderley Court who had noticed that Jessica Round had a regular male visitor. A description might be issued; someone might even have recognised Frank Ross. Her mind raced ahead at the thought of what conclusions the police might draw; her own nagging doubts came back to torment her, but for the moment she thrust them resolutely aside. She stood up and drew Sylvia to her feet.

'Now, Mother,' she said, doing her best to sound calm and practical. 'I suggest you go to bed and try to get some rest. What about a bath, and then a drink of hot milk? And perhaps you ought to take one of the pills the doctor gave you to help you sleep?'

'That sounds like a very good idea. You must be tired as well, dear — we'll both go to bed. You can use the bathroom first if you like.' Sylvia began bustling about checking doors and windows and giving instructions for turning off lights before shooing Melissa upstairs and bidding her goodnight in an unexpected and vaguely comic rush of maternal solicitude.

Later, when they had both settled down, Melissa switched on her mobile and keyed in Joe's number.

'How are things?' he asked.

'Grim.'

He listened in silence as she outlined the events of the day. 'What a ghastly shock for Sylvia!' he said as she came to the end of her account. 'How has she taken it?'

'She was shattered at first, but then she became . . . I can only describe her attitude as stroppy. And I don't think it did her any good when she jumped to the conclusion that Jessica Round was the victim when all the police said was that there'd been a murder at Alderley Court.'

'Oh dear!' Joe sounded dismayed. 'That won't have gone unnoticed.'

'Exactly.'

'I suppose there's no doubt that it was Jessica who'd been topped.'

'From the way the interview went from then on, none at all. And after the detectives had gone she made this extraordinary confession.' Once again Joe listened without interruption to Melissa's summary of her mother's revelations.

'I suppose that explains a lot,' he said when she had finished.

'If it's true.'

'Don't you believe it?'

'Joe, I'm so confused I hardly know what to believe.'

'What are you going to do now?'

'I'm hoping to see Eunice Lester again tomorrow, and possibly Mr Bell. Hopefully, one of them will come up with something useful. And I'd very much like to know why Denis Botting lost his entrée to Ross and Company. It might have nothing to do with the case, of course, but you never know.'

'Well, keep in touch.' A warm, intimate note crept into his voice as he added, 'Sleep well.'

'Thanks.' She switched off her light and snuggled down under the bedclothes, but it was some time before she fell asleep. When she did, she was haunted by dreams in which she was pursuing Sylvia along endless corridors, every so often catching up with her and saying, 'Tell me the truth, Mother,' and constantly getting the same reply, 'I don't know . . . I'm so confused.' Once she woke in the small hours with a question ringing so clearly in her head that she wondered if she had spoken it aloud: confused — or guilty?

Chapter Seventeen

'I do appreciate your giving up your lunch-hour like this,' said Melissa. She put two plates of sandwiches and two glasses of orange juice on the table — Eunice had firmly declined anything alcoholic — and sat down.

'No problem,' said Eunice. 'Most days I eat a sandwich in the office, but now and again I come here if I want a bit of peace. You'd be surprised how many people expect you to be at their beck and call at any old time, your lunch-hour included — especially when you're PA to the boss and they want you to put in a word for them over some pet project they're trying to promote.' She took a mouthful of juice before adding, 'I like it here because it doesn't seem to have been discovered by anyone else from the company.'

'It's very pleasant.' Melissa glanced round the cosy bar of the little pub. 'Very popular too, by the looks of it.' Although it was barely midday it was already busy, with more people – many of them apparently regulars from the familiar way they were greeted by the bar attendants – coming in all the time.

Eunice put down her glass and took a notebook from her handbag. 'I've had a few thoughts about what you said yesterday and for what it's worth I'll pass them on to you.'

'I'd be very grateful,' said Melissa. 'My brain's been going round in circles getting nowhere. By the way, one interesting thing happened. I was approached by a journalist called Denis Botting. I can see the name rings a bell with you,' she added as Eunice gave a slight start. 'He was one of a mob trying to get an interview with Mother and he buttonholed me after the rest of them had pushed off. He said he'd been trying to get the low-down on the possible takeover at Father's company and been shown the door.'

'He was lucky not to have been physically chucked out,' said Eunice heatedly.

'What happened?'

'Nothing that's relevant to this enquiry, if that's what you mean.' Eunice frowned and chewed at her sandwich. It was plain that her encounter with Botting had been far from pleasant and Melissa decided to keep to herself the pact she had, reluctantly, entered into with him.

When Eunice was free to speak again she said, 'Look, I don't want to rush you, but I don't have that much time.'

'I'm sorry, I shouldn't have digressed, but I just wondered.'

'It's all right. How is your mother, by the way?'

'Rather prone to mood swings, I'm afraid. She seems okay this morning, but she got very upset last night when she heard that Jessica Round had been murdered.' Melissa inspected the contents of her ham sandwich and added mustard before continuing. 'She'd been to see Jessica only that afternoon and a mutual acquaintance saw her there and mentioned it to the police. They called about nine o'clock as part of their house-to-house enquiries; all they wanted was to check the time of her visit and ask whether she'd seen anyone acting suspiciously and so on, but she thought at first she was a suspect and threw a real wobbly.'

'I'm not surprised — it must have been awful for her!'

'It was rather.'

'Do give her my best wishes.'

'I will, thank you. Now, I don't want to take up too much of your time, but there's one other thing I'm concerned about. Can you give me some idea of what's going to happen to the company now my father has gone? I understand from Mother that he'd already partially retired so there must have been some contingency plan and I'm anxious to know how she's been left financially.'

'Marcus Bell is the man to ask about that.'

'I'm seeing him this afternoon, but from the way he reacted when I rang to tell him about Father's murder I don't think he feels exactly warm towards me.'

'I've never known him to be warm towards anyone,' said Eunice with a wry grimace. 'He came to the office yesterday morning and addressed a meeting of the factory workers and office staff. He wouldn't answer any questions, he simply told them in essence that their jobs were safe for the time being and that the day-to-day business of the company would continue as usual. He then asked the other directors to attend a meeting at his own office in the afternoon.'

'Have you any idea what happened there?'

'I haven't spoken to them since, but I gather they weren't in the best of moods when they got back.'

'How many directors are there?'

'Now Mr Ross has gone there are three, including Marcus Bell who as you already know is also the company solicitor. The other two are Ivor Patmore and Tom Fingle; Ivor's in charge of production and Tom looks after sales. They're directors in name only; that is, they hold the statutory minimum number of shares and attend board meetings, but it's all a formality and they have no power to influence policy. They've both been with the company for years and they've always been very loyal to your father, but I know they were increasingly critical of the way he ran it; in particular they'd been trying to persuade him to think about diversification. When Metal Furniture made their offer they were dead keen for him at least to consider it because they could see enormous advantages for the business, but he wouldn't hear of it. That was typical, of course. You did things his way or you were out.' There was a faint, sardonic twist to Eunice's mouth as she took another bite from her sandwich.

'Yes, that figures,' Melissa agreed. 'Eunice, you said you'd had some thoughts of your own.'

'You want to hear them?'

'Please.'

Eunice wiped her fingers with a paper napkin and opened her notebook. Melissa, idly watching, noticed that unlike the previous day she was wearing rose-pink nail varnish and matching lipstick. 'I happen to know,' she began, 'that your father was beginning to have serious doubts about Ivor Patmore's competence. Twice it had been necessary to junk a batch of window catches because some fault in a machine hadn't been properly dealt with and he blamed Ivor for it.'

'How did Ivor take that?'

'He was pretty annoyed and to be honest, I couldn't blame him. It was a new machine and the problem turned out to be a design fault that had to be put right by the manufacturer.'

'But surely that would have exonerated him?'

'Not entirely – not according to FR, that is. He claimed Ivor should have spotted the trouble earlier.'

'That must have rankled.'

'I'm sure it did. The thing is, Ivor will reach retiring age next Easter, but he's still fit and active and he's made it clear he wants to carry on working for a few more years.'

'And my father thought he should go, is that it?'

'Yes.'

'Had he discussed it with Ivor?'

'I doubt it, that wasn't his way. The first I heard of it was about a week ago when he dictated a memo saying that he thought Ivor should leave on his sixty-fifth birthday and that his second-in-command should take over his job. He said he was going to talk it over with Marcus Bell before informing Ivor of his decision, but it was obvious his mind was already made up.'

'But Ivor wasn't aware of this?'

'Not officially.'

'How do you mean?' Melissa asked as Eunice hesitated.

'Well.' Eunice fiddled with her napkin; she seemed faintly reluctant to continue, but after a moment she said slowly. 'I hesitate to read too much into this and it could be nothing more than coincidence, but later that day I was in FR's office sorting out some papers and when I went back into my own room Ivor was there. He had a folder in his hand, the one I keep memos and correspondence in. It's clearly marked "FR Confidential" and I'd rather carelessly left it lying on my desk.' Eunice hesitated again before saying, 'There was just one sheet of paper in it — the memo about Ivor's retirement.'

'Do you think he'd been reading it?'

'I can't be sure. He jumped when I came in and dropped the folder as if it was red hot. He mumbled something about having accidentally knocked it off the corner of my desk.'

'Could that have been true?'

Eunice shrugged. 'I thought it sounded a bit thin, but as I'd been out of the room I couldn't say anything.'

'Did he seem upset or angry?'

'He certainly looked shaken, but I don't know whether it was because he'd been caught handling the folder or because he'd read the memo. In any case, I was a bit shaken myself at the thought of how careless I'd been and how the boss would react if he knew.'

'So what happened then?'

'Ivor said he wanted a word with FR. I told him he'd gone out and wasn't expected back that afternoon, so he left.'

Across the table, the two women's eyes met. Melissa drew a deep breath and said, 'So you think Ivor Patmore knew of the intention to get rid of him?'

'I think it's a definite possibility.'

'If so, it would give him a pretty strong motive for wanting Father out of the way.' Melissa felt the adrenalin beginning to flow at the realisation that here at last was a positive line of enquiry. 'Suppose he decided to have it out with him in private. I presume he knew where Father lived?'

'Of course.'

'He might have gone round there that afternoon, tried to reason with him, pleaded with him—' Melissa broke off and closed her eyes against the sickening picture her mind conjured up.

'And when he failed to move him, went for him with the axe.' Eunice shook her head in evident disbelief. 'You read of these things happening, but not to people you know.'

Melissa took a deep breath and swallowed hard before saying, 'Do you happen to know if there was any particular reason why Ivor was so reluctant to retire?

Did he have any financial responsibilities that he'd have found difficult to meet on a reduced income?'

'That I couldn't tell you. I don't know much about his private life except that he's married with one or two children and several grandchildren that he's very proud of.'

'That's something I could look into.' Melissa made notes of her own, thinking that here was something where Denis Botting's local knowledge might prove useful. 'What about Tom Fingle? I gather from what you said earlier that he felt himself in a bit of a strait-jacket due to Father's old-fashioned notions.'

'Very much so. Tom's a real eager beaver and he's got loads of ideas. To be fair to FR, he did accept some of them, but the more radical ones always met with a very definite no-no. I've seen Tom come out of his office fuming on several occasions.' Eunice gave a faint, slightly hollow laugh. 'He's in his early forties, but your father often referred to him as a boy and said he'd grow out of his "juvenile enthusiasms" as he used to call them.'

Someone else who might be worth investigating, Melissa thought as she scribbled more notes.

It was Eunice's turn to ask a question. 'Have you any idea how the police enquiries are going?'

'None at all. DI Adair never referred to Father's murder when she came round yesterday. Reading between the lines, I gather that house-to-house enquiries haven't come up with anything useful so far.'

'No one was seen visiting the house during the critical time?'

'If they were, I haven't been told. Not that I expect to be – DI Adair and I aren't exactly buddies.'

'Well, do keep in touch.' Eunice put away her note-book and stood up. 'I really have to get back, but please let me know if there's anything else I can do to help.' She bit her lip and blinked. 'I worked with him for a long time, you know, and I'd like to . . .'

'I understand.'

'Do you?' Eunice gave a sad little smile and left. Melissa watched as she zigzagged her way across the crowded bar towards the exit, a slim, upright figure with a purposeful air about her; a useful, dependable ally in an increasingly complex and bizarre situation.

A passing waiter took away the empty plates and glasses and asked if there was anything else she wanted. She ordered coffee; behind her a man's voice said, 'Make that a coffee and another pint of Old Peculier,' as Denis Botting walked round the table and slid into the chair Eunice had just vacated. He held an almost empty tankard which he drained noisily before handing it over to be refilled. He ran the back of his hand over his mouth and remarked, 'I see you've enlisted the aid of the lovely Eunice.'

'Have you been following me?' Melissa asked indignantly.

'Sheer coincidence. I just popped in for a jar and happened to spot the pair of you with your heads together,' he replied nonchalantly. 'Learn anything useful?'

'For a start, that you were chucked out of the Ross and

Company offices after saying or doing something to cause Eunice to get very hot under the collar. What was that about?'

Botting gave a wheezy chuckle. 'It happened a month or so ago, when I first got wind of the Metal Furniture bid. I thought I'd try and get the low-down, and as you've already found out, confidential secretaries can be very useful informants.'

'How did you hear about the takeover bid?'

'A little bird told me.' Botting gave a suggestive wink as he reached for the fresh tankard the waiter had just put in front of him, along with Melissa's coffee. He handed over a fiver saying, 'Take for that as well,' before she had a chance to open her purse. 'I reckon I'd have scored with the lovely Eunice, given time,' he went on, 'but her po-faced old sod of a boss came storming in and kicked up a fuss. Sorry, I forgot it's your old man I'm talking about.'

'Never mind.' Melissa poured cream into her coffee and stirred it, trying to picture the scene. On the face of it the claim was ludicrous, but she had to admit that there was an earthy sexuality about the man that would certainly appeal to some – but surely not the elegant, sophisticated Eunice. 'I wouldn't have thought you were her type,' she said pointedly.

Botting chuckled again. 'You'd be surprised – most women enjoy a bit of rough!' he said complacently.

'There are exceptions,' she countered.

'Okay, okay, no need to get shirty. My interest in you is strictly professional.'

'I'm relieved to hear that. Now, since we've so fortuitously met, maybe you'd like to know what I've managed to pick up so far.' She repeated the gist of her conversation with Eunice. 'It's clear that Patmore and Fingle have had serious disagreements with my father over the direction the company's taking and, on the face of it, Patmore had the most to lose. What I'd like to know is, just how much.'

'And whether it would have provided a strong enough motive for topping the old— for killing your father?'

'Exactly. By the way, you mentioned yesterday that a disgruntled employee is bringing a case for wrongful dismissal. Do you have any details?'

'Last I heard, there was talk of an out of court settlement, but no one seems to know where it's got to.'

'So we're back to Patmore as number one suspect, with Fingle a possibility?'

Botting shrugged. 'Assuming, of course, that the police are on the wrong trail.'

'What do you mean?'

'With all your experience of the way they work, you know very well what I mean. Their first thought is always, "Is this a domestic?" Yes?'

'I suppose so, but in this case—'

'Oh, I'm sure you don't believe your Mum could possibly be guilty, but the Old Bill aren't troubled by sentimental considerations, are they? I happen to know they're sniffing around among your Dad's friends and acquaintances, and I've also heard a rumour that the

Alderley Court murder victim is a friend of the widow. Is that true, by the way?'

After her earlier optimism, Melissa felt her spirits sinking again. 'Not a friend, but they are . . . were acquainted,' she admitted.

'Care to give me some details?'

'It's no secret. She was president of Mother's flower club, that's all.'

'Thanks.' Botting finished his beer, put down the empty glass and stood up. 'I'll be getting along now. I'll be in touch.'

'How long do you think your enquiries will take?'

'Hard to say. The name Fingle doesn't ring any bells, but it so happens that my mother goes to bingo with an old duck called Rosie Patmore. If she's related to Ivor we could get lucky quite soon.'

Chapter Eighteen

Marcus Bell and Partners, Solicitors, occupied a suite of offices in a converted Regency house in a leafy suburb less than a mile from the offices and factory of Frank Ross and Company. There was an air of solid prosperity about the property: the substantial, impeccably maintained building with its tall windows and ionic columns supporting a stone portico, the well-tended gardens planted with early-flowering trees and shrubs, and the neatly gravelled car park where a row of wrought-iron lamps ensured ease of manoeuvre on dark winter evenings. The thought passed through Melissa's head as she mounted the broad flight of shallow steps leading to the glossy white-painted front door that anyone who could afford offices in Stratford House must be doing very nicely thank you. As she searched for the right bellpush in the bank of highly-polished brass name-plates set in the wall, she noted that the other tenants included a firm of architects, a partnership of financial consultants and a chartered accountant.

The small reception area, where a pleasant, middle-aged woman invited her to take a seat and assured her that Mr Bell would be with her in a few minutes, was decorated in a discreet, mock-Regency style. She was idly reflecting on the contrast between the decor – crystal chandelier, striped wallpaper and reproduction chairs – and the banks of legal reference tomes bound in dark leather completely covering one wall and the cartoons of learned judges adorning the others, when a door opened and a grey-haired man in a grey suit emerged and said, 'Mrs Craig? Marcus Bell – how do you do?'

He was, she thought as she stood up and returned the formal greeting, very much as she had imagined him: tall and spare, with a sallow complexion, hollow cheeks and a thin nose supporting wire-framed spectacles. Out of politeness she extended a hand; his was dry and cool, the clasp brief but firm.

He led her into his office, which had bare white walls and a couple of low wooden bookcases, offered her a seat and sat down facing her across a surprisingly shabby desk that had more of a Dickensian than an elegant Regency air. 'Well, Mrs Craig,' he said, 'what can I do for you?'

'I'm really here on my mother's behalf,' she began and found herself immediately interrupted.

'Yes, she told me you would be coming to see me when I spoke to her yesterday. I dare say she mentioned our conversation?'

Melissa frowned. 'No, she didn't. I wonder why?'

'Perhaps it slipped her mind. She sounded a little distressed. I understand the press had been troubling her and she'd had to take refuge in a friend's house for a while.'

'That's right. Fortunately I was able to persuade them to leave her in peace, for the time being at any rate.'

'Yes, she told me that. She also confirmed that you are pursuing certain enquiries on her behalf. May I ask if you have made any progress? I take it there have been no further approaches from the police?'

'Not concerning my father's death, although the inspector in charge of the case did call on her last night in connection with another violent incident. It was merely a routine enquiry this time, but it was very upsetting for her as she had visited the victim only that afternoon.'

'Indeed?' Bell's thin eyebrows registered surprise and a desire to know more, but Melissa decided not to oblige him.

'Understandably, my mother has been thoroughly traumatised by the shock of finding my father's body and her subsequent questioning by the police. My immediate concern is for her physical and mental well-being, but I am also thinking of her future and I would like to satisfy myself that my father has left her properly provided for. I haven't broached the matter with her directly because to be honest I don't think she's in a fit state at the moment to discuss it rationally and in any case I have the impression that she has little grasp of business matters. That's one of the reasons why I've come to you.'

'Your concern is perfectly understandable.' By a total absence of warmth in his tone, Mr Bell managed to convey the impression that he suspected Melissa of a degree of self-interest. He coughed and pressed the fingertips of both hands together. 'The situation is really quite straight-forward. Your father made me his executor and trustee, which means I am responsible for the administration of both his business and his private affairs. His will makes provision for your mother to receive a sufficient regular income for her day-to-day needs whilst leaving in my hands control of all such matters as maintenance of her current residence, handling the sale of the property and the purchase of another should she wish to move house and so on. In order that I may effectively manage these matters without constant reference to her, which your father felt would cause her unnecessary anxiety, he instructed me to obtain from her an Enduring Power of Attorney in my favour. That was the purpose of my telephone call, to explain the situation and obtain her consent for me to go ahead with the preparation of the document.'

'And did she agree?'

'Naturally.' There was a touch of asperity in Bell's response. 'She is well aware that I have been legal adviser to Frank Ross and Company for over twenty years and that I have always enjoyed your father's complete confidence.'

'I'm not suggesting that she doesn't share that confidence,' said Melissa quickly. Despite being nettled by the man's attitude, she recognised the need to tread carefully if she wanted his co-operation. 'It's just that I would have expected her to at least mention the proposed arrangement to me.' It occurred to her to wonder if Sylvia might have expressed during her conversation with the solicitor an intention of doing just that, and been discouraged, but she kept the thought to herself.

'Perhaps if you had not been estranged for so many years—'

'That has really nothing to do with it,' Melissa said coldly. 'I shall certainly discuss it with her as soon as I get back.'

'I can assure you that everything will be done in accordance with your father's wishes.' Bell glanced at his thin gold wristwatch. 'Now, you suggested earlier that you have more than one reason for consulting me.'

'Yes, I have. This goes back to my own private investigation. You may recall that when we spoke on the telephone on Sunday evening—'

'When you advised me of the death of your father?'

'That's right. My mother was distraught because the detective in charge of the case had made it clear that she was the prime suspect and she had begged me to try to find the real killer. I asked you if you could think of anyone who would benefit from my father's death, but you declined to answer.'

'I remember.'

'Are you prepared to answer now?'

There was a short silence before Bell said, 'Perhaps you

would give me some idea of the kind of benefit you had in mind when you asked the question?'

'I suppose it was chiefly financial. You've explained the situation very clearly, except that you haven't mentioned whether my father made any special bequests—'

'That is something that would be revealed only to beneficiaries and at the appropriate time, and—'

This time it was Melissa's turn to interrupt. 'You've already made it clear that I'm not a beneficiary, and in any case that wasn't what I had in mind.' She was finding it increasingly difficult to conceal her irritation. 'At the time of asking I was completely in the dark about my father's affairs and the state of the company, but I've since learned of his determination to reject a substantial takeover bid which some or all of his fellow directors – of whom I know you are one – might have found attractive.'

'And how did you come by that information?'

It was clear from his sharply raised eyebrows that Bell was disconcerted by the extent of her knowledge and she was quick to take advantage of the fact. 'So it's true?' she said. He made no reply, but began fiddling with the blotter on his desk. 'May I ask if you share Father's attitude towards the proposed takeover?'

'That is a matter for me and my fellow directors and I fail to see how it can have any relevance to your enquiries.'

'It might have. Takeovers can mean different things for existing officers and employees of a company.' Having done some research on the subject for a book, Melissa found herself speaking with increasing confidence. 'Some are made redundant, often with substantial lump sums or other benefits; others are given promotion and end up with better jobs and fatter pay cheques than under the old regime. Now, I understand that as Father has left you in control of his affairs, you are in a position to decide whether or not to accept.'

Bell's colour rose. 'Just precisely what are you suggesting?' he demanded angrily. He put down the blotter and leaned forward, fixing her with a hostile stare. 'Do I understand that you suspect me of murdering my old and valued friend for personal gain? That's a perfectly monstrous accusation!'

'Mr Bell, I'm not accusing you of anything. What I have in mind is, could there be anyone who would benefit from the takeover and who had reason to believe that with Father out of the way it would be likely to go ahead? Someone who perhaps has financial difficulties, frustrated ambition or other possible motives, whose problems would be solved if Metal Furniture took control of Frank Ross and Company?'

'I am not a party to everyone's private affairs and I would certainly be unwilling to divulge anything revealed to me in confidence.'

'Not even to clear an innocent woman from the suspicion of murder?'

'You seem very sure of your mother's innocence.'

'I see no reason to doubt it.' *Please God*, she added silently before going on. 'Mr Bell, I believe someone else killed my father in his own workshop. Either that person went there with the deliberate intention of killing him or – what I suspect is the more likely – it was done in the heat of an argument. Admitting the possibility that that person stood to benefit from the takeover and saw Father as the one obstacle to its going ahead, all I'd like to know is, can you think of anyone—'

'I have already made it clear that I am not prepared to enter into any speculation on those lines. Now, if you will excuse me—' He stood up in a clear indication that the interview was at an end.

Melissa too got to her feet, but she fired one last shot before leaving. 'Your refusal to answer a simple question is capable of more than one interpretation,' she said crisply, and left the room without giving him time to reply. As she emerged, the ginger-haired girl from Frank Ross and Company was in the act of handing over a bulky envelope to the receptionist. She gave Melissa a friendly greeting, walked with her to the car park and used a remote control to unlock a dark blue Renault Mégane standing next to the Fiesta.

'Nice car,' Melissa commented. 'Looks new.'

'Not mine – if only!' the girl said cheerfully. 'Mr Patmore asked me to fill it up for him and said I could use it at the same time to deliver some papers to Mr Bell. Still, you never know,' she went on, 'maybe one day I'll join the ranks of the elite. I might even aspire to one of those.' She gestured towards a sleek, dark green Jaguar parked in one of the designated spaces alongside those reserved for visitors before climbing into the Renault and giving a mock-regal wave as she drove away.

To Melissa's surprise the front door of her mother's house was opened by Mrs Menzies who, in contrast to her unconcealed displeasure of the previous day, greeted her almost cordially. Melissa responded to the change in attitude with a warm smile and a heartfelt, 'Mrs Menzies, I'm so glad to see you. I was afraid—'

'Oh, please.' The woman appeared almost embarrassed. 'I should apologise; it was foolish of me to take offence like that when she's still not herself.'

Melissa felt a surge of anxiety. 'What do you mean?' she asked in a low voice.

'Nothing particular, just a little confused now and again, that's all. We've had a nice day together – we went for a walk in the park after lunch. She's watching the telly at the moment and I'm just about to make a cup of tea.' She bustled off into the kitchen and Melissa, relieved that good relations were restored but still vaguely troubled about her mother's state of mind, went into the sitting-room.

Sylvia was sitting comfortably in an armchair with her feet up, watching a game show. When she saw Melissa she gave a smile of delight and waved her to a seat. 'He's only got to get one more right to win the jackpot,' she declared excitedly, pointing to the young man on the screen. 'I do hope he . . . ooh, no!' She joined in the chorus of groans from the studio audience as a raucous buzz greeted an incorrect answer. She picked up the remote control, switched off the set and said, 'It's lovely to see you, Lissie. Have you had a good day?'

'Not bad. I had lunch with Eunice Lester and then I went to see Mr Bell. Eunice was quite helpful, but I didn't get much change out of Bell. He said he'd spoken to you, by the way. You never mentioned it.'

'Didn't I, dear?' Sylvia's tone was dismissive. 'It wasn't anything special – he's coming back here after the inquest to talk to me about your father's will. He's bringing a paper for me to sign so that he can look after everything for me, which will be such a relief. I don't understand the first thing about business.'

'Mother, I don't think you should sign anything without reading it very carefully and maybe letting me have a look at it first,' Melissa began, but Sylvia made a quick gesture of impatience.

'Mr Bell assures me that he's simply carrying out your Father's wishes,' she said with a frown.

'Can you be sure of that? Did Father ever mention it to you?'

'Of course he didn't – he didn't know he was going to be murdered, did he?' Sylvia's eyes grew misty.

'So how can you be sure?'

'Lissie, you aren't suggesting I can't trust Mr Bell, are you? He's known your father for years, he's the company solicitor.'

'Yes, I know. That's why I went to see him, to find out

if he could help me with my enquiries, but he wasn't very forthcoming.'

'I expect he was just being discreet. You know what these legal people are like,' said Sylvia with an air of worldly wisdom which Melissa might have found comical had she not been so uneasy.

At that moment, Mrs Menzies entered with the tea-tray and Melissa was forced to drop the subject. She gave non-committal replies to their questions about her own enquiries and it was only later, when Mrs Menzies had returned home with a promise to take Sylvia into town the following morning to help her choose a new summer outfit – 'I thought it might cheer her up,' she confided to Melissa as she left – that she tried again to raise the subject of Mr Bell and the Enduring Power of Attorney. Sylvia, however, refused point blank to enter into any further discussion and, sensing that insistence on her part would lead to the atmosphere becoming heated, Melissa allowed the matter to drop for the time being. Later, when they were both settled in bed, she called Joe and gave him an account of the day's events.

'You certainly seem to have made some progress,' he said when she had finished. 'Suspects springing up all over the place. How's your mother bearing up, by the way?'

'Almost too well. She seems more concerned by my misgivings over Mr Bell than any progress I might be making to track down the killer. I really can't make her out.'

'Give her time – anyone would act a bit irrationally now and again after what she's been through.'

'I suppose so.'

'What about you — are you quite sure you're okay? Would you like me to come down for the inquest?'

'That's sweet of you, but I don't think there's any need. Unless there are any dramatic developments within the next few hours it'll be opened and adjourned very quickly. I'm fine at the moment, Joe. Just so long as I can talk to you every day.'

'Call me at any hour, day or night. Has there been any further word from the police?'

'Not since they came to question Mother about her movements yesterday afternoon.'

'I take it you'll be passing them any information you dig up?'

'Eventually, but I don't expect any developments just yet.'

'Well, best of luck with the sleuthing!'

They chatted for a while and then said goodnight. Melissa soon fell asleep, but her slumber would have been less peaceful had she known that her own tentative enquiries were about to be overtaken by events outside her control.

Chapter Nineteen

'Splendid — a breakthrough at last!' With a smile of triumph, Detective Inspector Mollie Adair patted the report which Detective Constable Carole Sharwood had placed on her desk half an hour ago. 'As soon as the old bat let on she knew the Alderley Court victim was Jessica Round I had a gut feeling there was a connection between the two murders. Everything in here supports both theories; all we needed was a motive and at last we've got one.'

'You reckon there's enough here to justify pulling her in again, Guv?' Carole asked doubtfully.

'If we can get her to admit she knew what her old man was up to.' There was a zealous gleam in the inspector's hard blue eyes. 'I'm willing to bet that when we confront her with this little lot, she'll realise she hasn't a leg to stand on. First the faithless husband and then his lover . . . classic *crimes passionels* as they say in France.' She sounded each final 's' and pronounced *crime* like its English equivalent but Carole, despite a good A level in French, resisted the temptation to correct her.

'Let's see.' Adair glanced at the clock. 'It's half past eight. I'll have a word with the DCI and then we'll pay the lady a visit.'

'She may refuse to say anything without her brief,' Carole pointed out.

'Not if I handle her right. I might even get her to oblige us with an instant confession, but on second thoughts I doubt if she'll do that, not with that gorgon of a daughter breathing down her neck. No, the idea is to soften her up, drip-feed her these bits of evidence, get her thoroughly rattled and wait for her to put a foot wrong.'

'It might work,' Carole agreed.

'I intend to make it work.' And with a purposeful air, Detective Inspector Adair stood up and put on her coat.

'It's a lovely morning,' said Melissa, glancing out of the kitchen window at the sunlit garden as she washed up after breakfast. She found herself mentally contrasting the geometric arrangement of lawns and flower-beds, separated from the neighbouring properties by neatly clipped hedges, with the gentle informality of her own small plot at Hawthorn Cottage. There, the kitchen window afforded an open view of sloping pastures and woodland and the only other house within half a mile was the adjoining Elder Cottage. She felt a momentary stab of longing to be back in her Cotswold home, where spring meant clumps of primroses by the roadside and carpets of bluebells in beech woods, and the air was alive with the cries of young lambs and busy with the comings and goings of nesting birds. Here the predominant sounds were the hum of traffic from the nearby main road into town and the drone of aircraft on their way to and from Heathrow.

Her mother's voice brought her back to reality. 'Lovely,' she agreed. 'Nice and sunny but not too hot – ideal for a shopping trip. Why don't you come with us, Lissie?' she added as she plied the tea cloth.

'I don't think so. Mrs Menzies might think I was interfering and we don't want to offend her again.'

'That's true.' Sylvia looked troubled at the recollection. 'I didn't mean to upset her, truly I didn't. I don't know what gets into me these days, I keep saying things I don't really mean.'

'It's nothing to worry about. You've had a dreadful shock, we all understand.'

Sylvia's look of perplexity deepened. 'I'm not sure I do,' she said. 'There are times—' She was interrupted by the sound of the front doorbell. 'That'll be Mrs Menzies,' she said, putting down the tea towel. 'She's early – it's only just gone nine and I thought we agreed half past. Do you mind finishing here while I get ready?' she added over her shoulder as she went to answer.

'Of course not, you go ahead.' Melissa pulled out the plug and turned on the tap to rinse the sink. Over the sound of running water she became aware that the voice of the woman greeting her mother was not the one she expected to hear, but was nevertheless familiar – unpleasantly so.

Sylvia returned to the kitchen looking perturbed. 'It's those policewomen again,' she said in a low voice. 'They want to ask more questions.'

'I'm sure this won't take long.' Behind her, the crisp voice of DI Adair cut through the air like a sword. 'Just a few points we need to clear up; shall we go in here?' Without waiting for a reply, she led the way into the sitting-room followed by DC Sharwood while Sylvia and Melissa trailed in their wake.

'Only one or two points,' the inspector repeated as they all sat down. 'This isn't—'

'Just a moment,' Melissa broke in. 'I thought it was understood that if you wanted to question my mother further, it would be in the presence of her solicitor.'

'As I was about to say' – the words *before I was so rudely interrupted* remained unspoken but were clearly written in the frosty gaze that Adair turned on Melissa – 'this is not a formal interview and Mrs Ross is not under caution. We merely want her comments on one or two points that have arisen during our enquiries.'

'It's all right, dear.' Sylvia appeared to have recovered from her momentary loss of composure. 'Let's get it over quickly so that we can go and do our shopping.'

'I really think—' Melissa began, but her mother silenced her with an impatient gesture.

'Mrs Menzies will be here soon and I want to be ready or we'll miss our bus,' she said. She turned back to the inspector. 'Have you made any progress in your hunt for my husband's murderer?' she asked. 'Is that what you've come to tell us?'

'We think so, but as I said a moment ago, we'd appreciate your help over one or two things.'

'I'll do my best.'

'We really appreciate your co-operation.'

Melissa was not deceived by the sudden show of cosy friendliness, but she felt unable for the moment to do anything except listen and observe.

'I'm afraid this will be painful for you, but I'd like you to think back to last Friday afternoon,' the inspector continued. 'You told us' — she made a show of consulting a file she held in one hand — 'that you left the house a little before two o'clock and came back about four. That is correct, isn't it?'

'Yes.'

'And you did not return at any time in between?'

'No, of course not. I told you—'

'You did not, for example, pop back for a few minutes before catching the bus because you realised you'd forgotten something — your shopping list or your bus pass, for example?'

'No.'

'So you were not aware that your husband went out shortly after you left?'

Sylvia took a few moments to digest this information.

'He never told me he was going out,' she said with a frown. 'What makes you think he did?'

'We have a witness who claims to have seen his car outside the front gate a little after two o'clock, which seems to indicate that he left shortly after you did. Can you suggest where he might have gone?'

Sylvia licked her lips. 'I've absolutely no idea,' she said uneasily.

'You're quite sure?'

'Quite. He told me he was going to spend the afternoon in his workshop. Perhaps he found he needed something for his model-making and went out to buy it.'

'Perhaps that was it. Where would he have gone for that, do you suppose?'

'There's a shop in the High Street called the Model Shack.'

'Ah! I wonder. Perhaps he went there and possibly met someone he knew. Make a note to check that, Carole.' DI Adair waited a moment before adding casually, 'I believe you said you regularly go shopping on a Friday afternoon, Mrs Ross?'

'That's right.'

'And you always go by bus? Did your husband never drive you to the shops?'

'No. He hated supermarkets and I was quite happy to go on my own.'

'I see.' The inspector nodded thoughtfully. 'I presume that means that he could easily go out on any – or every – Friday afternoon without your knowledge?'

'I suppose he could, but why should he?' For a moment, Sylvia appeared disconcerted; then she added, with a touch of defiance, 'What's so unusual about that anyway?'

'Nothing at all.' The words were accompanied by what was obviously intended to be a reassuring smile. 'It was just a passing comment.'

Melissa had been listening intently to the apparently anodyne questioning and she felt her misgivings return. She was sufficiently familiar with police methods to recognise the technique: put the witness at ease and then without warning catch him or her off guard with a loaded question or a piece of incriminating evidence. She had no idea what the inspector had up her sleeve but the latest question, put almost as if the notion had only just occured to her, seemed to indicate that the danger point was fast approaching and that any minute now the trap could be sprung.

'Right,' DI Adair resumed. 'That's one more detail cleared up, thank you very much. Now, if I could just turn to the murder at Alderley Court. We've made some progress there as well and we think you might be able to help us narrow things down a little.'

'I don't see how.' Sylvia reached for Melissa's hand. 'I've told you all I know about that.'

DI Adair was still smiling her cosy, cat-like smile, but a touch of steel crept into her voice as she continued. 'A witness who lives on the floor below your friend – your late friend, I should say – has come forward to say that she overheard raised voices and what sounded like an altercation between two women at around the time you say you were there. Unfortunately, she couldn't be sure exactly when it was or even which flat it was coming from. Did you by any chance hear anything of that nature?'

Sylvia shook her head. 'No, I didn't.'

'You're quite sure?'

'Of course I am.'

'Did your friend happen to mention that she was expecting another caller?'

'No.'

'Now' – again, notes were ritually consulted – 'you gave us to understand that there was no particular purpose behind your own visit.'

Sylvia did not answer, but Melissa felt the pressure on her hand increase. The detective waited, eyebrows raised slightly, as if encouraging Sylvia to volunteer some additional information. When none came, she leaned forward and fixed her victim with an almost hypnotic stare.

This is it – here comes the crunch question, Melissa thought. She was frantically casting about for some way of fending it off without arousing suspicion when a ring at the doorbell gave them a momentary respite. Sylvia half rose, but without shifting her gaze DI Adair said sharply, 'See who that is, Carole.'

'Yes, Guv.'

As if the interruption had not taken place the inspector said, 'Mrs Ross, you are probably unaware that it is common gossip among certain residents of Alderley Court that your friend received regular Friday afternoon visits from a gentleman.'

Sylvia fidgeted and avoided her questioner's eye as she replied in a low voice, 'I don't know about any gossip.'

'Of course not – not living there, why should you?' There was the faintest pause before the inspector added, almost as an aside, 'They describe the gentleman as probably in his late sixties or early seventies, tall, on the thin side, with aquiline features and iron-grey hair.'

Like a cat pouncing on a mouse, it was done so stealthily, so subtly, that up to that moment Melissa had seen no point at which she could raise any valid objection. Sylvia let out a faint whimper as DI Adair delivered what was obviously intended to be her *coup de grâce*. Melissa opened her mouth to protest, but before she could speak there was a further distraction. From the hall a determined voice declared, 'I'm here to see my friend and you have no authority to prevent me,' and Mrs Menzies swept into the room, a formidable figure in a grey flannel coat and skirt with a matching felt hat adorned with a peacock blue feather. She glared at the two detectives. 'When are you going to stop harassing her?' she demanded. 'Hasn't she put up with enough from you? Look at her – she's white as a sheet! What have they been saying to you, dear?' She plumped down on the sofa beside Sylvia. 'I'm surprised at you allowing this,' she went on, speaking this time to Melissa. 'She shouldn't have to answer questions without her solicitor.'

'I pointed that out, but the inspector assured us that

she only wanted to check a few minor details, so Mother agreed,' Melissa protested lamely. 'I was just about to challenge the way things were going when you arrived.'

'She's trying to make out that Frank was seeing another woman,' Sylvia said. Obviously shaken by the suddenness of the attack, she still managed to convey a sense of righteous indignation.

'That's not quite—' the inspector began, but was stopped in her tracks by a wrathful Mrs Menzies.

'You call that a minor detail?' she exclaimed. 'It's outrageous! A more upright, God-fearing gentleman than Frank Ross you'd be hard put to find anywhere. How dare you besmirch the name of a man unable to defend himself!'

'Mrs Menzies, I am investigating two very violent murders.' DI Adair's colour rose under the attack, but she stood her ground. 'I assured Mrs Ross as soon as we arrived that she was not under caution. She freely agreed to the interview and she is at liberty to ask us to leave at any time. So far, she has been very helpful—'

'I dare say she has, and I dare say you've been leading her by the nose, trying to trip her up no doubt.' She turned back to Sylvia. 'What was it your Mr Fenton told you to say if she asked you anything you didn't want to talk about? "No comment" was it? Go on, tell her to get out!'

'Yes, I think perhaps you had better go.' Despite her distress, Sylvia spoke with a certain dignity. 'I've no further comment to make and if you want to talk to me again I'd be grateful if you'd arrange for Mr Fenton to be present.'

'Of course,' said the inspector stiffly. 'I won't take up any more of your time now, but you will be hearing from us again.'

She remained outwardly composed, but Melissa guessed that she was seething inwardly at being baulked of her prey and felt a gleeful satisfaction at the thought. 'I'll see you out,' she said with an ingratiating smile which, unsurprisingly, was not returned. At the door she asked, 'Inspector, can you be absolutely sure that the car your witness saw was my father's?'

'She's a neighbour and she described it sufficiently accurately to satisfy us that it was. Why do you ask?'

'Many modern cars look surprisingly similar and she could have been mistaken. It occurs to me that it might have belonged to the killer.'

'Most unlikely.' The inspector's lip curled in contempt at the notion. 'I suggest you keep your red herrings for your thrillers.'

'We nearly had her!' said DI Adair through her teeth as she buckled her seat belt. 'Sod that Mrs Menzies!'

By way of smoothing her superior's ruffled plumage, Carole said, 'At least her reaction seems to confirm that you were right. Anyone could see that she knew perfectly well what her old man was up to.'

'And if that old battleaxe hadn't come barging in like that we'd have got her to admit it.'

A glance at the furious profile next to her warned Carole, as she started the engine and pulled away from the kerb, that this was not the moment to point out that even without Mrs Menzies' ill-timed arrival, their suspect's daughter had quite obviously been on the point of intervening. 'So what do you plan to do next?' she asked. 'We showed our witness at Alderley Court a photo of Frank Ross and she seemed fairly sure it was him, but she's elderly and wears thick glasses.'

DI Adair's mouth set in a hard line. 'I'll think of something,' she muttered.

Chapter Twenty

As Melissa closed the front door behind the two detectives she overheard Mrs Menzies saying, 'It's positively disgraceful! If you take my advice, you'll make a formal complaint. Don't you agree, Mrs Craig?' she added as Melissa re-entered the sitting-room. 'You know about such matters — wouldn't you say this was harassment? They've already had to admit that your mother had nothing to do with your poor father's terrible death.'

Only too aware that the police had in fact done nothing of the kind, Melissa said cautiously, 'It might be worth mentioning it to Mr Fenton, but—'

'Please,' Sylvia interposed, 'let's forget all about it and go and do our shopping, shall we?' She was still pale, but surprisingly composed. 'It's such a lovely morning – don't let's have any more unpleasantness.'

'Unpleasantness!' snorted Mrs Menzies. 'That woman cast an unforgivable slur on your dear husband's memory.'

'It wasn't quite like that, was it, Lissie?'

Reading the plea in her mother's eyes, Melissa said quickly, 'The inspector said that the woman who was murdered at Alderley Court sometimes had visits from a gentleman. The description she gave could have applied to my father, but she never actually said it was him.'

'There you are!' said Sylvia, as if that resolved the matter once and for all. 'It was just a coincidence and for a moment I took it the wrong way.' She stood up and smoothed her skirt. 'I don't want to talk about it any more. You heard what I said: no more questions without my solicitor – or should I say "without my brief"?' she added with a giggle. 'That's what people say in your books, isn't it, Lissie?'

'Well, if you're sure . . .' Mrs Menzies said dubiously.

'Quite sure,' said Sylvia firmly. 'By the way, Lissie, talking about Father's car – it's still in the garage and I don't drive so you might as well use it instead of the one you're hiring.'

'I suppose I could, if there are no objections.'

'Who's going to object?'

'I don't know – the police maybe.'

'Oh, bother the police! You take it, dear. It's a lovely car, almost new. I'll give you the key, and you'd better have his house keys as well. They're in the kitchen.' She bustled out of the room, returning a moment later with an assortment of keys that she proceeded to identify one by one: front door, back door, side gate, garage door. The car key was on a separate ring; Melissa felt a twinge of excitement on seeing the logo embossed on the fob but she made no comment, merely saying, 'Thank you,' and putting them in her pocket.

'Now, if you'll excuse me,' said Sylvia, 'I'll go and get ready and then we'll be off.'

The moment she was out of the room, Mrs Menzies said, 'Isn't there anything you can do to stop them pestering her?'

'I'll have a word with Mr Fenton,' Melissa promised. 'Only please don't tell her or she'll start throwing another wobbly. She's in a very volatile state — I've a good mind to speak to the doctor again.'

'That's a very good idea.'

'There's one thing you may be able to help me with,' Melissa went on. 'According to DI Adair, someone — a neighbour, presumably — told the police they saw Father's car outside the house around the time Mother left home on Friday afternoon. Have you any idea who that might have been?'

Mrs Menzies thought for a moment. 'Most of our immediate neighbours would have been out then. It might have been Mrs Seymour at number fifteen; she's got children of school age and a two-year-old at home so she doesn't go out to work. Is it important, do you think?'

'I'm not sure; it might be.'

At that moment Sylvia returned wearing a cream linen jacket over her plain blue dress. She had changed her slippers for smart cream court shoes, carried a matching handbag and, to Melissa's surprise, had put on a little make-up. She twirled round before them like a model on a catwalk. 'How do I look?' she asked with a simper.

'Very smart,' said Melissa. She forced herself to return the smile, but inwardly she felt a stab of apprehension at this further change of mood. 'I hope you have a successful trip.'

'Thank you, dear.' Sylvia gave her a peck on the cheek. 'I hope you have a nice morning too; have you any plans?'

'Only to carry on with my enquiries.'

'Oh?' Sylvia looked puzzled. 'What enquiries are those?'

'I'm supposed to be trying to find out who killed Father, remember?'

'Really, dear? I thought the police were doing that.'

'I thought I might give them a little help.'

'Oh well, I suppose it might be useful for one of your books. Bye-bye, dear, see you later.'

'What time do you plan to be back?'

'We'll be home in time for an early lunch,' said Mrs Menzies firmly.

'But I thought we might have lunch out,' Sylvia protested. 'I was looking forward—'

'You'll need to have a lie down before the inquest.'

'Mrs Menzies is quite right,' said Melissa. 'You mustn't get overtired. Go along now or you'll miss your bus.'

Sylvia pouted. 'Oh very well,' she said sulkily.

The first thing Melissa did when they had gone was call the surgery. By a stroke of luck, Doctor Newton was between patients and agreed to speak to her. 'She has quite noticeable mood swings and her memory seems very capricious,' she explained. 'She has to attend the inquest this afternoon and I'm really concerned that the strain of it will be too much for her.'

'Would you like me to call round and see her?'

'I'd be very grateful. She's out shopping with a neighbour at the moment, but they promised to be home by lunch-time.'

'What time is the inquest?'

'It opens at half past three.'

'I'll be round soon after two.'

'Thank you very much.'

Melissa left the house, crossed the road and rang the bell at number fifteen. A young woman with a thumb-sucking toddler clinging to her skirt opened the door and said, 'Yes?'

'Mrs Seymour?'

'That's right.'

'I'm sorry to bother you. My name's Melissa Craig and I'm Frank Ross's daughter.'

'Frank Ross?' For a moment the name did not appear to register; then the woman said, her round face register-ing mingled enlightenment and concern, 'You mean, the gentleman over the road who was . . .' The word 'murdered' appeared to stick in her throat and she bent down to wipe the child's nose with a paper handkerchief as if to conceal her embarrassment.

'That's right,' said Melissa. 'May I come in for a moment?'

'Of course.' Mrs Seymour held the door wide open to allow her to step into the hall. 'I was just making myself a cup of coffee – would you like one?'

'No thank you, I won't keep you long. I was wondering, was it you who told the police you'd seen my father's car outside the house at about two o'clock last Friday afternoon?'

'Yes, it was. I do hope I didn't—'

'No, that's all right. What I want to ask you is, are you absolutely certain it was his car?'

'Well, I . . .' Mrs Seymour looked nonplussed for a moment. 'It certainly looked like his car,' she said. 'It was outside his house so I assumed it was his.'

'Can you describe it?'

'It's dark blue. I've seen it lots of times before, either going out or coming back.'

'Do you happen to know the registration number?'

'Well, no, not actually. I mean, I don't think I've ever noticed it. I know it's fairly new, but . . .'

'What make is it?'

Again, Mrs Seymour hesitated. 'I think it's a Citroën, or is it a Renault that has the diamond-shaped badge on the bonnet?'

'Like this?' Melissa held up the car key her mother had given her and displayed the badge on the fob.

Mrs Seymour nodded in immediate recognition. 'That's the one.'

'So all you can be sure of is that the car you saw was a newish dark-blue Renault? Forgive me, but if you don't know the registration number, how can you be certain that it was my father's car and not another one the same make and colour?'

From looking perplexed, Mrs Seymour began to show signs of distress. 'Oh dear,' she said anxiously. 'Do you suppose I made a mistake? I was so sure at the time. It never occurred to me . . . I do hope I haven't caused any trouble.'

'On the contrary, I think you may have been very helpful,' Melissa assured her. 'Thank you very much, that's all I wanted to know.'

She turned towards the door. Mrs Seymour reached out to open it, then paused. 'I've just thought of something,' she said. 'That badge – I mentioned it because when I saw the car on Friday it was parked facing up the road so I could see the front.'

'What's so strange about that?'

'Only that this road doesn't lead anywhere in particular. The road into town is in the other direction. Nine times out of ten, that's the way people go.'

'Did you mention that to the police?'

'Well, no. I never thought of it at the time.'

'I see. Well, thank you once again, Mrs Seymour.'

Melissa's heart was thumping with excitement as she hurried back and opened the garage door at number twelve Brimley Road. It came as no surprise that the car inside was a dark blue Mégane, identical as far as she could see with the one in Marcus Bell's car park, the one driven by the ginger-haired girl from Frank

Ross and Company but according to her belonging to
Ivor Patmore.

Back indoors, she was fishing in her handbag for Denis
Botting's card when her mobile rang. Botting himself was
on the line. 'I think I might be on to something,' he said.

'Me too. I was just about to call you. The police came
again this morning, and—'

'Let's not discuss things on the phone, you never know
who might be listening. Can we meet at the Crown?'

'All right. Is that the pub where we met yesterday?'

'That's the one. Eleven o'clock, okay? See you there.'
There was a click as he ended the call without waiting for
a reply.

The Crown had been open for only a few minutes, but
already there was a sprinkling of regulars. Their quiet
chatter, combined with subdued background music, meant
that conversation at the corner table Botting indicated was
unlikely to be overheard.

'You go first,' he said as he put down a pint of beer and a
glass of fruit juice before settling in a chair opposite Melissa.

'It started when the police arrived first thing this
morning,' she began. He listened without interruption
as she recounted events without making any reference to
her mother's erratic behaviour. 'The fact that the car the
neighbour saw was pointing up the road suggests to me
that it belonged to someone calling at the house,' she said
when she had finished her narrative. 'What do you think?'

'Could be. D'you happen to know where your Dad bought his car?'

'From a dealer called Southway Motors.' She pulled out the key and showed him the fob.

Botting nodded. 'I know them. Any idea of the registration number?'

'I wrote it down.' She passed him a slip of paper. 'What have you got in mind?'

'Just a thought. Don't you want to hear my news?'

'Of course – please go ahead.'

'Last night Mum was at bingo and who should be there but Rosie Patmore. Had a lot on her mind, did Rosie.' Botting broke off to take a long pull from his beer. He put down the glass, belched and gave a sigh of content. 'That's better.'

'You were saying?' said Melissa, trying not to show her impatience.

'Ah yes, Rosie Patmore. Seems that last time Mum spoke to her she was very worried; her old man was being made to retire even though he was keen to stay on for another couple of years so's he could pay off the mortgage and carry on shelling out for school fees for one of the grandchildren who's got learning difficulties. The kid was at a special school, but the local authority closed it down and he had to go to a comprehensive where he was bullied something rotten, so Ivor and Rosie have been paying for him to go private.'

'And presumably they wouldn't have been able to afford it if Ivor had to retire?'

'Right. Now, here's the interesting part. According to Rosie, it was your Dad who decreed that Ivor should retire and he's had some pretty hard things to say about him, so you'd have thought he'd have been relieved when the man responsible for his problems got topped, but she told Mum he's been moodier than ever these past few days. Guilty conscience, d'you reckon?' Botting drained his glass and stood up. 'Think I'll have a refill – how about you?'

'No thanks.' While he was at the bar, Melissa was busy organising her thoughts. Botting's news confirmed Eunice's suspicion that Ivor Patmore knew of the decision to force him to retire and that his personal circumstances gave him a strong motive for wanting her father out of the way. Mrs Seymour's evidence suggested that he could have paid him a visit on the afternoon of his death; someone should check on his movements that day. It was an obvious task for the police, but it was unlikely that DI Adair would take the suggestion seriously. Since Botting was already *persona non grata* at the company she would have to undertake it herself. She made a mental note to consult Eunice.

The moment Botting returned with his second pint and before he had a chance to sit down, she said excitedly, 'It all seems to fit. Ivor Patmore must have decided to tackle Father about the proposed retirement away from the office. He went round to see him, pleaded his cause, got nowhere, lost his temper, saw the axe and—'

'Let's not get too carried away.' He lowered his stocky

form into his chair and raised his glass to his mouth. 'The guy may have a perfectly sound alibi.'

'I've thought of that. Eunice Lester might be able to help.'

'Ah yes, the lovely Eunice.' Botting leered, took a lusty swallow and gave another belch. 'Want me to tackle her?'

'I thought you'd been barred from Ross and Company.'

'I might try again, now you-know-who's out of the way.'

Recalling Eunice's expression of distaste at the mention of Botting's name, Melissa said diplomatically, 'I think, if you don't mind my saying so, she's more likely to talk to me. One woman to another and all that.'

He shrugged. 'Suit yourself. By the way, I've got a mate who works at Southway Motors. It's possible they supplied both those cars – your Dad's and Patmore's. I'll ask him.'

'If they did, how will that help us?'

'You never know,' he said vaguely. 'One thing's just struck me,' he went on after a further swallow and the inevitable belch. 'Patmore might have had a motive for topping your old man, but why Jessica Round? The police have contacted her relatives so they released her name to the press this morning,' he added by way of an aside. 'It'll be in tonight's edition.'

'Have they revealed the cause of death? There was speculation it was a stabbing, but DI Adair wouldn't comment.'

'A single knife wound through the heart. Whoever did it either struck lucky or had some knowledge of anatomy. Your Mum ever studied medicine?' he added facetiously.

Melissa ignored the question and returned to that of motive. 'You're probably right about Patmore. That would upset DI Adair's calculations, wouldn't it? She's never said in so many words that she thinks the two killings were carried out by the same person, but from the way she keeps chipping away at Mother it's pretty obvious she'd love to pin both of them on her.'

Botting nodded. 'That ties in with what the police spokeswoman said at this morning's briefing: "A connection between the two crimes has not been ruled out." Wonder what motive Adair has in mind for the Round killing? Rumour has it that she was having it off with an older bloke, but the description doesn't fit Patmore.' A lascivious glitter in the journalist's eye taunted Melissa over the rim of his glass, but she ignored the remark. 'Well,' he went on, seeing that she had no intention of rising to the bait, 'if we can pin your Dad's murder on Patmore, Mollie Adair will have to look around for a second killer, won't she?' He appeared to relish the thought. 'I take it you and your Mum'll be at the inquest this afternoon?'

'Of course.'

'Right.' He finished his beer and stood up. 'See you there. Maybe I'll have some further news by then.' He was gone before she had a chance to ask what he had in mind.

As she made her way back to her car, her mobile rang. An agitated Mrs Menzies was on the line.

'Oh Mrs Craig!' she said. 'I'm calling from the hospital – your mother's been taken ill. Can you come here right away?'

Chapter Twenty-One

'She's in there. There's a doctor and a nurse with her.' Mrs Menzies, sitting stiffly upright on a chair beside the ward reception desk – for the moment unmanned despite the persistent shrilling of a telephone – indicated the closed door opposite. 'I've been waiting out here for ages,' she complained. 'Everyone's disappeared; there's nobody about to tell you what's going on.' Her face was drawn with anxiety and her gloved hands fiddled with the strap of her handbag.

Melissa went over to the door and tried to peer through the window, but it was obscured by a blind. 'What happened?' she asked.

'She complained of a headache, so I suggested a cup of coffee to give her a chance to have a rest. We'd finished the shopping; she bought a lovely dress and jacket and shoes and a hat to match.' Mrs Menzies indicated a cluster of plastic carrier bags on the floor beside her chair. 'I thought she'd probably overdone it a bit on top of all that upset with the police so as we had plenty of time before the bus we went into a café in the arcade. I left her at a table while I popped into the chemist next door for some aspirins. She took a couple and drank her coffee, but she said the headache was getting worse. She looked very pale so I thought we'd better get a taxi home instead of waiting for the bus; I was just about to go and phone for one when she gave a little groan and passed out. She fell off her chair and banged the side of her head against the next table. I wasn't quick enough to catch her and I feel as if it's all my fault . . .' During her recital Mrs Menzies' voice became more and more unsteady; at the end it failed altogether.

'Please, you mustn't blame yourself,' said Melissa. She spoke mechanically; her attention was elsewhere, her eyes fixed on the closed door. 'This is her second fainting fit; she had one on Saturday, remember? They didn't seem to attach much importance to it, but now . . .'

'I didn't know what to do for the moment.' It was clear that Mrs Menzies, too, had been only half listening. 'It was such a shock you see.'

'It must have been. I'm thankful you were with her.'

'It's kind of you to say that. I've been thinking ever since it happened, perhaps I shouldn't have encouraged her to go on this shopping trip. I thought it would take her mind off things and she seemed so excited at the prospect. If only she'd stayed quietly at home . . .'

'If she had, it might have happened when she was on her own.'

'I suppose so, but if only I'd been quicker . . .'

'You mustn't blame yourself,' Melissa repeated. 'It's been plain to me ever since I came that she's far from well. I wish there was someone who could give us some information.' She glanced in frustration at the deserted desk where, after a momentary silence, the telephone began ringing again. This time a nurse appeared to answer it. She spoke for a few minutes, put the instrument down, made some notes and was about to hurry away again when Melissa intercepted her. 'Excuse me, I'm Mrs Craig and my mother, Mrs Ross, was brought in a short time ago,' she said, aware that her own voice was shaking. She pointed to the door, which was still firmly closed. 'I understand she's in there. Can you please tell me——'

'I'm afraid you'll have to wait till Doctor Freeman has completed her examination.' Harassed and overworked as she evidently was, the nurse's manner was sympathetic and she showed no sign of impatience. 'You'd be more comfortable waiting in the day room. You'll be sent for as soon as there's something to report.'

'If there's no objection, I'd rather wait here.'

'No problem.' With an encouraging smile, the woman bustled away and Melissa looked round for another chair.

Mrs Menzies stood up. 'Have this one,' she said. 'Mrs Craig, I don't want to seem unfeeling, but I really have to go and have something to eat. I'm diabetic you see and if I go too long without food . . .' Her tone was apologetic, as if she was confessing to some misdemeanour.

It was Melissa's turn to feel guilty. 'Goodness, I had no

idea! Why don't you go home, get some lunch and have a rest. You've had a shock as well.' She realised with a pang of conscience that ever since her arrival she had come to regard Mrs Menzies as a rock amid the shifting sands of her mother's erratic behaviour in the wake of her father's murder – more so than ever since Joe returned to London.

'If you're sure you don't mind.'

'Of course I don't mind. I'll stay here as long as I have to and I'll let you know as soon as there's anything to report.' A card pinned to a notice board, advertising a taxi service, caught Melissa's eye. She took out her mobile and keyed in the number. 'I'm calling a cab for you.'

'Please don't bother – there's sure to be a bus.'

'Nonsense, I'm not having you hanging around at bus stops. I'll pay the fare – no, I insist. You wouldn't be in this situation if you hadn't been looking after Mother.'

When Melissa returned to the ward after installing Mrs Menzies and the shopping in a cab and, ignoring her protests, paying the fare in advance, she found a middle-aged, white-coated woman with a stethoscope in one hand in consultation with a nurse. The door to the side ward was still closed, but the blind was open. Resisting an urgent desire to peer through, she said tentatively, 'Are you Doctor Freeman?'

'That's right. And you are . . .?'

'Melissa Craig. I believe Mrs Ross is in there – I'm her daughter.'

'Ah, Mrs Craig, I'm glad you're here.' The doctor spoke in a brisk, no-nonsense manner, but with an underlying warmth that was comforting. 'I've just completed my initial examination of your mother.'

'How is she? May I see her?'

'There's mild concussion, but otherwise I don't think the actual fall did any damage. She's comfortable and you can see her in a minute, but I'd like a word with you first. If you wouldn't mind coming this way.' She led Melissa to a small, barely furnished room behind the nurses' station, closed the door behind them and invited her with a gesture to sit down. 'I'd like some information about your mother's medical history,' she began. 'Do you happen to know the name of her GP?'

'It's Doctor Newton. Oh, my goodness!' Melissa put a hand to her forehead. 'I clean forgot. I spoke to him earlier and he's supposed to be coming to see her at two o'clock.'

'I'll get a message to him. Do I understand your mother's condition has been giving cause for anxiety before this?'

'Very much so.' Melissa spent several minutes explaining the background while Doctor Freeman made notes. 'As you can imagine, the strain on her has been terrible and we thought—'

'That her symptoms have been due to trauma,' the doctor said with a nod. 'Quite understandable in the circumstances, but we have to consider other possible causes for these fainting fits. I've arranged for your mother to have a brain scan. It may reveal an aneurism, which would account for the sudden headache—' She broke off in mid sentence, as if she had been about to continue but changed her mind.

'But you suspect something else?' Melissa felt her already low spirits take a further dive. 'Please, don't keep me in the dark.'

'Very well. I don't want to cause you unnecessary alarm, but erratic behaviour such as you have been describing is sometimes symptomatic of a brain tumour. I think we have to be prepared for that possibility.'

'I see.' Melissa felt her own brain go numb. 'How long before you get the result of the scan?'

'I've asked for it to be done urgently; with luck, we should know within twenty-four hours. Meanwhile, we'll keep her in for observation. Where can we contact you?'

Melissa wrote down her mother's address and phone number on the back of one of her business cards. Doctor Freeman's eyebrows lifted at the sight of the printed inscription. 'So you're the famous Mel Craig!' she exclaimed. 'I'm so pleased to meet you — I'm a great admirer of your books.'

'Thank you.' It was something she had heard many times and it had never before failed to give her pleasure; today it seemed of little importance. 'May I see my mother now?'

'Just for a few minutes. She's under sedation and very drowsy, so don't expect too much.' Without warning, the doctor reached across the table and grasped Melissa's wrist. 'Your pulse is steady,' she said after consulting her watch for a minute, 'but you're looking very pale. Are you feeling all right?'

'Just a little shaken. The past few days have been a bit of a nightmare, one way and the other.'

'Is there anyone at home to keep you company?'

'There's Mother's next-door neighbour; she's been a brick, but she's not a hundred per cent fit herself.'

'If it's possible, I advise you to arrange for a friend to stay with you for a few days.'

At the suggestion, the cloud of desolation that had threatened to engulf Melissa dispersed a little. The assurance Joe had given during their conversation the previous night rang in her head with the comforting certainty of church bells: *Call me at any hour, day or night.* She knew that he meant it, the way he meant everything else he said.

'Yes,' she said shakily, 'yes, I'll do that – right away.'

When, tired and emotionally drained, Melissa turned into Brimley Road after the inquest, she was almost overwhelmed by a surge of relief at the sight of Joe's car outside the house. The double gates were already standing open and she drove straight in and parked the Fiesta on the drive. The moment she switched off the ignition he opened the door, one hand extended to help her out. It closed over hers, warm, firm, reassuring. 'I got here as soon as I could,' he said.

Her throat seized up; all she could manage in response was a watery smile of pure gratitude. The moment they were inside the house she almost fell against him; too exhausted even to weep, she leaned her head on his shoulder, absorbing the strength of his encircling arms, saying in a muffled voice, 'Oh Joe, I'm so thankful you're here . . . so thankful.'

'I'm thankful you sent for me.' After a few moments he gently disengaged and said, 'Now, let me make some tea while you tell me what happened at the inquest.'

'Nothing much.' She slipped off her jacket and followed him into the kitchen. 'The coroner heard statements from the forensic pathologist and the police, but because the principal witness — that's Mother, of course — was unable to give evidence it had to be adjourned almost immediately. I wish you could have seen DI Adair's face!' Melissa gave an involuntary chuckle as she recalled the detective's look of frustration; it was the first time that the funny side of the situation had struck her and the realisation that her sense of humour was alive and well was an additional comfort. 'It was wonderful of you to come at a moment's notice like this, Joe,' she said huskily. 'I can't tell you how good it is to have you here. Was it terribly inconvenient, dropping everything at a moment's notice?'

'No problem; nothing that couldn't wait.' He was setting out cups and saucers; beside him, the kettle was starting to sing. 'Now, what's on the programme for this evening? Do you want to go back to the hospital?'

'I suppose I ought to take her nightdress and toilet things, but I don't think there'd be any point in staying. She was only just about conscious when I saw her and they're keeping her under sedation. They said they didn't expect any change in her condition overnight, but they'd call me if there was.'

'We ought to be thinking about food. Would you like to eat out?'

'I'd rather not; we can shop for something on our way back from the hospital. Would you mind if I asked Mrs Menzies to join us? She's been so good to Mother and I don't like to think of her in there on her own, fretting. I must have a word with her anyway. I promised to let her know how things were.'

'Invite her by all means.' Joe put two cups of tea on the table and sat down beside her. 'You're such a kind soul, Mel,' he said softly. 'That's one of the things I love about you.'

To her consternation, his words induced another rush of emotion and she gave all her attention to drinking her tea until she had it under control. Then she said, 'I'd better consult her before we decide what to eat – she's probably on some sort of diet.'

It was while the three of them were drinking coffee after a meal of grilled chicken with stir-fried vegetables, followed by sliced bananas and yoghurt, that Melissa remembered Sylvia's offer of her father's car. 'I might as well use it and return the Fiesta,' she said. 'It's costing a small fortune.'

'I do hope you'll look after it,' said Mrs Menzies. Her sudden flush of embarrassment betrayed the fact that she had spoken on impulse and she hurried on, 'Forgive me, that must sound impertinent, but he took such care of it, you know.'

'Yes, I remember.' Melissa's mind flew back over the years. 'His car was always his pride and joy. He'd never let anyone else drive it. I remember being very miffed when he wouldn't even take me out for extra practice before I took my test. He did all the maintenance himself, kept a detailed record every time he filled it up so he could check on his fuel consumption.'

'He kept that up right to the end.' Mrs Menzies brushed a hand across her eyes. 'So meticulous in everything, he was.' She glanced at the clock on the mantelpiece, finished her coffee and stood up. 'If you'll excuse me, I think I'll be going home — I like to be in bed by ten. Thank you for the meal; I really appreciate your invitation.' At the front door she renewed her thanks and added, 'You will keep me informed of your mother's progress, won't you, Mrs Craig?'

'Of course.'

With his usual courtesy, Joe escorted her to her own house. When he returned he was chuckling.

'What's the joke?' Melissa asked.

'Are you expecting me to spend tonight in a hotel?'

'No, of course not. What gave you that idea?'

'Your puritanical neighbour does. I'm afraid your reputation will be irretrievably damaged when she sees my car still here in the morning.'

'Too bad.' She was in the kitchen, stacking dishes on

the draining board, and she made a point of keeping her back to him as she added, 'I'll sleep in Mother's bed and you can have the spare room.'

'Thank you.' If he was disappointed at the response, he gave no sign. 'Perhaps before we turn in we ought to be thinking about plans for tomorrow,' he suggested.

'Good idea. I'll call the hospital first thing and find out how things are with Mother and then I'll have a word with Eunice to see if she can help me check on Ivor Patmore's movements last Friday.'

'What about returning the Fiesta? I could follow you to the garage and bring you back here to pick up the Renault.'

'That'd be great. Speaking of cars, I forgot in all the anxiety over Mother to mention that Botting phoned to tell me all the company cars come from Southway Motors. During recent months they've supplied four Méganes, all identical. Incidentally, the original order was for three, but they increased it later.'

'Maybe your Dad negotiated a quantity discount,' Joe grinned. 'Four, eh?' he went on, becoming serious again. 'You mentioned there were four directors. Presumably they had one each.'

'Probably. Which means, in theory, that if the one Mrs Seymour spotted wasn't Father's — and I'm pretty sure it wasn't — it could have belonged to any of the others.'

'So now we have three suspects, not just the one?'

'Ivor Patmore seems the most likely at the moment,

but yes, you're right.' A thought flashed into Melissa's mind. 'I wonder. That record Father kept—'

'What about it?'

'He used to make a note of every journey he made, and the mileage. He entered it in a diary and kept it in the car. If he still did that, it would tell us—'

They found the diary in the glove compartment and brought it indoors. Melissa uttered an exclamation of triumph at sight of the final entry in her father's neat, precise hand, made the day before he was murdered. It indicated that he had driven to the factory and back and that the mileage at the end of the journey was the same as that registered on the odometer.

'So he didn't go anywhere on Friday!' Melissa exclaimed. 'This proves it wasn't his car that Mrs Seymour saw, doesn't it?'

'Not conclusively,' said Joe. 'He might have been intending to go somewhere, got the car out and then for some reason changed his mind.'

'But it was facing the wrong way. Remember what Mrs Seymour said? No, I'm convinced it wasn't his. All we have to do now is establish which of the other three it was.'

'We? Aren't you going to hand this over to the police?'

'Not likely! I want the next thing I give DI Mollie Adair to be the name of the person who killed my father.'

Chapter Twenty-Two

Melissa lay awake for a long time that night. It felt strange to be sleeping in the big double bed that her parents had shared; it recalled memories of being soothed when sick or frightened by a bad dream. Tonight there was no such comfort. Anxiety about her mother, excitement over the discovery of the mileage record, possible ways of approaching the problem of checking Ivor Patmore's movements on the day of her father's murder, jostled for attention in her over-active brain. Deliberately thrust to the back of her mind was the thought of Joe, asleep in the room next door. Part of her longed for him; she knew beyond doubt that the smallest sign from her would have brought him to her side, but instinctively she had held back. And as if he recognised that she was emotionally spent, that this was not the time, his 'goodnight' had been almost deliberately casual, without so much as a hand on her arm or the lightest kiss on her cheek.

She forced her thoughts back to her goal of tracking down her father's killer, mentally running over all the information she had gleaned so far. As things stood it all seemed to point in the same direction, yet the more she thought about it, the more uneasily convinced she became that somewhere along the line there was something significant that she had overlooked. It lurked just beyond the edge of her consciousness, tantalising her, a shadow defying all her efforts to nail the substance. She was no nearer to identifying it when at last she fell into a restless sleep.

A light tap on the door aroused her. 'Tea downstairs in ten minutes,' Joe called. There came the sound of his footsteps descending the stairs, the gush of water from the tap in the kitchen, the clatter of crockery, the click of the refrigerator door opening and closing. She got out of bed, put on her dressing-gown and slippers and padded quietly along the landing to the bathroom. Back in the bedroom she drew back the curtains, blinking slightly in the early morning sunlight, and sat down at her mother's dressing-table to comb her hair. Her cheeks were paler than usual and there were faint smudges under her eyes that had not been there when she left Gloucestershire, but otherwise the face that stared back at her from the mirror looked surprisingly normal. She stayed there for several minutes, idly fingering the few toilet items: a tortoiseshell-backed brush and comb, a crystal trinket set, a jar of hand cream, a manicure set in a brown leather case. She picked up a silver frame containing a photograph of her parents in the garden of their old home. A stab of emotion brought a gush of tears to her eyes; as she put it down and reached for a handkerchief it slid along the polished surface and fell to the floor. She stooped and picked it up; as she did so, the back fell off revealing a second, much older, photograph underneath. Two young women in nurses' uniforms smiled up at her. She turned it over; on the back was written 'Harmley Hospital, August 1948' in her mother's handwriting. She examined the two faded faces more closely and caught her breath as she recognised one of them. The realisation of what her discovery might mean sent her flying downstairs in a panic.

Joe had evidently been up some time; he was freshly shaved and clad in a checked shirt and casual fawn trousers. As she entered the kitchen he looked up from pouring tea into pottery mugs and greeted her with a smile that swiftly turned to consternation. 'Whatever's the matter?' he asked.

'This.' Dumbly, she held out the photograph.

He studied it for a moment before handing it back. 'One of the girls looks like your mother,' he remarked.

'It is my mother.'

'Where did you find it?'

'It was behind another picture on her dressing-table. I dropped the frame and it fell out.'

'It seems to have given you quite a turn. Here, drink this.' He put a mug of tea on the table and pulled out a chair for her; she made no move to sit down but continued to stare in horrified fascination at the photograph.

'Don't you see what this means? Don't you remember what Botting told me?' she said, her voice hoarse with dread. 'The police reckon that whoever killed Jessica Round might have had some medical knowledge. I knew there was something I'd forgotten. I lay awake for ages last night trying to think what it was. As soon as I saw this I remembered; Mother trained as a nurse after leaving school. She never took her final exams, said she realised in the end that it wasn't the right career for her, but she must have learned enough to . . . oh Joe, she might have—'

He stepped forward and grasped her by the shoulders. 'Mel, don't say that, don't even think it!' he commanded. 'It doesn't mean a thing, it's just a coincidence.'

'How can you be sure?' Yet again, all the doubts that she had tried so hard to suppress came back to torment her. 'What if the police find out? DI Adair won't give up enquiring into Mother's background just because she's been hospitalised.'

'Is she likely to probe that far back into her past?'

'She's made up her mind Mother's guilty and she'll go to any lengths to—'

'So what if she does find out? It won't prove anything.'

'But Joe, supposing—'

'Supposing you drink that before it gets cold.' He pushed her firmly into the chair and placed the mug of tea in her hands. She obeyed without protest, shivering a little, grateful for the warmth. When she had finished he took the empty mug away and sat down beside her. 'Now, just listen to me,' he said. 'You promised your mother you'd try to find out who killed your father, you've been doing your best to keep that promise and yesterday you uncovered one very important piece of evidence. You could be on the verge of a breakthrough and you're not going to give up now.' It was neither a command nor a plea, but a simple statement of fact, a recognition that, whatever setbacks she might encounter, it was not in her nature to quit.

She knew that as well, but the one overriding fear remained like a leaden weight in her brain. 'Supposing I find out that she did it after all — what then?' she whispered.

'I don't believe you will. From what I've seen of Sylvia, I find it almost impossible to believe she's capable of that kind of violence.'

'You never can tell; everyone has their limits. Joe, what will I do if—'

'If the worst comes to the worst, you'll be given the strength to face up to it,' he said. His arm slid round her shoulders, promising without words that part of the strength would come from him. After a moment he stood up and said, 'Now, let's be practical. We'll have some breakfast and then decide how to organise our day.'

After speaking to the ward sister and being assured that her mother had passed a comfortable night and would shortly be undergoing the promised brain scan, and having later returned the Fiesta to the garage where she had hired it, Melissa drove in her father's car to the premises of Frank Ross and Company and parked in one of a row of bays marked 'Visitors'. A short distance away she noticed an empty bay labelled 'Chairman' alongside three others simply designated 'Director'. They too were empty, but as she switched off the ignition and released her seat belt an identical dark blue Mégane slid into one of them. The driver, a tall man with iron-grey hair, got out, reached across to the passenger seat for a briefcase and slammed the driver's door. On impulse, Melissa called, 'Excuse me, are you Mr Patmore?'

The man swung round in surprise. For the first time, she saw his face; he was younger than she had supposed, tanned and athletic-looking. She realised her mistake even before he said, 'No, my name's Fingle.' He glanced along the empty bays. 'I don't think Ivor Patmore's in yet. Have you an—' He stopped short. 'Forgive me for asking, but isn't that Frank Ross's car?'

'Yes.' She stepped forward. 'I'm his daughter, Melissa Craig.'

'His daughter?' Raised eyebrows and a note of surprise in his voice indicated that he had been unaware of her existence, but all he said as he took her outstretched hand was, 'I'm so sorry about your father – it must have been a terrible shock to you and your mother.' He turned away for a moment to lock his own car before remarking, 'It was quite a shock for me to come back to.'

'You've been away?'

'On holiday in Switzerland. I only arrived home on Tuesday night, and when I got to the office yesterday morning . . .' He shook his head as if he still found it difficult to believe what had happened. 'Frank Ross, of all people. How's your mother taken it?'

'She's pretty badly shaken. As a matter of fact, she's in hospital at the moment, having some tests; she's had a couple of fainting fits.'

'That's hardly surprising. Do give her my condolences when you see her.'

'Thank you, I will.'

'Have the police any idea who did it?'

Deducing from the question that Eunice Lester had not betrayed her confidence, Melissa shook her head. 'They're following one line of enquiry, but I think they're on the wrong track,' she said and added, after a moment's hesitation, 'I don't suppose you can think of anyone who might have had a grudge against my father?'

Fingle appeared uncomfortable at the question. After a moment, speaking with apparent reluctance, he said, 'I have to be honest, he wasn't the most popular man in the company, but I find it difficult to believe that anyone here felt strongly enough to murder him.'

Something forthright and basically honest about his manner made Melissa decide to put her cards on the table. 'The fact is, the detective in charge of the investigation seems to have made up her mind that my mother did it,' she said.

He stared at her open-mouthed. 'You've got to be kidding!' he exclaimed.

'You don't believe it either?'

'Not for a moment. A quiet, gentle person like Sylvia Ross – she wouldn't hurt a fly.'

'That's what I think.'

'So you've decided to do a little private sleuthing and make the lady cop eat her words? Fancy that, now!'

'Something like that,' Melissa admitted with a smile. His sympathetic tone and a total absence of condescension in his manner had robbed his remarks of any possible offence. 'Let me explain why I'm here. A neighbour saw what she believed to be my father's car outside the house on the afternoon his body was discovered. For reasons I won't go into now, Detective Inspector Adair is convinced this supports her theory, but enquiries I've made since make me almost certain that it wasn't his car at all.'

'Well, as you can see, mine's identical – but I'm afraid you'll have to consider me eliminated from your enquiries. My alibi for last Friday is unassailable.' He gave an infectious grin, displaying teeth that shone white against his tan, then became suddenly serious. 'Ivor Patmore has the same model as well. That was your father's choice, of course; he was a bit like Henry Ford when allocating company cars. We could have any model we liked as long as it was the same as his.' He shot her a keen look and said, 'I assume you knew that – is that why you want to see Ivor?'

'Well, yes. I've reason to believe that he was in dispute with Father over his prospective retirement.'

Fingle looked impressed. 'You've certainly been doing

your homework!' he said with a hint of admiration. 'He was sounding off to me about it the day before I went on leave. He claimed to have inside knowledge that FR was planning to edge him out on his sixty-fifth birthday and he was pretty upset, but I never thought for a moment – I mean, Ivor's got a quick temper, but I wouldn't have thought him capable of violence.' He broke off and looked at Melissa with a slightly puzzled expression. 'Forgive me, but why don't you tell the police of your suspicions?'

'I've already crossed swords with Detective Inspector Adair. She told me in so many words to leave the investigation to her and I'm not going back to her with half a story.'

'I take your point.' Fingle thought for a moment, then said, 'How about if I do a spot of sleuthing for you? I can easily check on Ivor's movements last Friday if you like – would that help?' The notion seemed to appeal to his sense of adventure; a gleam of excitement shone in his eyes, reminding Melissa of what Eunice had said about her father's opinion of his 'boyish enthusiasms'.

'Is that a serious offer?' she asked cautiously.

'Dead serious. I have to be honest, I don't think for a moment that Ivor did it, but at least I might be able to eliminate him for you.'

'That would be very useful.' To have Ivor Patmore eliminated was not quite what Melissa had in mind, but she felt it would be inappropriate to say so. 'If it's not too much trouble,' she said politely.

'Happy to be of service.' Fingle glanced at his wristwatch. 'Sorry, must dash – I've a meeting in ten minutes. Where can I contact you?' He made a note of the numbers she gave him, promised to be in touch and hurried away.

Deciding that there was now no point in trying to speak to Eunice, Melissa went back to the car. As she was buckling on her seat belt, a dark green Jaguar, similar to the one she had noticed outside the building where Marcus Bell had his offices, drove into the car park and swept into the bay marked 'Chairman'. At the wheel was Marcus Bell himself.

'You realise what this means, don't you?' said Melissa. 'We have to eliminate Marcus Bell straight away.'

Joe looked up from his task of cracking eggs for their lunch-time omelettes. He put a lump of butter in a pan and set it on the stove. 'Not necessarily,' he said after a moment's thought.

'What do you mean? Bell drives a Jag so it couldn't have been his car Mrs Seymour saw.'

'Do we know how long he's had the Jag? He might have objected to having someone else's choice foisted on him and turned the Renault in the minute your father was out of the way.'

Melissa shook her head, frowning. 'That sounds a bit improbable to me. Don't forget, although he's a director of the company, he's not an employee in the way the other two are – he's a solicitor with an independent practice. He can drive any car he likes.'

'True.' Joe poured beaten egg into the hot pan and began gently prodding the edges with a spatula. 'I see the point you're making. If the fourth car wasn't for him, it was for somebody else – somebody we haven't even considered.'

'Exactly.' Resignedly, Melissa faced up to the fact that her investigation was in danger of being blown off course. 'We still have Ivor Patmore as our prime suspect, but if Tom Fingle's enquiries put him in the clear we're back to square one.'

Joe folded the omelette, slid it on to a plate and put it in front of her. As he poured more eggs into the pan he remarked, 'Didn't you say something about a disgruntled employee who was claiming unfair dismissal? Maybe he's been sitting at home nursing a grudge, unable to find another job.'

'You're right!' Melissa paused with a forkful of omelette halfway to her mouth as disappointment gave way to renewed optimism. 'According to Denis Botting they were trying to negotiate an out of court settlement and a new car could have been part of the deal. That would account for the fourth Renault Mégane. Joe, I think you've hit it!'

Chapter Twenty-Three

'So how do you propose to set about tracking down the mysterious fourth suspect?' asked Joe between mouthfuls of omelette.

'I've been thinking about that,' said Melissa. 'Eunice Lester might be able to help. I'll give her a call when we've finished our lunch.' She laid down her fork and pushed away her empty plate. 'Joe, that was absolutely scrumptious. I had no idea you were such an accomplished cook.'

'My culinary talents are pretty limited I'm afraid, but I do pride myself on my omelettes,' he said. 'What would you like to follow?'

'Just some fruit, and then coffee and a biscuit.' She fetched the fruit bowl, sat down again and began peeling a banana. 'I still think Patmore's our man,' she went on thoughtfully, 'but it would be interesting to find out where that other car went.'

'If Patmore's eliminated it'll be more than interesting –

it'll be vital information.' He finished his omelette, put their plates and cutlery in the sink and filled the kettle before bringing out coffee, mugs, cafetière and biscuits.

Noting the confident way in which he located every item, Melissa remarked with a smile, 'You've certainly made yourself at home in this kitchen.'

'Given a little encouragement, I can make myself at home anywhere.'

The glance he directed at her was full of meaning, but she chose to ignore it. 'I'll see if I can catch Eunice now,' she said. 'She usually eats a packed lunch in her office.'

Luck was with her; Eunice was there, but she seemed nonplussed by the question. 'I'm afraid I don't have the answer to that one,' she said after a brief pause for thought. 'The case was brought some while ago; it was dealt with in Mr Bell's office and all I know is that they were hoping to settle out of court. The last thing FR would have wanted would have been adverse publicity.'

'You don't happen to know if there was talk of including a car in any settlement deal?'

'I've no idea. Is it important?'

'It might be, if it was the right sort of car.' Eunice listened in silence as, without revealing Botting as her source, Melissa explained that she had found out that the company had taken delivery of four identical cars and was almost certain that the one seen by Mrs Seymour was not the one driven by her father. 'That left three to account for,' she said. 'I assumed the other three directors had one each, but when I saw Mr Bell driving a Jag it was obvious the fourth one had gone elsewhere.'

'I see.' Eunice sounded impressed. 'I only wish I could help you.'

'Would it be too much trouble for you to check with Mr Bell? I'd do it myself, but he's made it pretty clear he isn't too well disposed towards me.'

'I'm sorry, but that's out of the question,' Eunice said quickly. She hesitated for a moment before continuing. 'The fact is, one of Mr Bell's staff saw me talking to you in the Crown and when he heard about it he was very angry. He said if you made any further approach to me I was to refer you directly to him. I shouldn't really be speaking to you now – he'd be furious if he knew.'

'Did he give a reason?'

'No. I really am terribly sorry. I can't afford to risk losing my job.'

'No, of course not. Well thanks anyway. Sorry to have disturbed your lunch hour.'

'No joy?' said Joe as she ended the call. He put two mugs of coffee and a plate of biscuits on the table and sat down. 'Are you sure it isn't worth tackling Bell yourself?' he suggested when she had relayed the conversation. 'It seems a harmless enough question.'

Melissa shook her head. 'I've got a better idea – Denis Botting. If he wants an exclusive we may as well make him work for it. He's probably in the pub, having his usual liquid lunch.'

She punched out Botting's number. He answered

immediately; from the background noise she deduced that her surmise was correct. 'Made a breakthrough yet?' he asked. 'I've got my piece partly written up; all I need is a few essential details and the name of the killer – but don't tell me on the phone! You never know—'

'I haven't solved the case yet, but I'm making progress.'

'Great! Come and join me for a jar and bring me up to date. I'm in the Crown.'

'Sorry, no time, but thanks anyway. Look, there's something I'd like you to check for me.'

'Go ahead, but remember, no names.'

'All right, masterspy. You mentioned a certain case of alleged unfair dismissal – you know the one I mean?'

'I'm with you; what about it?'

'Can you find out if it's been settled and if so, exactly what the deal was?'

'You mean, how much?'

'That, and whether anything else was thrown in – like a new Renault Mégane?'

There was a brief pause as if Botting was digesting the significance of the question. Then he gave a low whistle. 'That sounds like an interesting new twist!' He sounded almost excited. 'I'll see what I can dig up. Leave it with me.'

'The man's paranoid!' Melissa commented as she ended the call. 'He's terrified there are rivals tuned into his mobile, waiting to pirate his story. I shudder to think what he's going to write, but it's going to be pretty sensational stuff if we do manage to crack this case before the police do. The headline will probably be something like, "Crime Writer Beats Police in Hunt for Father's Killer". You'd just love that, wouldn't you, Joe?'

'Of course! Loads of publicity, up go your sales — and my commission! Great!' Joe rubbed his hands in mock anticipation and helped himself to a biscuit. For a moment, the clouds hanging over them were forgotten as they chuckled over the time-honoured joke they had shared since the aftermath of Melissa's first encounter with a real-life murderer had sent the sales of her crime novels rocketing.

A glance at the kitchen clock brought her back to reality with a jerk. 'Two o'clock; it's time I checked with the hospital.' She made the call, exchanged a few words with the ward sister and put the phone down. 'The results of the tests have come through and Doctor Freeman wants to discuss them with me,' she said soberly.

'You reckon it's serious?'

'Sister was very non-committal, but yes, I have a feeling it is.'

'Then we'll go to the hospital straight away.'

Immediately on their arrival, they were shown into Doctor Freeman's office. 'As I half suspected, there's a brain tumour,' she informed Melissa. 'It's operable, but we can't tell at this stage whether it's malignant or not. I've discussed her case with our consultant neurologist and he recommends immediate surgery, but as her next of kin we need your consent. She's rather confused, you see; she's told us to do whatever is necessary, but we can't be sure she fully understands what's involved.'

'What are her chances?'

'Of surviving the operation — quite good. As for the long-term prognosis, it's impossible to say at this stage.'

'And if she doesn't have the operation?'

'We can't be certain, of course, but there's a strong possibility that the tumour will enlarge, in which case the headaches and confusion will get progressively worse and the condition will eventually become inoperable.'

'I see.' Melissa felt as if she had received a physical blow to the stomach and her voice seemed to come from somewhere outside her head. 'If you don't mind, I'd like a few minutes to talk it over with my friend.'

'Of course.' Doctor Freeman stood up. 'Let Sister know when you've come to a decision.'

The minute the door closed behind her, Melissa turned to Joe in something close to despair. 'This is an awful responsibility they're giving me,' she said shakily. 'Whatever am I going to do?'

He had been sitting beside her in silence while the doctor explained the situation; at one point he had taken her hand and was still holding it. 'I think in your heart you know the answer to that one, don't you?' he said quietly.

She nodded miserably. 'It seems so cruel. After all these years, it takes a murder to bring us together again . . . and now there's a chance I may lose her for ever. I've been secretly telling myself that once we find the real killer and things have settled down, we'll be able to spend some time . . . to make up for . . . but now . . .' The remaining words were washed away under a rising tide of emotion.

'Now come on, this is no time for tears.' Joe's tone was kind, but firm. 'You have a vital decision to make on your mother's behalf and you must try to think calmly.'

'Joe, please help me; tell me what *you* think,' she begged.

'It seems to me there's a simple choice,' he said. 'Either you condemn her to a very real risk of steady deterioration and eventual death, or you give her a fighting chance of a few more years of normal life. If you were the patient, which would you go for?'

Melissa managed a grateful, if tremulous smile. 'Put that way, there's only one answer, isn't there?'

'I'm sure you've made the right decision,' said Doctor Freeman. 'I have the form ready for you to sign.'

'I would like to see my mother first, if you don't mind.'

'Of course. This way.'

Sylvia lay supine on a heap of pillows. Her eyes were closed and her features pale but relaxed. She wore an expression of childlike innocence that brought the lump back into Melissa's throat. 'Mother, are you asleep? Can you hear me?' she whispered.

Sylvia's eyes fluttered open. 'Lissie, is that you?' she said. Her voice had a dream-like quality, as if she was talking in her sleep.

'Yes, it's me. How do you feel?'

'Dopey.' A faint smile played about the colourless mouth. 'Lissie, they want to look inside my head.'

'Yes, they told me.'

'Are you going to let them?'

'What do you think?'

'I don't know, dear, you decide.' Sylvia gave a weary little sigh and her eyes closed again.

Melissa dropped a kiss on her forehead and said huskily, 'It'll be all right. You won't know a thing about it, and I'll be here when you wake up.'

'Promise?'

'I promise.'

After Melissa had signed the consent form and learned that the operation was scheduled for nine o'clock the following morning, Joe drove her back to the house. They had been indoors less than five minutes when the telephone rang.

'Melissa?' It was a woman's voice, soft and slightly anxious. 'It's Lottie Haynes. I feel I owe you an apology.'

'Oh – why's that?' Melissa felt a pang of guilt herself; she had a vague recollection of having promised to let Lottie know how she was getting on with her enquiries and realised that she had been so overwhelmed by events that she had hardly given her a thought since.

'For not having been in touch before, to ask after your mother,' Lottie explained. 'I've been away again, you see; my niece was rushed into hospital for an emergency operation and I've been looking after her children. Her parents were away on holiday so I stepped into the breach – they're back now so I'm home again. It's not that I haven't thought about Sylvia,' she hurried on, apparently without drawing breath and giving Melissa no chance to utter a word. 'I've really been very worried about her; it said in last night's paper that she wasn't well enough to attend the inquest on your father. Please, how is she? Is it anything serious?'

'I'm afraid it is.' Melissa explained, to the accompaniment of exclamations of distress.

'Oh my dear, I'm so very sorry.' There was no doubt about the sincerity of Lottie's concern. 'Do let me know how things go, won't you?'

'Yes, of course.'

'And what dreadful news about Jessica Round! I'd heard about the murder at Alderley Court, but what with Emma being ill and everything . . . it was only this morning when I found time to read last night's paper that I realised it was Jess. Such a dreadful thing, so soon after what happened to your poor father; it must have been a terrible shock for your mother—' The torrent of words ceased momentarily as Lottie paused for breath.

'It has been a very stressful time for her,' Melissa agreed. *And you don't know the half of it*, she added mentally. 'It's really very kind of you to call,' she went on. 'I'm sorry I haven't—'

But Lottie was once more in full flow. 'You said you were trying to find out who killed your father – have you made any progress? It said in the paper that the police hadn't ruled out a connection between the two murders. Whatever can they mean by that?'

'I haven't had time to give it much thought, I'm afraid.' Melissa was aware that she was skating round the truth, but she had no intention of revealing the nature and extent of the police suspicions. 'All I can think about at the moment is tomorrow and Mother's operation.'

Immediately, Lottie was all contrition. 'My dear, I quite understand. I'll leave you in peace for now. I hope all goes well; perhaps I may visit Sylvia when she's feeling up to it? I'll do a special arrangement for her.'

'That's very kind. I'm sure she'll love that.'

Melissa had no time to put Joe in the picture before the phone rang for a second time. Tom Fingle was on the line.

'I thought I'd let you know straight away that I've managed to eliminate another suspect for you!' he said with a note of triumph in his voice. 'Ivor Patmore was at a meeting in Birmingham for most of Friday. He's got relatives there and stayed overnight with them before driving back on Saturday.'

'Well, thank you for letting me know so quickly.'

'No trouble! Anything else I can do, just say the word. Bye.'

'Patmore appears to have an alibi,' said Melissa as she put down the phone. Realising that she had mentally become convinced that he was the man they were seeking, she experienced a sharp stab of disappointment.

Joe considered for a moment, then said, 'That makes three down, one to go. It's up to Denis Botting now to deliver the goods.'

*   *   *

It was several hours before Botting called, and when he did Melissa's hopes were dashed still further. 'Sorry, but you appear to be barking up the wrong tree,' he told her. 'It was a cash settlement and your man blued part of it on a cruise starting last Thursday. And in any case, he doesn't drive.'

Chapter Twenty-Four

'What you need is a good stiff drink,' said Joe as he opened the bottle of gin that, with other essential supplies, they had picked up in the supermarket on their way home from the hospital. He poured out two measures, added tonic, ice and lemon, tipped the contents of a packet of crisps into a dish and sat down beside Melissa at the table in the kitchen.

'Bless you!' she said gratefully. 'I don't know what Father would say if he could see us quaffing strong liquor in his house — he always declared it was the invention of the devil.'

'I'm sure he'd forgive you, in the circumstances.'

Melissa gave a wistful smile. 'I doubt it, but as he's not here to object . . .' She reached for her glass, but before she had a chance to drink from it there was a ring at the doorbell. 'Oh Lord!' she exclaimed in dismay. 'You know who that is, don't you? I promised to keep her posted, but it went right out of my head.' She half rose, but Joe put a hand on her shoulder.

'I'll go,' he said.

He went out into the hall, returning moments later preceded by a dour-faced Mrs Menzies. 'I seem to recall asking to be kept informed of my friend's progress,' she said, ignoring Joe and looking accusingly at Melissa. 'I telephoned the hospital to enquire, but all they would say is that your mother was comfortable.'

'I really am most awfully sorry,' Melissa said earnestly. 'It wasn't intentional, it's just that I've had so many other things on my mind.'

'So it would seem.' Mrs Menzies shot a brief glance in Joe's direction; the insinuation was obvious.

Somewhat unwisely, Melissa felt, he reached for the gin bottle and said, 'As you can see, we're just having a pre-prandial snifter. Melissa's had a very stressful day and I thought it would do her good. Would you care to join us?'

'No thank you, Mr Martin, and I'm surprised at you' – the reproachful gaze fastened once more on Melissa – 'allowing alcohol in your late father's house.'

Looking abashed, Joe put down the bottle and said, 'My fault, I'm afraid,' but all he got in return was a disdainful sniff.

'I know Father wouldn't have approved,' said Melissa humbly, 'but Joe's right, it has been a very worrying day. I went back to the hospital this afternoon and saw the doctor again.' She went on to explain the situation; as she spoke, the expression of disapproval softened to one of sympathetic concern.

'I can understand your anxiety,' said Mrs Menzies in a gentler tone. She made a slightly helpless gesture. 'I wish there was something I could do.'

'Your support and friendship have been a tremendous comfort to her,' Melissa assured her warmly.

Mrs Menzies brushed a hand over her eyes. 'She can rely on me at all times,' she said huskily. 'I shall pray for her – and for you. I'll go now and let you get on with your supper.'

Melissa felt obliged to respond by saying, 'Why don't you stay and have something with us?' but was relieved when the offer was politely declined. At the door, she renewed her apologies and promised to report as soon as there was any news after the operation.

Back in the kitchen, she slid into her chair, grabbed her drink and took a long swallow. 'Boy, did I need that!' she said fervently, then gave a slightly hysterical giggle. 'You really put your foot in it, offering the old duck a G and T!'

Joe gave a rueful grin. 'It was a bit tactless, wasn't it? He picked up his own glass. 'Anyway, here's to Sylvia's complete recovery – and the success of your investigation.'

'Amen to both of those.' They drank without speaking for several moments. Then Melissa said with a sigh, 'Where do we go from here, Joe? I'd been pinning everything on tracking down the driver of that fourth Renault.'

'Has it occurred to you that your friend Botting might

have been given inaccurate information and there never were more than three?'

'But Mrs Seymour saw it, and we've eliminated all the others.'

'It's quite a popular model. Isn't it possible that what she saw was a very similar car belonging to a complete stranger who has nothing to do with the case? Because it happened to have been left outside your parents' house for some reason, she may have jumped to the wrong conclusion.'

Melissa shook her head. 'That's surely too much of a coincidence. No, I'm positive there is a fourth car and somehow we need to find out who's got it.' She picked up a teaspoon that was lying on the table and moodily prodded at her slice of lemon, her mind sifting through possible avenues of enquiry.

'Maybe another employee in the company was given the opportunity to take advantage of some special discount arrangements,' Joe suggested.

'That would imply someone else with a grudge against Father,' said Melissa, a shade wearily. 'I suppose it's a possibility, though. How do I set about finding out?'

'Eunice?'

'She might know, but she's been warned off speaking to me.'

'What about your friend Tom Fingle?'

'Good idea! Perhaps he could check it for me. I'll see if I can catch him before he leaves the office.' Her optimism momentarily renewed, she punched out the number, then put down the phone in exasperation on hearing the recorded message. 'Too late, they're already closed,' she grumbled.

'You can try again first thing in the morning. Meanwhile, let's get on with preparing our dinner. You're in charge. What's my first job?'

'You can light the oven and then start crushing peppercorns for the *steak au poivre* if you like.' She finished her drink and began unpacking the rest of their shopping, put frozen chips into a baking dish, unwrapped a parcel of steaks and put a bottle of red wine on the table. 'Would you mind opening this – and take a brownie point for remembering to buy a corkscrew. I'll bet there isn't such a thing in the place.'

They went about their tasks for a while in silence. Then Joe said, a little diffidently, 'You aren't going to like this, Mel, but don't you think perhaps this is the time to pass on what you know to the police? Presumably they're still working on the theory that it's your Dad's car that Mrs Seymour spotted, and that it helps support their case against your mother. At least you're in a position to shake their confidence in it, even if you can't actually disprove it.'

'That's true, but I'm reluctant to—'

Joe gave a sympathetic nod. 'I know, you want to present DI Adair with a cut-and-dried solution that will blow her theory out of the water.'

'It would give me a lot of pleasure to cut her down to size,' Melissa admitted.

'It's understandable, but don't lose sight of your main objective, will you?'

'Dear Joe, how wise you are,' she said softly. He took a quick breath as if about to say something, but instead returned to his operations with the pestle and mortar.

'You know,' she went on thoughtfully as she flattened the steaks, brushed them with oil and began smothering them with the crushed peppercorns, 'I'm beginning to think that somewhere along the way I've picked up a scrap of information that didn't seem important at the time, but is somehow connected with something I heard later.' She frowned, dredging her memory, but nothing significant emerged. 'Everything's a blur at the moment.'

'That's hardly surprising in view of all the anxiety about your mother.'

'It's on her account I so badly want to track down Father's killer. On the way back from the hospital, I thought how wonderful it would be if when she wakes up after the op I could tell her it's all over, that I've managed to prove her innocence, but I just don't seem to be getting anywhere.' She went to the sink to wash her hands, dabbing her eyes surreptitiously with a towel as she battled with a sudden gush of tears at the memory of Sylvia's pale, tired face. She took a couple of tumblers from a cupboard and put them on the table; her voice was unsteady as she said with an attempt at a smile, 'We'll have to drink our plonk from these, I'm afraid. Wine glasses are taboo here.'

'No problem.'

As they sat down to their meal, Joe said, 'How about if

we do a recap of everything so far? You've been keeping me up to date on the essentials, but if you were to go over it again in a bit more detail, something might crop up to jog your memory.'

'So it might,' she agreed. 'We'll do that. Where do I start?'

'At the beginning, but not until we've finished eating and you're feeling more relaxed.'

But by the time their dinner was over and they had cleared everything away, the combination of weariness and anxiety proved too much for Melissa. 'It's no good, I'll have to go to bed. I can barely keep my eyes open,' she declared, yawning. 'That was a good idea, but I'm afraid it'll have to wait till tomorrow.'

'It mightn't be a bad thing to sleep on it,' Joe agreed. 'Maybe your subconscious will get to work during the night.'

Despite her physical tiredness, Melissa's brain refused to relax. The minute she put out her bedside light it went into overdrive, churning over every detail that she could recall of her enquiries so far, searching in vain for the missing piece of the puzzle. She was no nearer a solution when she fell asleep at last from sheer exhaustion, but shortly after she awoke the following morning the solution flashed into her head like a bolt of lightning. She was out of bed in a moment, banging on Joe's door and shouting, 'My subconscious came up trumps. I think I know who murdered both Father and Jessica Round!'

*   *   *

They sat in the kitchen drinking tea while Joe listened in growing astonishment and admiration as Melissa explained the clues that had led her to what she was now convinced was the identity of the killer. 'I can't think how I didn't tumble to it before,' she said when she had finished. 'I suppose it was because half my mind has been distracted by Mother's problems.'

'I'm sure that's it,' Joe agreed. 'Now, all you have to do is get the evidence to prove it.'

'Once I know for certain who that car went to it'll be proof enough for me. I'll call the office as soon as it's open and speak to Tom Fingle.'

Joe poured out second cups of tea and said tentatively, 'I don't want to sound discouraging, Mel, but it may not be proof enough for DI Adair.'

'Why not?'

'Because, like her evidence against your mother, yours is purely circumstantial.'

'I suppose so, but at least she'll have to listen to me. Then it'll be up to her.'

'So you are going to tell her about it?'

'Of course.'

'I'm relieved to hear that. I was afraid for a moment that you were planning a dramatic face-to-face encounter with the killer.'

'Not likely, I don't want to risk a knife in my ribs!'

On the stroke of nine o'clock, Melissa called the office of Frank Ross and Company and asked for Tom Fingle. He came on the line almost immediately.

'Hallo, how's the investigation going?' he asked bree-zily. 'Picked up any more clues?'

'I think I might have done. Can you check if anyone in the company besides you and Ivor Patmore drives the same make and model of car as my father?'

'I can tell you that right away.' She felt a surge of adrenalin as he gave her the name she expected to hear. Then he said, in obvious disbelief, 'For goodness' sake, you surely don't think—'

'I not only think,' she interrupted in triumph, 'I'm nearly a hundred per cent certain, but please, keep it to yourself for the time being!'

After a perfunctory greeting, DI Adair said, 'I hope your mother's feeling better. I need to talk to her again as soon as possible.'

'I'm afraid you'll have to wait some time for that,' said Melissa coldly.

When she had explained the nature of Sylvia's illness, the detective's manner softened slightly. 'I'm very sorry to hear that,' she said. 'I hope you understand that I have a job to do, and—'

'That's why I'm here,' Melissa interrupted. 'I may be able to help. I've been doing a bit of ferreting around, and I think I've turned up something—'

It was DI Adair's turn to interrupt. Her expression hardened again as she said curtly, 'I thought I made it clear that I wanted you to leave the investigation to us.

Valuable evidence can often be destroyed as the result of amateur meddling.'

'I'm not a complete amateur,' Melissa retorted, 'and I assure you, I haven't destroyed any evidence.' Briefly, she outlined her case, but she had barely finished when a uniformed officer put his head round the door and said, 'DCI Franks wants an urgent word, Guv.'

'I'll come at once.' DI Adair got to her feet. 'I'm afraid you'll have to excuse me, Mrs Craig,' she said dismissively. 'I'll bear in mind what you've told me.'

'Well, thanks for nothing,' Melissa muttered under her breath as she made her way back to where Joe was waiting for her in the car park.

'How did she take it?' he asked.

'She didn't exactly fall on my neck with tears of gratitude. In fact, I've a feeling she was relieved when she was called away before she had time to think up a way of shooting me down in flames.' Feeling utterly deflated, Melissa sat back in her seat and closed her eyes, then opened them again as her mobile phone rang. Tom Fingle was on the line and he sounded concerned.

'I thought perhaps you should know that your suspect went home early yesterday complaining of feeling unwell and hasn't put in an appearance this morning,' he said. 'The girl on reception has rung several times to enquire, but there's no reply. Remembering what you said, I haven't breathed a word to anyone about what you told me earlier, but d'you suppose . . .?'

'Do you know the address?' He gave it to her and she said, 'I think it could be serious. Can you meet us there?'

'I'm on my way.'

The house was at the end of a terrace of small dwellings that Melissa guessed had once been labourers' cottages but which now bore signs of recent gentrification, with replacement windows, glazed porches and neatly tended gardens. There were no garages; cars were parked outside several of the houses, but there was no sign of the fourth Renault. Moments after Melissa and Joe arrived, Tom Fingle's car appeared and drew up behind them. The three of them hurried up the front path; Fingle began hammering on the door, but there was no response.

After a minute or two the door of the adjoining house opened and an elderly woman with her hair in rollers appeared on the doorstep. 'You're making enough noise to wake the dead,' she complained. 'There's no one there . . . went off half an hour ago . . . driving like a looney . . . swerving all over the place, drunk as like as not . . . turned the wrong way at the end of the road.'

'How do you know it was the wrong way?'

'Only leads to the old quarry, doesn't it? No one goes along there now, only courting couples and kids up to mischief.' Muttering under her breath, the crone stooped to pick up a bottle of milk from her doorstep, went inside and slammed her door.

'We'll take my car.' Fingle jumped into the driver's seat

and started the engine while the others scrambled in behind him. He made a three-point turn, put his foot to the floor and tore up to the junction where he stamped on the brakes before taking a wild swing to the left with his passengers clinging on for dear life. After about a quarter of a mile the tarmac surface of the road began to disappear under a layer of stone-coloured dust; a couple of hundred yards further on the way was barred by a pair of heavy metal gates bearing a faded sign reading, 'Danger – Keep Out'. The gates were intact, but on one side a gap had been torn through the rusted iron fencing. Fragments of gravel flew in all directions as the car skidded to a stop. The three of them leapt out and rushed forward, then pulled up in horror at the sight of the rear end of a dark-blue Renault Mégane protruding over the edge of the quarry.

'I'll go. You two wait here,' said Fingle grimly. The others held their breath as, by clinging to the branch of an overhanging tree, he managed to reach a point level with the driver's window. His face was green as he scrambled back to rejoin them. 'It's Eunice all right,' he said shakily. 'She looks pretty badly hurt, but she's still alive. We must get help.' He took out his mobile phone and began jabbing buttons. 'She ran straight into the trunk of that tree; if she'd missed that, she'd have gone crashing to the bottom.'

The other two exchanged glances. 'I've no doubt that was her intention,' Melissa said sadly.

Chapter Twenty-Five

'Whatever put you on to Eunice?' asked Tom Fingle. 'I thought you said she'd been quite helpful to your investigations.'

'So she had,' Melissa agreed, 'until I started enquiring about the fourth Renault when I called her yesterday lunchtime. She seemed perfectly happy to accept my call, but at that point she suddenly remembered she'd been forbidden by Marcus Bell to have any further contact with me. It didn't strike me as particularly odd then – in fact, it's no more than I'd have expected from him, going on past experience – but when I was lying in bed last night, raking over everything in my head for the umpteenth time, it occurred to me to wonder why she hadn't said so straight away.'

'But surely that in itself wasn't enough to make you suspect her?'

'No, it wasn't. I think at that point I must have fallen asleep; it was when I woke up and started asking myself what had prompted that change in attitude that I suddenly remembered something much more significant. When Lottie Haynes — she's a friend of my mother's — phoned to enquire after her yesterday she mentioned having only just learned from Wednesday evening's paper that the Alderley Court murder victim was Jessica Round, whom they both knew through the flower club.'

'So?'

'After the inquest on my father on Wednesday afternoon, I was talking to a local journalist called Denis Botting. He happened to mention in passing that the police had released Jessica's name that morning and it would appear in the evening paper. He already knew it, of course, and so no doubt did the other local media hounds, but only unofficially, so up to then it hadn't been published. The thing is, Eunice knew the day before.'

'How did you figure that out?'

'Because when I met her for lunch on Tuesday, I said something about Jessica's murder being very upsetting for Mother and she agreed it must have been. I never gave it a thought at the time, but the point is, when I asked her on Monday if my father had ever mentioned Jessica Round she said no and asked who she was. I told her about the flower club, but nothing else and certainly not where Jessica lived or that I'd spoken to her. Then it came to me in a flash: the name of the Alderley Court murder victim hadn't been released, so the only way she could have known it was Jessica was because she herself had killed her.'

Fingle ran his fingers through his hair, a puzzled expression on his face. 'I'm afraid you've lost me,' he said. 'Is there some connection between the two killings, I mean—' He looked away, his colour rising in embarrassment as the implication dawned on him.

'I'm afraid there is,' said Melissa sadly, realising that there was no way of preventing the whole story from becoming public. 'I believe that my father was having an affair with Eunice and that he ended it when he met Jessica. My guess is that she killed him in a fit of jealous anger and then went after the woman who'd stolen him from her.'

Fingle shook his head in disbelief. 'Frank Ross, of all people – I'd never have believed it! It's not easy to keep that sort of thing quiet, but I've never heard so much as a whisper in the company.'

'And I suppose,' said Joe, 'when she realised that one way or the other you were bound to find out that she had the fourth car, and that a witness had seen it outside the house at about the critical time, she knew the game was up and decided to take what she saw as the only way out.' It was the first time he had spoken for several minutes; having already heard the story from Melissa, he had listened without comment as she repeated it for Fingle's benefit. 'Up to that point,' he went on thoughtfully, 'she must have been kidding herself she was going to get away with it. She might have done if she'd kept her cool; after all, if no one actually saw her, or got the number of the car, there was no way of proving that it was hers.'

The three of them lapsed into silence. Barely an hour had passed since a combined crew of firemen, police and paramedics had hauled the crumpled Renault from its precarious position on the lip of the quarry, cut free its semi-conscious occupant and rushed her to hospital. Having given preliminary statements to the police, they were sitting in a subdued group waiting for news while doctors were assessing the injuries sustained by the woman they now believed had killed twice over. Melissa's thoughts returned to her mother, at that very moment undergoing surgery in the same hospital. She had managed to establish that the operation was still in progress and to extract a promise that she would be kept informed and sent for as soon as the patient showed signs of regaining consciousness. The knowledge had yet to sink in that her fantasy of being able to greet her with the news that the real killer had been caught might soon become a reality.

After an interval, Fingle said, 'She must have gone completely to pieces. Funny, that – I wouldn't have thought she was the type to panic.'

With an effort, Melissa switched her mind back to Eunice. 'That surprises me as well,' she agreed. 'Thinking back, I can't believe how controlled she's been all along. She seemed quite eager to help me clear my mother's name. In fact, she was the one who suggested Ivor Patmore as a likely suspect, but of course that was just a red herring, to put me off the scent.'

'The cold-blooded bitch!' Fingle muttered through his teeth.

'Not completely. I believe she was genuinely disturbed at the thought that Mother was under suspicion. Perhaps that was what made her decide to put the finger on Ivor Patmore, although her common sense should have told her nothing could make it stick.'

'Common sense doesn't seem to have played a very large part in her scheme of things,' Fingle commented. 'I wonder if we'll ever know the full story.'

'If she doesn't pull through we shan't.' For a moment, Melissa found herself wondering whether she would prefer to have Eunice's secret die with her, rather than watch her parents' private lives becoming food for sensation-hungry journalists and their readers. Yet in her heart she knew there was no way of concealing the whole, pitiful story of betrayal and vengeance.

Fingle glanced at his watch and stood up. 'I'd better get back to the office,' he said. 'It may be some time before there's any news, and I've got things to attend to. The police and the hospital want to know her next of kin. I've promised to check her file.'

When he had gone, Joe said, 'There's a cafeteria on the ground floor — why don't we go and get a sandwich and some coffee? We can tell the nurses where we are and they can page us if—'

Melissa shook her head. 'I'd rather stay here and wait for news of Mother,' she said.

'But it's nearly lunch-time and you ate hardly any breakfast.'

She was about to refuse for a second time when

Doctor Freeman entered the waiting-room. She was smiling. 'Mrs Craig, I thought you'd like to know right away that the operation is over and your mother has come through it satisfactorily,' she said before Melissa had a chance to speak. 'We need to carry out further tests before we can give you a firm prognosis, but in the meantime we feel there are grounds for optimism.'

'Oh, thank God!' Melissa exclaimed, her voice weak with emotion. 'Is she conscious? Can I see her?'

'It will be a while before she wakes up, so I suggest you have a bite to eat and come back in an hour or so.'

'That's just what I've been telling her,' said Joe. He took Melissa by the arm. 'Thank you, Doctor, I'll make sure she takes your advice.'

In spite of Doctor Freeman's assurances, it was all Joe could do to persuade Melissa to stay in the cafeteria for the twenty minutes or so it took to gobble a hasty snack. The moment she swallowed the last of her coffee she was on her feet. 'I promised her I'd be there when she wakes up,' she insisted.

They had been waiting at the bedside in the intensive therapy unit for almost two hours before Sylvia's eyes fluttered open. For a few moments they stared unfocused at the ceiling. Melissa grasped her hand and said softly, 'Mother, it's Lissie — can you hear me?'

'Is it over?' The words were barely audible. 'Am I going to be all right?'

'It's over and you're going to be fine. How do you feel?'

'Sleepy.' It was some minutes before she spoke again.

Then she said, in a surprisingly clear but anxious whisper, 'Lissie, do the police still think I killed your father?'

'No, Mother, they know now that you didn't.'

Sylvia gave a tired smile, squeezed her daughter's hand, and closed her eyes. A nurse who had been hovering in the background stepped forward and whispered in Melissa's ear, 'She'll probably sleep for several hours now. You look exhausted. Why don't you go home and get some rest?'

'All right.' Melissa turned to Joe. 'What about Eunice?' she said. 'Shouldn't we—'

'I don't want to sound callous, but Eunice isn't our concern any more,' he said firmly. 'The police will let us know in due course how things go.'

'I suppose so.'

That night, Melissa slept more soundly than she had done for a week. The evening had passed in a blur of weariness; after supper she fulfilled her promise to keep Mrs Menzies and Lottie Haynes informed of her mother's progress, took a bath and fell into bed, leaving Joe – at his insistence – to clear away and lock up the house for the night. It was after nine o'clock the following morning when she was awakened by a soft tap at the door and his voice saying, 'Tea's made. Shall I bring you a cup?'

'No thanks, I'll come down.'

In the kitchen, while she was drinking the tea that he had poured out for her, he said, 'I've been thinking, Mel. There are some things I should be attending to in the office next week. Do you think you can manage without me for a while? I'll come back straight away if there are any problems.'

He spoke a little jerkily, not meeting her eye as he bustled about taking items for their breakfast from cupboards and drawers. She sensed that he was uncomfortable with what he was saying and hastened to reassure him. 'Of course I can manage. I should really be going home for a couple of days myself, once Mother's out of immediate danger. Gloria, my lovely cleaning lady, will be wondering what on earth's become of me and there'll be a mountain of post and e-mail to deal with. There's a book waiting to be finished as well; you must be getting worried about your cut from the advance!' she added mischievously.

There was no answering smile as he said, 'Hadn't given it a thought.'

'Is something bugging you?' she asked.

'No, what makes you think that?'

'Oh, nothing. I'll have to come back and make some arrangements for convalescence,' Melissa went on, almost thinking aloud. 'And there'll be Father's funeral, of course, once they release his body. I'm sure Mrs Menzies will be only too happy to lend a hand; she seems really anxious to do whatever she can for Mother.'

'So you're sure it's all right if I—?'

'Quite sure.'

After breakfast Melissa checked with the hospital and was told that her mother had passed a comfortable night and would be visited by the consultant at eleven o'clock. At half past ten, just as she and Joe were preparing to leave for the hospital, the telephone rang. Detective Inspector Adair was on the line. Without preamble she said, 'Eunice Lester is less seriously injured than was feared. In fact, she's well enough to be interviewed.'

'Well, that's good news,' said Melissa. 'Has she confessed all?'

There was no mistaking the resentment in the detective's voice as she went on, 'She refuses point blank to say a word to us or make any kind of statement until she's had a chance to speak to you in private.'

'He had ten years of my life and then he dumped me.' Eunice Lester's eyes filled with tears at the memory. 'He never actually said he cared, but it went on for so long, and he seemed to need me so badly, I really believed he had some feeling for me.'

'How did it start?' asked Melissa.

A faintly cynical smile flickered briefly among the bandages that swathed the injured woman's head and face. 'The way a lot of office affairs start, I suppose. We were working late one evening to get a job finished and when we'd done he offered to buy me supper. I'd arranged to go to the cinema with a friend so I said, "No thanks" – but all of a sudden our eyes met and it was like a chemical explosion. We began kissing as if there was no tomorrow; he said he'd wanted me since I started in the job a few months before and I found myself saying I wanted him too. The next minute we were rolling on the floor in his office. It was crazy, we never gave a thought to who might come barging in, but everyone else had gone home and by a miracle the cleaner hadn't shown up because she was sick, so we got away with it.'

Melissa made no comment, but sat passively waiting for Eunice to continue. She was conscious of a curious feeling of detachment, as if what she was hearing concerned strangers with whom she had no emotional tie.

After a few moments, Eunice went on. 'After that, he used to come to my house. Not regularly, and not during office hours; it was usually when his wife was at one of her various clubs: flower arranging, Women's Institute, that sort of thing.' There was a hint of disdain in her voice as if such mundane interests were beneath her. 'He was desperate to keep our affair a secret. Although no one else from the company lives anywhere near me, he even used to leave the car up the road leading to the quarry, just in case.'

There was a long silence. Eunice lay with her eyes closed, her bandaged hands moving restlessly on the covers. When she spoke again, her voice took on a new note and for the first time, Melissa caught a hint of the suppressed rage that had turned love to hatred.

'You're probably wondering why I'm telling you all this. Well,' she went on as Melissa remained silent, 'I thought you had a right to hear it from me first that your father wasn't exactly the goody-two-shoes he liked the world and his wife to believe.'

'I'd already found that out for myself,' said Melissa drily. She stood up. 'I think I'll go now.'

'No, wait, you might as well hear it all.' Reluctantly, Melissa sat down again. 'He suddenly stopped coming,' Eunice said harshly. 'Wouldn't talk about it, just said it was over. But I wasn't going to let him go without a fight. I knew he was on his own that afternoon. I phoned to say I had to see him urgently — I concocted a story about something needing his signature. He let me in through the side gate and showed me into his workshop. I pleaded with him, I begged him to come back to me. But all he said was, "Can't you get it into your head — it's over. I've met someone I really care for, someone I'm truly happy with. And Jessica feels the same way. I'm very grateful for what you've done for me," he said. Grateful!' The word was almost a snarl. 'As if he was thanking me for working a couple of hours' overtime! After ten years, all he could offer me was gratitude! I did everything he asked of me, I even gave up wearing make-up in the office because he didn't approve. And he'd never cared, never even had any respect for me as a woman — he was just using me. The few presents, the discount on the car that he arranged, to him they were nothing but payment for services rendered. For ten years he'd been treating me little better than a prostitute.'

'And that's why you killed him?'

'Yes.' The word was a drawn out, almost feline hiss. 'I saw the axe lying on the floor and . . . well, you can guess what happened next, can't you?'

Her voice broke into a high-pitched sob on the final words and the sound brought a nurse hurrying to the bedside. 'I hope you aren't upsetting the patient, she needs to be kept quiet,' she said severely. She checked Eunice's pulse, gave her a drink of water and plumped up her pillows. 'If it happens again I shall have to ask you to leave.'

'My fault, I got carried away,' Eunice told her. 'I'm okay. I promise not to do it again.' As the door closed behind the nurse her mood underwent a swift, terrifying change. In a tone of exultation that made Melissa shudder she said, 'You can't imagine how good I felt as I drove back to the office. Cleansed, liberated!' Her breathing became faster and she showed signs of renewed agitation. 'And then of course I realised the job was only half-finished. There was something else to be done.'

'You mean, kill Jessica Round?' Stunned by the enormity of what she was hearing, even though it was merely confirmation of her own suspicions, Melissa found it an effort to utter the words.

'Of course. That way, the account would be closed. I didn't know her full name then, but—'

'Oh, dear God!' A fresh wave of horror swept over Melissa as she recalled the question she had, in all innocence, put to Eunice at their first meeting. 'I asked you if my father ever mentioned her in connection with Mother's flower club. I was the one who told you. I put you on to her!'

A tigerish smile played round the half-concealed mouth. 'I wouldn't lose any sleep over it,' said Eunice. 'I'd have tracked her down sooner or later.'

Epilogue

It was agreed that Joe would return to London on Sunday morning. On Saturday evening, at his somewhat diffident suggestion, they went to the Beverley Court for dinner. After studying the menu for a few minutes, Melissa threw it down and said, 'It's no use, I can't make up my mind. You order for me.'

'What's wrong?'

She spread her hands in a helpless gesture. 'I suppose it's partly reaction to all the pressures of the past week, but I can't shake off my feelings of guilt over giving Jessica Round's name to Eunice.'

'That's understandable.' The sympathy in his voice and the look of compassion in his eyes almost brought tears to her own. 'Try not to dwell on it,' he said gently. 'You told me what Eunice said and I'm sure she meant it. It would have been just a matter of time before—'

'I know, but . . . Joe, you should have seen the look in

her eyes. It was horrible – like all three Furies rolled into one.' The memory brought a chill and she shivered, despite the warmth of the dining-room. 'It's not only that,' she went on, crumbling a bread roll with restless fingers. 'I can't seem to focus on anything. There's going to be so much to arrange and so many decisions to make once Mother's well enough to leave hospital. And when she's fully recovered there's the long-term problem of what's to become of her. She can't go on living in that house on her own and Hawthorn Cottage isn't big enough for the two of us. Besides, I'm still going to need a life of my own. Oh, I'm sorry!' She gave an apologetic smile. 'I didn't mean to spend the evening whingeing.'

'You're not whingeing, just stating the problems. What you really need is someone to share them with, someone to look after you. You know how I feel about you. I'd do all that and more besides if you'd marry me, but you've made it pretty clear . . .' A shadow passed over his face and he resumed his study of the menu as if there was no more to be said.

From feeling cold, Melissa experienced a warm glow that enveloped every part of her body. *This is it*, she told herself. *This is the moment . . . you were right to wait. Now go for it!* She took a deep breath and said, 'You could try asking me.'

Melissa got out of the car and went over to the gate leading into the field opposite her front door. She turned to look back at the cottage; the hawthorn tree that gave it its name was a froth of white and the reflection of the late afternoon sun set the windows aflame. From along the valley came the sound of lambs calling their mothers; birds darted to and fro with food for their young. She took deep breaths of the fresh Cotswold air, rejoicing in the feel of the breeze playing softly on her face.

'Oh, it's so good to be home!' she exclaimed. 'I feel as if I've been away for a year instead of a mere ten days.'

Joe came and stood beside her. 'You love it here, don't you?' he said.

'I've put down roots. Joe, I can't bear the thought of parting with Hawthorn Cottage.'

'I'm sure we can work something out,' he said, drawing her close.

Lost for the moment in their own world, neither of them noticed the door to the adjoining Elder Cottage being opened. It was only when a familiar voice called 'Yoohoo!' that they became aware that they were not alone.

'Iris!' Melissa ran forward and flung her arms round her friend. 'What a super surprise!'

'Surprise nothing. Here for an exhibition. Sent e-mails, left messages, no response. Been too busy I suppose.' Iris's sharp grey eyes glinted with sardonic humour as they darted from the solitaire diamond on her friend's engagement finger to the man standing quietly behind her.

'You could say that,' Melissa admitted with a smile. 'I'm afraid it hasn't all been good news, but—'

'Tell me later about the bad news. Let's talk about the good.' Iris detached herself from Melissa's embrace and offered Joe a thin, brown hand. 'Joe Martin, isn't it? Seen you once or twice on your visits . . . never met you properly . . . heard all about you though. Always felt you were the one for her,' she added gruffly. 'Glad you've got her to see sense at last!'

BETTY ROWLANDS

THE MAN AT THE WINDOW

Graham Shipley has come to the Cotswolds to take up a new teaching appointment and to make a fresh start after the break-up of his marriage. He is made welcome by the Head of St Monica's Preparatory School and by his new neighbour in Upper Benbury, crime writer Melissa Craig.

But shortly after his arrival a young girl is found drowned. Foul play is suspected and Graham's past threatens to catch up with him. In desperation, he turns for help to Melissa who soon discovers that this is not a simple case of murder – there are other more complex and sinister influences at work in the village.

'A clearly gifted and knowledgeable writer, never less than engaging and readable'

Financial Times

HODDER AND STOUGHTON PAPERBACKS

BETTY ROWLANDS

THE CHERRY PICKERS

The Cotswold village of Upper Benbury is buzzing with rumour and gossip. The body of a young gipsy girl has been found in a discarded freezer, recently stolen from outside the house of one of its most prominent residents.

A local newshound persuades Melissa Craig, the crime writer with a reputation for solving real crimes, to accompany him to the gipsy encampment. When she learns that members of the victim's family are planning to administer their own brand of justice, Melissa's investigation lands her in grave danger and exposes dark secrets in unexpected places.

'Fresh and lively . . . an enjoyable read with a gratifying array of twists'

Shots

HODDER AND STOUGHTON PAPERBACKS